SHADOW OF THE RAVEN

THE MORGUES OF CHARLIE BRAND: BOOK ONE

JOE COOKE

CPG

Cannon Publishing Group

Shadow of the Raven

ISBN 978-9766291-1-5

Library of Congress Control Number: 2009904967

CPG

Cannon Publishing Group

Printed in the United States of America

1 2 3 4 5 6 7 8 9

SHADOW OF THE RAVEN

The Morgues of Charlie Brand: Book One

By Joe Cooke

Preface

Charlie Brand's life came to me in a morgue.

By the arrival of these thirteen cardboard crates; white, square and unmarked except for my address written long-hand in Charlie's unmistakable script, I assumed that he had likely "passed on," as they say. Why he sent these millstones to me was at first unclear, since I had only worked with Brand on a slight number of occasions, early in his career, and really, nothing came of it. Although he made somewhat of a living from his journalism, as a freelance writer he was not what I considered to be a novelist. A passable author, I suppose, if I may be so bold as to use that title, but not brilliant. He did, of course, have a penchant for sticking his nose into the most unusual of circumstances, and it was that, most likely, rather than his proficiency at writing, that kept some bread on the table (a bad cliché, especially since I found out later that he did not eat bread) and booze in the cabinets, when necessary.

Admittedly, this baker's dozen that held Brand's secrets sat here, tucked not-so-neatly away in the corner of my office, for a long time. And when I say 'a long time' I mean years, not weeks or months. Seven years, to be precise. Seven years, three months and some odd days, to be even more precise.

Somewhere near the end of that repose, I hired a new assistant, an intern actually, and not really hired as much as taken on. Kate lived in Greenwich Village, attended NYU on a full scholarship and studied English Literature with a minor in sociology. Dark hair, dark eyes and freckles that gave her a perennially young look. Petite, witty and mostly happy to the point of being vivacious, except when talk turned to the elderly and death. Despite her twenty-one years, she looked all of fifteen. She worked for experience and college credit, although I often gave her gift certificates and bought her pizza and lattes in exchange for some long hours and late nights spent mostly cleaning and organizing the accumulated clutter of fifteen years in the publishing business, all of them from this same New York office. Needless to say, she mentioned the unopened boxes several times, wondering what they contained and what my intentions were toward them.

It was late in the afternoon, a cup of coffee on my desk, that I stared at those boxes, pondering them, wanting more than anything to be rid of them and yet reticent to throw away what seemed to be all that remained of a life, flotsam and jetsam that it was. I decided that, before I called the janitorial staff, I would at least read a bit from at least one box, out of respect for the presumed dead.

So, with a bit of morbid curiosity, I popped one open, flipped through some of the dusty pages, became almost immediately uninterested, and promptly shoved the containers into the corner for disposal. Harsh as it sounds, I have no room in my office for a stack of loose journals roughly the width and breadth of a coffin.

It was Kate who saved them.

She asked if she could paw through them a bit, and with no more interest in them myself, and supposing Brand to be beyond caring, I said, "Knock yourself out," or words to that effect. She did, diving in while I toiled through a surprisingly tedious manuscript from one of my better clients. As we proceeded through our tasks, we would often stop and chat for a few moments about life, her school, my family, the economy.

It was upon the opening of the third box, and the random rifling through of it, that Kate became silent for a long while, sitting cross-legged on the floor, papers strewn about her. Quiet was an unusual state for my protégé, and after an hour and a half of nothing but the clock ticking down toward six in the evening, I realized that she had come upon something and that I had not.

I put my project aside, stretched, fetched two fresh cups of coffee and then sat down on the floor next to Kate, saying nothing. I put her cup next to her. She handed me a sheaf of papers and I began to read.

There turned out to be no real order to these journals, and gaps resplendent, when, for long periods of time, Brand would simply forget or ignore his personal writing. This more than likely happened during those times of personal tragedy. Thus, what we have been able to piece together of this particular time during Brand's life, comes from his journals, for some part, letters both to and from Brand, and from drafts of articles that appear to never have been published, along with recordings mostly on micro-cassette for which Kate had to spend most of a day shopping local thrift shops in order to find a suitable player. As we strung this series of events together, I found myself more and more compelled to outline, and then to fill in, as best I could, the details of his experience. By necessity, we had to sort information, setting much aside that may or may not have been germane to the thread we followed. It was a confusing, messy morass of details and gaps, mostly the latter, which made reading and listening like trying to draw a picture of the night sky through breaks in a heavy cloud cover.

As a publisher, I often criticize the rough novels and non-fiction manuscripts I receive, by the hundreds each month, and those being filtered first by my staff, so that I am only reading the *crème de la crème*, and yet, now that I have spent so many hours digging through Charlie's life, compiling, sorting, organizing and transcribing, I find a new appreciation for those novelists and journalists who send me such a proliferation of letters, words, paragraphs and chapters.

From what we found, we know that Charlie Brand was born in Seattle, Washington, on a rainy October day in 1960. I know it was raining because Charlie's mother taught her young boy to journal everything. Taught not by lecture, but by demonstration. I have then, Charlie's life, and that of his mother, and by proxy, that of his father and the few friends that his family managed to maintain; all captured in musty spiral-bound notebooks of every shape, size and color; heavy, black-bound journals; loose sheaves of paper and notes, notes, notes, taken in journalistic style; as well as some final product – clippings, magazines and print-outs. However, most of Charlie's published material is obscure, hard-to-find and, occasionally, impossible to locate, as if it had been completely redacted from the seemingly endless morgues of recent human memory.

As we dug deeper into Brand's journals, I found myself becoming more and more upset. Vague feelings of dread seemed to pervade my thoughts, and at night I would lay in bed, staring at the ceiling, unable to even think of the specifics that I was reading, and all the more convinced that Charlie Brand suffered from some unique ailment, a curse of being in the wrong place at the wrong time, of being sent to this earth perhaps to see and experience things that the rest of us are better off not knowing; us, tucked into our condos and suburban housing, tending to our yards and our children, watching the news, disturbed and depressed, but not directly involved. We turn down the sound, or turn the damned TV off altogether, and sit down to our salads and summer squash and grilled ribs, our pies and meat loaves and strawberry ice cream.

Brand did note some moments of joy, perhaps made all the more splendid by the overall tone of his life, the overall struggle to find himself, to cope with his gifts and the shadows that haunted him.

Even now, as I write this preface, I can feel a presence in the darkness around me, a tangible knowledge left by Brand and his notes. The knowledge that life is not as simple as it seems, perhaps not as safe as we would like to believe, and certainly that danger is not as distant or removed from us as we think.

What purpose I propose to serve with all of this somewhat superfluous explanation is unclear to me. Perhaps I am attempting to delay the inevitable; the story. As I mentioned, compiled from Brand's own notes, filled in by my research, discreet interviews, some educated guesses and some anonymous tips.

I have yet to open all those boxes, now more afraid of them than annoyed. I relate this portion of his life, not for anyone but myself, simply because we dipped our hands into his life here, first. And it then became these days and weeks that we discovered, through Brand's legacy. And therefore, these days and weeks are the hours that now occupy these pages, beginning on a rainy afternoon in October, in Seattle, during the fall of 1995; they are here, as we have best deduced them from the runes and incantations of language left by a dead hand, these perspectives of events surrounding the Raven and his tribe from thirteen boxes – the journals of Charlie Brand.

ONE

Seattle, Washington

October 13, 1995 – 5:08PM

Brand stood at an open window, staring down at the street. Dark clouds made the afternoon look like night. A wave of Buicks and Mercedes and Hondas in all states of shiny and dull hissed by, tires throwing mist off the pavement. A siren wailed in the distance and the pungent smell of wet concrete and oil penetrated the air. He winced and closed his eyes for a moment, trying to remember the feel of a rough wooden wall against his back, his Justin boots, dusty brown, grounded in straw, the musty smell of Holsteins and Morgans in his nose, the sound of rain pattering on a tin roof, but the city overwhelmed everything and only reminded him of how much he hated the crowds and the concrete and the hookers on Fourth Avenue that always said the same thing, 'Can I walk with you boy?'

He'd always been here, except for those few months in Montana, a few months getting clean and sober and finding out how wrong the city was for him but knowing that he was trapped there. It held him like a prison, cordoned him in, separated him from the life he wanted as if he was a train running headlong on the wrong track, no way to jump to the other, even though it seemed so close.

Just outside the window, an old double-sided sign shaped like an arched doorway revolved slowly in its bracket. The big sign rotated toward the window. The frame was the same as it had always been, gunmetal gray, but the time tattered purple background and silhouette of Fred Astaire had been replaced by the black and red symbol of the YMCA. Brand wanted to leave, felt out of place here in this weird dance room, when he should be down at the dojo practicing Shudokan, couldn't remember what strange nudge led him up here to cardio-kick with the after-work ladies, other than that sidelong voice mail left by Krystal McCain, but knew those nudges and knew to follow them, even when they seemed a bit ludicrous, like turning left instead of right and meeting up with just the right person at the right time. Over the years though, maybe these nudges had been more trouble than luck, but here he was, back in the dance studio he'd grown up in. Sick about it. He hoped Ren would take him up on his invite.

Back in the seventies, this room had been the hub of the disco scene; the premier dance studio in the Northwest, where the best Latin Hustle aficionados came to learn from greats like Paulo Giraldez and Sarah Gulick. But the crazy nights of social dancing died in the eighties and the FADS franchise suffered a slow death along with the foxtrot and the two-step. The dancers left never-never land and went on to become accountants and lawyers and retail clerks, or they simply bled along with the dying industry until they collapsed into lifeless husks that could do nothing more than stare at a television and dream of days gone by. Brand was just a kid back then, but he still remembered crouching under elegant tables watching the smooth dancers clad in black tailcoats and the Latin dancers in sequined costumes that clung like a second skin as they spun and leapt like gazelles around the ballroom. But it was all a façade, because for all the beauty on the surface, there was little money in ballroom dancing, and Brand and his mother lived their days and nights wondering where the next meal would come from, wondering when dad would get home, and hoping that when he did, he would pass out quickly on the couch.

A gust of wind blew a surge of briny air from the Puget Sound across Brand's face and for a moment he could taste the good part of Seattle. There was no other city on earth that could give the fresh and foamy and fishy and gritty all at the same time. It was the one thing that never changed about his city. That and the relentless rain.

Across the street, the rain fell in sheets across the front of the Mayflower Hotel, a monster of concrete block, the kind of building that defied all logic, just as all of Seattle did, defied sinking into a hundred feet of mud and organic refuse, the underpinnings of a city built long ago on a floating quagmire. And beyond the Mayflower, a thousand more blocky buildings nestled up along the steep eastern slope of Elliot Bay, lined up like motley characters in a never-ending play with no plot, standing patiently along avenues shining with salty sea-air that blew in from the piers below.

Brand slid the window shut and leaned against the sill. He looked into the hard glass at a face that melted into the gray of the sky beyond. The extreme doses of silver he had been taking had gravitated to his epidermis and collected there, giving his skin a dead, gray look, almost like wet pavement. Argyria was incurable, although some people with mild cases had used dermabrasion to scrub off the outer layers of facial skin.

He pulled the hood of his sweatshirt up so that it flopped over his forehead, leaving his hollow cheeks and leaden eyes hidden in shadow.

A woman came into the room. The maple flooring clicked and squealed under her Reeboks. She peeled off her sweatshirt and threw it into the far corner. She placed her water bottle on the floor near her left foot and grabbed her ankle all in one movement.

Another woman came in, and then another, and then Brand was the only man in a gathering crowd of women. Most worked close by, probably within walking distance. Had to be that way, in order for them to get out of their workday attire and into workout clothes by five minutes after five. Brand moved over to the west wall and leaned against a ballet barre. The wood flexed and groaned as he pressed it with the small of his back.

A few feet away, two ladies. A dark-haired, petite girl, about thirty-five. Carol. Waitress at Outback. Two kids. Divorced. Sexy but reserved. One of the few on her way to work instead of home. Shift started at six-thirty. She'd respond to Brand's questions, but never initiated a conversation. Probably got hit on a lot. But then she always wore makeup and pulled her hair back tight and shiny, and stuffed her bosom into a French-cut Danskin that accentuated the bulge of her hips. The leotard was black, always black, and she finished off with white tights and leg warmers bunched up around her calves. She must have owned fifty pairs of cross-trainers, each one with a different colored stripe and a matching loop for her ponytail. Fuchsia today.

Carol stood with her arms crossed, one bony hip jutting out to the side, nodding as she listened to a taller, blond woman with a blotchy complexion. The blond became more and more agitated as she ruminated. Brand got the gist of what she was saying by watching her lips and catching a few random words. Carol shot a glance at Brand, and he turned his head. He knew what they were talking about. Not cheating husbands and empty bank accounts, or the way the mechanic wouldn't listen to them or the price of gas. Right now, in the emerald city, where crime usually sat in a box like the baseball scores; murder 14, robbery 29, rape 12, incest 4, embezzlement 7, another young couple missing 2.

Bones found. Not picked clean, but chewed on, like you might chew on a short rib or a T-bone.

Morning news picked it up and all the stations had been beating it to death all day. The media loved a mystery more than they did a bloodbath. Only thing they liked better was war. These deaths were local, close to home, right in the heart of the city. The media played them so hard that it was getting to the point folks didn't want to come downtown at night anymore. Brand couldn't blame them. He closed his eyes and tried to chase the thought of death out of his head, but his mood was like a shadow over him.

A woman skating out along Alki point, pushing a bike-wheeled pram with her twins. The dad reported them missing. Police found the cart and the wife's blades in the bushes, but no sign of the bodies. A month later it was ombudsman Wade Harris and his new bride, already a scandal because of his messy divorce, suddenly turned up missing. Both of them. Brand kept clippings of all the disappearances in Seattle and King County. Some of them fit the profile, some didn't. But there were more and more of them clustering around the urban area. Only one witness so far. One survivor. A kid.

His interest was like a compulsion, an addiction. OCD was what his shrink called it. If he wasn't fixated on one thing, he replaced it with another. Replaced alcohol with Jule, replaced Jule with alcohol, replaced alcohol with death. He opened his eyes again and pushed away from the wall. A big Bulova on the wall read after five and Brand looked around for the instructor. Still no sign of her. The schedule listed her as Laci Keller. New gal. Brand hoped she was tough. He was in the mood for a good workout.

A young lady in baggy sweats and a blue tee shirt re-opened the window along the back wall of the old ballroom, and the patter of afternoon rain on the sill mixed in with the quiet voices of the dozen women that milled around waiting with Brand.

Brand turned away from them and pressed his palms against the barre. He rolled his shoulders back and forth. The past, the city, the rain, the news. It all got him tensed up, and tension increase the pain.

"God, I need to get out of the city," he muttered again.

As he tipped his head from side to side, stretching the tendons in his neck, the entire front bank of florescent lights flickered off. Brand watched as everyone's eyes turned toward the back of the room. He tried to stay calm and casually ignore the woman who strode across the floor to the front corner, where a CD player sat waiting. Tall, lean, muscular. Hair as black as India ink and thick and shiny like oiled silk. Little, round dark glasses covered her eyes, hugging close to her face. She dropped her black bag on the floor and crouched into a tailor's squat in front of the stereo. She pushed a stray bundle of hair back behind her ear and adjusted a microphone strap across her head. The mouthpiece hovered in front of her lips, almost touching them. Her bare midriff was stark white against the black Lycra of her pants and the tattered hem of her black tee shirt. Her biceps bugled with rock hard muscle. There was nothing loose on her body.

Renata Rhodes came up beside him and took a perch, resting her back against the wooden rail. She'd pulled her straw-blond hair back through the opening on her red ball cap, exposing her thin neck. A short, tight top covered her chest, but she concealed her hips and legs under a baggy pair of nylon parachute pants. The dim light gleamed off her white shoulders and her shoulder blades seemed as if they were about to pop through her skin.

She cocked her head to the side, in a certain way she had, and then she'd fixed her eyes on Brand. "I thought maybe you'd fallen off the face of the earth," she said. "I haven't heard from you since..."

Brand felt a sting; it must have shown in his face.

"Sorry," she said. Brand took a breath and waved it off. Ren looked up at the ceiling. "Why is it so dark in here?"

Brand glanced at Ren and then shrugged. He turned to watch the lithe body of the instructor as she unpacked her workout bag, looking for something.

11

Renata smiled and then noticed that Brand was preoccupied. She took a good, hard look at the woman that had Brand's attention.

"Speaking of Jule," Renata said.

"Not even," Brand said.

Renata's eyes took on an evil look. She shook her head and then her face and tone turned serious.

"So," she said. "How are you doing?"

"Fine."

"Yeah?"

"Going on eight months now." Brand.

"Is that good?" Ren asked.

Brand shrugged. "Guess it depends," he said. His eyes kept drifting back towards the front of the room. The instructor poked at the stereo controls.

Renata glanced toward the front, following Brand's gaze. "I think we're talking about two different things."

Brand brought his eyes back to Ren. "Or three."

"What's the third?"

"Drinking?"

"Ah, that. I guess I was talking about the other thing."

"Seems to be under control, I guess."

"And Jule?"

"That's the big problem."

Ren crossed her arms and tipped her head just a bit. "Well, if it's any consolation, I know how you feel. I went into a funk when my husband walked out on me."

"How long did it last?" Brand asked.

"The marriage or the funk?" Renata countered.

"The funk."

"I'm still funky," she said. "Been over ten years."

"Great," Brand said.

The music started up and Renata winced. She glanced at the instructor again. "Even her taste in music is harsh," she said.

The teacher started weaving and bobbing from side to side with her hands held up high, in front of her face. Her steel-blue eyes flicked toward Brand's image for a moment as his eyes locked on her reflection in the mirror. People moved forward and took their places around the room, lining up naturally, like soldiers behind a sergeant.

"It's five-fifteen," she called out. "Let's get started. Side step." Her voice rang out over the music, digitized and amplified, but still somehow soft and alluring. Brand slid over till he was just behind her right shoulder. Renata took the spot to the right of Brand, frowning at him for a moment before she fixed her attention on the mirrors in front of her. The whole class was there, in an alternate reality, and Brand was an observer, watching the crowd from within.

"My name is Laci," the instructor said. "And I'll be your teacher today. This is cardio-kick, level two. I'll show you level one options as well, so if you can't keep up, just keep moving."

She stopped swaying and spread her legs wide. She bent her knees and brought her arms low and in front of her body.

"Take a deep breath," she said. She straightened her legs and reached for the sky, then bent to the right and reached her left arm toward the far right wall. The class followed her movements. "Again," she said, repeating the movement.

"Flat back," she said. She turned so that she was staring at the floor, with her feet still spread wide and her back parallel to the ceiling. Her left arm turned gracefully as she swung it toward the front of the room, her body following. She rolled into an upright stance again and repeated the action to the other side. Renata slid over and bumped up against Brand.

"She even dances like Jule," she whispered.

Brand nodded.

"Sorry about the lights," Laci said. "But I have a problem with my eyes. Light sensitive." She flexed her left foot and bent forward at the waist for a hamstring stretch, following it with a right foot stretch. The class mimicked her.

"Bob and weave," Laci called out as she took a crouched defensive stance. She warmed them up for ten minutes with boxer's shuffle and side steps before she moved to lunges and jump rope. After they were sweating and breathing hard, she dropped for three sets of sixteen pushups.

"Chest to the floor, but not on it," Laci yelled. "Give me two sets of eight and count 'em."

Brand glanced over at Laci. She was doing hers one-handed, with her right arm behind her back. He was tempted to copy her, but instead he just closed his eyes and concentrated on his breathing. In through the nose, tongue to the roof of his mouth, out through his nose, a sound like the ocean from his throat. He felt a surge of adrenaline, the gut-wrenching anticipation of the change; fought it down against his own will. He thought about the silver in his blood, in his body, enough to kill a man, or, he hoped, enough to subdue something else. The feeling subsided, slowly, as Brand slipped into the rhythm of the push-ups, but the strength in his body remained. He felt light, eager to get outside, into the rain, to run wild. The need became an ache; an itch he could not scratch.

They took a break and stretched their arms before they dropped forward for sixteen more. Brand let the endorphins run through his bloodstream and into his skull, where they dulled the pain slightly. This was the only relief he could get.

"Get your butt up," Laci said. Her voice boomed through the PA. Brand slid his hands in toward the center of his chest and did the last set touching his breastbone to the diamond made by his thumbs and fingers. He pushed slow and hard, using muscle against muscle. Laci got them back on their feet and went back to bob and weave, and then right into left and right jabs.

"Keep you eyes on your target," she said, glancing at Brand. "And keep your hands up, here." She raised her own fists up a bit higher to catch his attention. Brand brought his fists up in front of his nose.

"Protect yourself," Laci said. "And your target is your reflection in the mirror. Hit it."

Brand's arms ached a bit, but as he looked at his reflection, he found new energy. The energy produced more endorphins, and the endorphins masked the pain. He would pay for it later, but for now he was grateful for the relief. He focused on the stupid looking geek in the mirror with the gray face and baggy blue sweats. He punched at himself and ground his teeth together, following Laci's own intensity. Hooks followed jabs, and crosses followed hooks, then front kicks and sidekicks and combinations. Laci flowed through the movements like a dancer, every movement controlled and easy as she kicked invisible heads and punched the air around her, her hands always returning to her face.

Her eyes caught Brand's as he jabbed at the mirrors like a madman.

"Conceal your strength," she said as she pulled her arms in against her chest. "And when you strike, strike hard." She threw a right cross followed by two uppercuts and the class followed suit.

They fought themselves for an hour, interspersing three more minutes of speed jumping and three more sets of sixteen pushups before they cooled down with ab crunches and stabilization. Brand clenched his teeth together and made it through by staying focused on Laci's straps and the way she watched over the class like a mother bird, and the way that her black pants fit against her hips and thighs.

As the class wound down, Brand felt his sweatshirt hanging wet on his chest. Laci had only a trace of dark moisture around her neck, but her skin glistened. Brand spoke to her reflection. "Thanks."

The rest of the group started to disperse. Behind him, Brand could feel Renata watching, waiting, and he sensed her eyes rolling. He closed his mouth and focused his attention on Laci.

She turned around and wiped her neck with a towel. Laci stared at Brand with black pupils rimmed with just a thin line of blue.

"Pull off your hood," she said.

Brand pushed his hood back with one hand. Laci stared at his face, tipped her head to one side, and then pursed her lips.

"Argyria?" she asked. Brand nodded.

"Are you a doctor too?" Brand asked.

"In a past life," she said. "Are you afraid of vampires, Mr. Brand?"

"No."

She reached down and picked up her bag.

"You've been ingesting a lot of silver," she said.

"A bit."

"Does it do you any good?"

"Not that I can tell."

"What is it you're trying to stave off?" she asked.

"Something bad."

Laci nodded.

"What are you taking for that skin condition?" she asked.

"Nothing," Brand said. "It's irreversible."

Laci reached into her bag and dug out a pen and a small pad of paper. She dropped the bag on the floor and held the pad close to her chest as she wrote.

"Do this," she said. "Two thousand IU of vitamin E, or up to four thousand if you're otherwise healthy. The risk is that it could thin your blood a bit. Two teaspoons of sulfur and two hundred micrograms of selenium, plus a good isotonic mineral supplement. The selenium and sulfur will bind with the silver and will help pull it from your body. Drink tons of water to help flush it out."

She ripped the top sheet off the pad and handed it to Brand. He could barely read the scribbles.

"Vitamin E is a chelating agent," she said. "Do this every day until you've purged all that silver. Unless you like the dead look."

Brand just stared at the scratches on the paper, trying to remember what they meant. *Sulfur, selenium, vitamin E.*

"I've got to go now," she said.

"Thanks," Brand said. He was still staring at the paper.

"I didn't catch your name," she said.

"Brand," he said. "Charles Brand."

"Brand," Laci said. "You the Charlie Brand that's been writing those pieces on the Gryphons for the P.I.?"

"Yeah, that's me."

Laci's eyes narrowed a bit. When she spoke, her voice was so quiet Brand could barely hear her say, "You're a hack."

She spun around and walked into the storage room leaving Brand standing alone in the empty, dark ballroom. He could see just inside the door, where small dumbbells rested neatly one on top of another in racks against the far wall, along with rubber tubes and jump ropes. Stacks of Radia steps in green and white obscured the opposite wall, and along the far end, big rubber balls towered way above the top of the bin that was supposed to hold them. Laci dropped her bag on the floor and pushed up on the unruly stack of balls. She ignored Brand's curious gaze. He stood for a minute, watching the storeroom door, before he turned and left. As he passed a wastebasket in the hallway, he crumpled up the note Laci had written and tossed it.

Renata caught up with him. "Why do you always go for the buff hippy types?"

"She's not a hippie," Brand said.

"No," Renata said. "Not like a San Francisco hippy. I mean, hippy." Renata slapped her own narrow butt with the palm of her hand. "You know? Big hips."

"She doesn't have big hips," Brand said. "Those are muscles."

"Can't hardly tell, it's so dark in here," Ren said.

"Her pupils are so dilated, they make her eyes look black," Brand said.

"Drugs?" Ren asked.

Brand shook his head. "I don't think so. She's too fit to be into controlled substances. Unless maybe amphetamines or something."

"Well, whatever," Renata said. "In any case, she's a real piece of work."

She paused for a moment and waited for Brand to respond.

"Speaking of work," Renata said.

Brand waited for her to go on.

"You called me," she said.

"Maybe I just wanted to see you," Brand said.

"Here?" Ren asked.

Brand frowned. "A nudge."

"Oh, shit," Ren said. "I'll bet you got a nudge. A nudge in your pants."

"Jesus you're crude," Brand said.

"Hey," Renata bumped his shoulder with hers. "Five older brothers and a dad who's a hockey coach. Whadaya expect?"

"Some respect," Brand said. "When have my hunches not paid off."

"Oh, let us count the times," Renata said.

"Stop it," Brand said. "I'm serious."

They stopped at the entrance to the locker rooms. Brand stood in front of the door to the men's and Renata stood a few feet away, poised to enter the women's.

"You still driving that dirty white van thing?" she asked.

"Yeah. It's parked out in the surface lot."

"I'll meet you there," she said.

Brand pushed on the door and took one step before Renata's voice stopped him.

"Brand," she said.

He turned back and raised his eyebrows. "Yeah?"

"Maybe you should leave that one alone." Ren hooked her thumb back in the direction of the workout room.

He smiled. "Don't worry. I'm just a guy, you know?"

Renata's smile didn't reach into her eyes.

In the locker room, Brand peeled off his sweaty clothes and put on a pair of paper thongs. He took a long, hot shower but he dried off quickly. He stood on a clean white towel as he put on jeans and a cotton t-shirt, socks, boots, dark blue sweatshirt, grabbed his blue Nordica nylon coat, stuffed his damp workout clothes into his bag and stepped into the hallway. He paused for a moment, looked back toward the ballroom, leaned against the wall, took a step, paused again, wandered over to the drinking fountain but didn't touch it, and finally took a deep breath and walked back to the ballroom. Dropped his bag on the floor. Out of habit, he pulled his hood up over his head and yanked it down around his face. The light from the old sign outside rippled across the maple flooring and the steady patter of rain mixed with the hum of a big fan somewhere unseen. Brand glimpsed something moving, so he poked his head inside the door and stopped.

The dim light leaking in from outside swelled and receded like a tide. Laci stood right in the middle of the room with her flat, hard belly facing him and her eyes closed. She had stripped off her shirt and shoes. Her bag was sitting on the floor next to the bank of mirrors.

Brand stared, almost hypnotized by a dark tattoo across her chest.

That was the thing. The tattoo.

Its wings extended across her sharp collarbones and onto her corded shoulders, and its legs and feet slipped under the center of her black sports bra as they reached toward the end of her sternum.

As Brand stared, Laci reached up into the air with both hands and balanced on her right foot as she brought her left knee up to her chest. From there, she extended her lower leg till her toes almost touched her hands, all in one, long, graceful movement. She stood like that, in a vertical split, as solid and still as stone. Her muscles were like sculpted iron.

As if it knew he was there, one beaded eye of the beast on her chest regarded Brand with an angry stare. The thing was so much a part of her that Brand could see it breathing. Laci suddenly opened her eyes and immediately clutched her hands over her chest. Her leg dropped back to the ground with the speed of a pouncing spider.

"What the fuck?" she said.

She turned away from him and grabbed her bag. Brand swallowed and watched the muscles in her back as they rippled like sand being defined by an ocean wave. Brand's natural curiosity got the best of him.

"That's a helluva tattoo," Brand said. "Does it have some kind of meaning?"

She leaned over and grabbed a fresh black shirt out of her bag. She glanced at him from under her arm, and her eyes turned as hard as her body.

"No."

"It's very complex," he said.

"It's just one of those things that happens when you think you're in love."

Laci turned around and her eyes focused on Brand, as if she were looking into his soul. She held her shirt around her wrists and stood like a stone, letting Brand's eyes suck in the black thing on her chest.

Brand cocked his head to one side as he puzzled over the black design.

"Looks almost like the Tsimshian Sun God," he said.

She watched him for a moment longer and then pulled her tee-shirt over her head. She yanked on the lower hem to make sure that her chest was completely covered.

"You didn't answer my question," Laci said. Her voice and her eyes softened, as if she was too tired to hold up her hard exterior. Brand tried to regain his composure. His throat was dry and the bones in his upper legs felt like water balloons. Laci expelled a breath of air from between her lips and looked away. She turned her eyes back toward Brand and crossed her arms in front of her body. Brand took a deep breath and tried to relax his shoulders.

"I was just admiring the way you fight"

Laci just stared at him for a moment.

"Yeah, you and every other guy I've ever met."

"Shudokan karate," Brand said.

"Ah," Laci added quickly. She picked up her bag and stared at Brand. Her eyes, large, dark, penetrating. "I could tell you're not a dancer."

Brand nodded and walked away, resisting the urge to glance over his shoulder as the door to the ballroom swung closed behind him.

TWO

By the time Brand got to the parking lot, Renata Rhodes was standing beside the van, cowering under the hood of her rain jacket. Brand opened her door first and she crawled in. He threw his workout bag in the back and settled into the driver's seat.

"What took you so long?" Renata asked.

Brand kept thinking about Laci Keller, about a Tsimshian Sun God, carved black against her white skin. The native American raven. Ravens. Raptors. Gryphons. Vultures. Scavengers. Missing people and bones. He rubbed the back of his neck and then slammed the door of the ugly Chevy van. The inside stank of mildew and rust.

"You look like hell," Renata said.

Brand gripped the steering wheel and then glanced at his hand. Skin like wet pavement against the black plastic. He noted Renata's use of the expletive, felt a sense of her wanting to reach out, knew she wouldn't, but it was there, between them. Brand felt like a ghost. Felt as if he was the rain. Cold, gray and lifeless. A corpse, still walking, as if his body and mind did not know that his soul had died. His stomach turned over and his tongue scraped rough against the roof of his mouth. Renata's voice brought him back from the edge of his thoughts.

"Is it working?"

Brand didn't even pause. "Have you been reading the news?"

"That's not you," she said. "Besides, the full moon was a week ago."

"You tracking the moon now?"

"Mariners won," Ren said. "Don't you read the news?"

"Not if I can help it."

"Geez, Brand. We beat the Yankees. Best game ever played. Six-five in eleven innings. Won the division title. On the night of a full moon. The town was crazy. Where the heck were you?"

"It has nothing to do with that."

"With what? Baseball or the full moon?"

They sat and watched the rain spatter on the windshield, dark drops against a darker night.

"You got a plan?" Renata asked.

Brand frowned. "Plan for?"

"Work."

They sat for a while in silence.

"What day is it?" Brand asked.

"It's Saturday," Ren said. "Oh, yeah. Happy birthday."

Brand grunted. "No plan, really," he said.

"You called me," Ren reminded him.

"I know," he said.

Ren rummaged in her bag and pulled out a black camera body. It looked oversized as her small fingers turned it over. Brand noticed the delicate blue lines along the backs of her hands, the way her wrist bone jutted out where she had broken it as a child. He knew the whole story, of falling off the back of the tractor where she wasn't supposed to play, of how frightened she was to tell her father, of how she forced herself not to cry so that she wouldn't get spanked, of how that was the first time she'd felt fear in her father. From stories she'd told him, he knew the look and feel and smell of the old farm house she'd lived in then, with her uncle and her father. Long nights spent talking with Ren. Nights that might have led somewhere if not for Jule. If not for the accident. If not for a lot of things. Brand stared at the gray skin of his hand. Ren knew more about him than anyone else in the world. Knew the truth about him. It was like having her inside his mind, but gently. Not harsh, like Jule.

"I thought maybe we could go over to Memorial," Ren said.

Brand took a breath, realized he'd been holding it.

Ren continued. "I could take some head shots for your piece on botox," she said. "Then maybe we could get started on the Season of Non-Violence. Maybe follow some of the peace rally kids around. They're doing a Million-Man march in D.C. this weekend." She snapped a fifty millimeter lens onto her Ricoh along with a bounce flash.

"Jule sent me a bottle of Haig and Haig," Brand said.

Renata glanced at him, raised an eyebrow and then busied herself in her camera bag. "So, what's up?"

Brand sat for a minute before he spoke again. "Fletcher's at the U of W doing a symposium on exit wounds."

"Sounds fascinating. Is that all you've got on line right now?"

"News is slow," Brand said. "Seems like everyone is just in a holding pattern till Dash gets here."

"God," Renata almost gasped the word. "I hate the pols. And Clayton Dash is like the worst of the worst."

"You don't even know him," Brand reminded her.

"Don't want to," she said. "He's a career democrat, and since most of the democrats in the senate are corrupt, likely he is too. Worse that he's likely going to be our next VP. Only guy I'm more afraid of than Dash is the President."

"You are way cynical," Brand said, shaking his head. "Besides, Dash plays the house, not the senate." Brand pursed his lips and studied Renata's face for a moment. A beam of late afternoon light traced fine lines next to her eyes and framed her brown hair with an earthy glow.

"Maybe you should hang out with Vreman for a while," Brand said. "He's working the suburban beat. Very posh. No politics. No violence."

"You trying to get rid of me?" she asked.

"Nope. Just trying to figure you out."

"What's his angle?"

"Who's angle?"

"Vremen's."

"Hell if I know."

"Nah," Renata said. She turned and stared out the window. "I'll hang out with you today. Stories follow you around like horseflies. Vremen writes fluff. Who wants to shoot housewives in bunny slippers?"

"Your choice," Brand said. He turned the van down Fifth Avenue and drove along under the monorail toward the Seattle Center. The Space Needle guided them like a lighthouse.

"Why are you frowning?" Renata asked.

Brand tried to shake off the heavy feeling that had descended on him.

"Sorry," he said. "Hey, maybe we'll get to see some Griffs tonight. They'd be just the kind to be hanging around a peace rally. Making trouble."

"God, I hope not," Renata said.

"What? This coming from a veteran of two gulf wars?"

"The Gryphons give me the creeps."

"They're just a cult," Brand assured her. "Like the vampires and the shredders and the Latter Day Saints."

She shot him a killer look and he chuckled. Despite her sometimes crude behavior, she took pride in her conversion to Mormonism, and Brand knew that she didn't like to be teased about it. He'd made that mistake last time they'd worked together.

"What are you shooting today?" Brand asked, changing the subject.

Renata hung the big Ricoh over her neck and rummaged in her bag for a moment. Her hair hung down, tan streaked with darker browns. It covered her face and swung back and forth as the van lurched around a corner.

"I've got two-hundred in the Ricoh. Color balanced. And a roll of Panachrome in the AE-1. I'll shoot that out this afternoon and then switch to four-hundred black and white. And maybe eight-hundred in the Ricoh."

"I expect most of the good shots will be after dark," Brand said.

"Yeah. I'm a lousy night shooter."

"You won an award for long-exposure," Brand reminded her. "That's why I called you in for this gig." He pulled into a parking spot and stuck his press pass on the dash.

"Well, maybe you can get the demonstrators to hold really, really still for me."

They got out and Renata pulled her parka around her camera. Her black bag bumped against her hip as she trotted to keep up with Brand's long strides. Brand slipped his hood up over his head and stuck his hands in his pockets. His fingers closed around the little micro recorder. A single cassette could hold up to two hours of recorded material. Greatest invention ever.

By the time they got to the main building, the afternoon had gone silver-gray, but the warehouse-sized building that housed the international food pavilion was lit up like mid-day.

"I don't think I've ever seen this many people here," Renata said.

"You need to come tomorrow afternoon for the Polka festival."

"Bet this is a different crowd," she mused. The indoor courtyard was a sea of spiked coats and sopping sweatshirts, low-rider pants and navel rings. Nearby, a blue Mohawk waited in line for a chance at German pocket breads stuffed with ground beef and cabbage, a skinny shredder counted out quarters and pennies to pay for phad thai to split with his vampire girlfriend, and a group of granolas sat sipping Chai tea. One of the girls waved at a friend across the way and Renata gagged at the wad of black hair under her arm.

"Yuk," Renata said. "Buy a razor."

Brand poked her with his elbow and she glared at him.

"Look," he said. "There are some of your friends." The crowd parted as a small group of black, leather clad warriors strode along the main walkway. They all wore dark glasses and heavy boots, like a gang of bikers. Renata started to move toward them, but Brand grabbed her arm.

"They're harmless, right?" Renata said. "Just another cult."

Renata brought her camera up and popped the flash three times before Brand could stop her. The black leather kids didn't even miss a beat, they just turned like a flock of evil geese and bore down on Renata. The soles of their boots slapped the tile floor and their capes flapped like wings.

"Oh, shit," Renata said.

"Shit is right," Brand added.

"Stay calm," Renata whispered. "Don't let them see you sweat."

Brand clenched his teeth and cursed Ren under his breath, but he shoved his hands into his pockets and waited with her in the middle of the concourse.

The point man was a kid with a sparse stubble of beard that looked like mange. The bridge of his black-rimmed dark glasses rested on a beaked nose. He was as tall as Brand, maybe six feet, but lanky. He walked with a lurch in his shoulders, almost as if he imagined he was an ape. As he swaggered along, drops of water flicked out and left shining trails along the faux marble.

Brand watched the thin film of rain as it ran off the slick leather like blood from a slit throat.

People nearby stepped back and made a human amphitheater as the kid slowed down and stopped in front of Brand, holding out his arms so that his cape billowed like the wings of a bat. His group stopped behind him, posing like tough runway models, hands on hips, hips thrust to the side, heads cocked and jaws set. The kid's right hand man was a girl with tiny round sunglasses that fit tight into her eye sockets, making her gaunt face look like a scull. A long-scar on her cheek and shaved eyebrows, and only a light fuzz for hair finished off the illusion. The guy to her left was a sweet-faced boy with tangled blond hair. His dark glasses rested on rosy cheeks, but as he turned his head, the light flashed off razor blades that dangled from his ears, and Brand could see a black tattoo of cryptic running runes that ran up his neck and into his scalp. The boy bared his lips and spit on the ground, right in front of the table of earth muffins, and Brand caught a glimpse of the boy's pink tongue as it pressed up against an empty space where two front teeth should have been. In an instant, the cherub became a gargoyle, and then returned again. Behind the first three, five more gang members stood staring at Brand with wet, shining faces and twitching lips. All eyes were obscured behind dark lenses.

The kid waited. Brand's fingers touched the recorder in his pocket. He found the record button and pressed it lightly, felt it click.

"You two got a problem?" the kid said. A little lisping, sibilant sound tickled Brand's cheek, but he focused on the kid's face and kept stern and serious. His heart was pounding but he knew enough to stay cool on the outside.

"I'm doing a story on pigeons. Not very interesting though. Pigeons are just pests, you know. You guys know anything about pigeons? Or pests?"

The skin just above the kid's shades wrinkled and his leather gloves groaned as he balled his hands into fists. Renata stood her ground with her hand in her bag, clutching the Canon, finger hovering above the shutter control.

"Mister, you got some kind of death wish?" The lisp whispered out through parted lips that gave just a glimpse of pointed teeth, filed to an unnatural sharpness. The pause between them punctuated the unnatural silence of the pavilion. The kid leaned forward just a bit. His brow wrinkled with a frown. "What's the matter with you anyway. You look like a dead man."

Brand brought his hands out of his pockets and crossed his arms across his chest. His stomach shook and the muscles behind his shoulder blades ached.

"Yeah," he said. "I already got my death wish. What about you."

"We live on death," he said.

"Ah," Brand said. "So, you're not pigeons after all."

"Gryphons," said the kid.

"And you must be the head Griff," Brand said.

A soft chuckle rose out of the group as the kid turned and smiled at his girl. She grinned and showed a set of nice, white pointed teeth, but Brand noticed an etched line across her lower left canine. Parents that could afford braces. Little girl hadn't taken care of her teeth though, and decay set in along the bands. Now she was hanging out with the trikers in black leather. Mom and dad were probably holed up in a quarter of a million dollar shack in Bothell wondering where little Becky was. Maybe they weren't even home from work yet. Attorneys with latch key kids. A BMW in the driveway and a daughter hanging out with hookers and drug dealers.

The sweet-faced boy with razor-blade earrings looked Renata up and down and then licked his lips. Brand felt Renata press against his arm.

"There ain't no head Griff," the kid said. He stepped up close to Brand and then turned his body slightly so that he passed by like a busker squeezing by a turnstile in the underground. The others followed him; the sweet boy pushing against Ren's body as he passed. Brand stiffened his back and closed his eyes. The girl lagged a bit, brushing her fingers against Brand's leg.

"Whew," Brand said. "You guys are rank."

The girl turned and smiled, letting Brand's eyes linger on her pointed teeth. "Well, we are Griffs," she said. A burly Griff yanked on her arm and she skipped a step to catch up with her tribe.

"Cute kid," Renata said as she collapsed against Brand's chest.

"They file their teeth," Brand said.

"They scare the shit out of me."

"But they're all so cherubic," Brand said. He wiped a bead of sweat from his upper lip.

"Is it hot in here?" Renata asked. "Or did I just shoot up straight ephedrine."

"Got the shakes?" Brand asked. He stuck his own trembling hands into his pockets. They both watched as the Gryphons opened a path to the south exit.

When the kid got to the double doors, he hit both crash bars with his hands and threw the doors wide open. As he did, the back of his coat fanned out, and Brand froze. Emblazoned in bas relief in the shining leather was a Tsimshian Sun God, trickster deity from Native American lore.

"Jesus," Brand said.

"What is it?" Renata asked. Her body was stiff and upright again.

"Look at that marking on the back of Riff's coat."

"Who's Riff?" Renata asked.

The head Gryphon stepped out into the night, followed by his flock, and the doors slammed closed behind them. Even the vamp let go of a breath as the room slowly came back to life. The chatter rose steadily, but there was an undercurrent of tension in it, the aftermath of a few thousand straight shots of adrenaline.

"Who's Riff?" Renata asked again.

"Nobody is Riff," Brand said. "I just called him that. Ever seen West Side Story?"

"Oh," she said, nodding.

"Did you see the thing on the back of his coat?"

Renata shook her head. "What was it?"

"Kind of an emblem. Native American totem."

"So?"

"Second time today I've seen it."

"Does that mean something?"

Brand was still staring at the doors.

"Maybe."

"Like what?"

Brand just shook his head. He glanced at Renata. She was still staring at the doors, but when she felt his gaze, she turned and studied his face.

"Where did you see it before?" she asked.

"Um," Brand pressed his lips together and shifted his gaze back toward the doors.

Renata's eyes prowled Brand's face like a cat watching a juicy bird.

"Come on," she said. "Fess up."

Brand started walking toward the doors and Renata followed him a few steps back.

"Do you trust my instincts?" he asked.

Renata's shoulders dropped an inch. "Oh, no."

"I smell a story."

"God," Renata said, staring at the metal rafters. "Why do I do this?"

"Because," Brand said. "You're good. You have a gift. Now, come on. Let's see where the little birds are off to."

THREE

Brand and Renata stepped outside and followed the flashing lights to their left.

"Looks like a circus," Renata said. They were looking at a dozen or more cruisers lit up like Christmas. Blue and red flashes lit up the windows along the base of the needle and bounced off the flaring SkyLine level a hundred feet above.

"Follow me," Brand said. He skirted the action wide and headed toward one of the concrete towers that supported the monorail. The single track trains ran from the base of the needle to Fifth Avenue just about three blocks from the Y every hour from seven till midnight. Been doing that since the World's Fair in the sixties, back when the Fred Astaire Dance Studio was the hub of ballroom dancing, and Arthur Murray's ran a far second place, back when Eddie Brand was still a struggling dance director, pressing his pelvis up against blue-haired ladies to get them to buy three-thousand dollar dance programs so he could squeak out a living for Sheryl and his little boy, back when they lived in a little downtown apartment with a shared bathroom down the hall. Brand wondered sometimes if he could still find that old building somewhere downtown, and wondered if he would recognize it if he did. Maybe he walked by it every day.

A steady sheet of rainwater coursed off the tracks above, and as they ducked underneath the raised passenger platform, they heard the grinding scream of an arriving coach as the brakes caught hold and slowed it down. They stepped out on the far side of the needle's wide base and nearly tripped over a mess of cables that looked like a giant bowl of spilled black king snakes. A white truck sat squatting on its stabilizers with its radio mast sticking up in the air and the side door wide open. The swirling blue and red lights hit Brand in the eyes and he winced. Over by the van, a sleek brunette in a Givenchy trench coat stopped and stared for a moment, and then waved.

"Ugh," Renata whispered. Brand smiled.

The brunette came over in seven big strides, heels clicking like typewriter keys on the black pavement. As she walked, she held her hood up above her hair.

"Ever notice how her hair never moves," Renata said.

The Givenchy girl came right up to Brand and smiled with big, white teeth and sparkling eyes. "Hi, Charlie," she said.

"Krystal," Brand replied. "We interrupting a big social event?"

"I do hard news now," she replied. "Who's your little friend?"

"You remember Renata," Brand said.

"Oh, of course," Krystal said. She let go of one side of her hood and reached out with a kid leather glove. Renata barely touched her as they shook. Krystal's hand shot back up to her hood and rescued the lagging side so that it would not touch her dark, brown helmet of hair.

"So, what did you do so bad that they sent you out here today?" Brand asked.

"Don't you have your scanner on?" she asked. She glanced at Renata as if she was exchanging a sympathetic womanly insight.

"Scanner's on the fritz," Brand said.

Krystal glanced up into the drizzle. The graceful curves of the skeletal Space Needle towered above them. The saucer-shaped top was almost lost in the mist, five hundred feet above.

"Jumper," she said. "He's made it to the outer edge, beyond the retaining fence."

"That's a hell of a note," Brand said. "I can't even remember the last time we had a jumper up there."

"Nineteen seventy-eight," Krystal said. "Only two before that. Both in seventy four. After the seventy eight jump, they put the suicide cage around it."

"Did you cover all those jumps too?" Renata asked.

Krystal shook off the insult like a duck shakes off water. "I was in fourth grade," she said. She turned back toward Brand. "You're looking good. Well, better, anyway. I guess. Been working out?"

"Yeah," Brand said. "At the Y."

"Got my message then," Krystal said. "See anything you like?"

"A tattoo."

Krystal nodded and then tucked her chin against her chest. Brand noticed the cords in her neck standing out. Thought of her as another one of those vain women that worked out till she almost looked like a man.

"Well, whatever," she said. "Anyway, you're really not looking good. You gotta stop drinking that shit concoction of yours." She paused. "Ever see Jule around? I haven't seen her in ages."

Renata winced. Brand kept a stoic look on his face, but inside he could feel the sting.

"No. We don't stay in contact."

"I heard she's getting re-married."

"I wish her well," Brand said.

"Well, I've gotta go," Krystal said. "Let's do lunch sometime."

"Sure," Brand said. "I'll call you."

"Call me Wednesday," she said. "I'll fit you in." She winked at him.

"Yeah," Brand said. "I'll do that."

"Great," she said. She smiled and moistened her lips. She took a step backward as the conversation paused for a moment.

"Hey, Krystal," Brand said.

"Yes?"

Brand tried to settle his heart down and get back to business.

"Did you see a bunch of scary looking kids go by?"

"You mean the Gryphons?"

"Yeah."

"Uh-huh," she nodded. "They're standing over in the peace garden. Waiting to see what happens."

"Figures," Brand said.

Krystal took another step backward, smiled at Brand and winked again, and then turned and skipped lightly between the snaked cables. She stopped at the van and peered inside.

"She's a slippery vixen," Renata said. "And she's got a hard on for you."

"Can't imagine why," Brand said.

"Because you're so damn unbreakable," Renata said. "Women find that appealing. Even if you do work out at the Y and drink silver till you turn blue."

"Even just lunch with her could be dangerous," Brand said.

"Lunch with her is code for hump. She wants to do you."

"Not in a million years," Brand said. "Who would be that stupid?"

"Some guys are."

"Come on," Brand said. He stepped across a cable and peered around the corner of the low building that formed the base of the tower. Renata stuck her head around his shoulder so she could see as well.

"Where are all the cops?" she asked. The cars sat vacant. The only human activity was around the news van. Brand walked along the wall and stepped around the next corner and then pulled up short. A line of city cops stood staring up into the rain. The security lights along the top of the base gift shop glimmered on the row of dark blue parkas. Brand took a step back, but one of the cops saw him and started over. Brand froze. Renata stayed behind him with her camera ready.

"Is this the peace rally?" Brand asked. "I'm here to cover the rally. On assignment for the P.I."

"I know you," the cop said.

"Oh, hey. Captain Devers. What's going on?"

"Jumper," he said. "You can't be here. Now, get back where you belong before I have to get someone to escort you."

"You sound all police-like," Brand said.

"I am all police-like," Devers said.

"KING 5 is here," Brand said.

"They've got an exclusive," Devers said.

"I see Marshall's wife is covering the story," Brand said.

"Yeah, whatever. Now, get lost."

"She invited me to lunch," Brand said. Devers' eyes narrowed. "How about you?" Brand asked. "You ever been to lunch with Krystal Marshall?"

Devers stepped up to Brand. Their chests almost touched. A drip of rain hovered on the end of the captain's nose. Brand stared at it.

"If you don't get the fuck off this piece of ground right now, I'll grind you under the heel of my boot like a piece of shit. Got it?"

Brand touched the recorder in his pocket and nodded. "I got it," he said. He stepped back and tripped over Renata. She hit the auto shutter and took ten frames of the captain's glare as she backed away. Brand caught her arm and pulled her along. Devers watched them go with his hands on his hips.

"Maybe he has had lunch with Krystal Marshall," Renata said. She kept chattering as she trotted along behind Brand. "What's the record? Didn't Wilt the Stilt say that he had sex with twenty thousand women? Let's see, three hundred sixty five days in a year, maybe three hundred sixty lunch-humps, jeepers, it'll take her almost sixty years at that rate. Is that right?"

"Wilt did two a day," Brand said.

"How did he do that and still have legs to jump?"

"Wilt didn't have to jump. Not in basketball anyway."

Brand pulled her up short and they stopped to listen to Krystal talk to the bright light of the hand held. She stared into the camera with a look of concern and spoke slowly and clearly. The cameraman stood like a statue, and the tech in the van hunched over a thousand blinking lights. The red and blue and white flashes from the patrol car shot out like shafts through the drizzle. Krystal's voice was clear but soft.

"Sources within the department indicate that this young man may be one of the gang members called the Gryphons. His black leather garb is consistent with the culture of that gang, although there is no clear indication about why he is perched in such a precarious and dangerous situation."

She paused and nodded as the anchor asked her a question, and then continued.

"This does not appear to be related to the peace rally scheduled to begin here tonight, Robert. But certainly this does throw a dark shadow over the rally itself. Of course, we'll stay with this situation at the Space Needle in downtown Seattle until it is resolved. This is Krystal Marshall, live, at the Seattle Center. Back to you, Robert."

"Krystal's in her element," Renata said.

"So are we," Brand said. "Birds of a feather."

"Gryphons again," Renata said. She stared at the puddles on the pavement.

"You don't spook that easy," Brand said.

"They spook me."

"Get out."

"No, really. Even in the gulf, at least we felt reasonably safe at night. I mean, there was all this open space. Here, in the city, it's like these things can just lurk in the shadows. I hate it. And they bite. I hate things that bite."

Brand cleared his throat a bit.

"Sorry," Ren whispered. They stopped in a dark, narrow walkway between three rhodies and a concrete wall.

"Can't you just blind them with your flash?" Brand said.

"Don't tease me, Brand. They give me the chills. I wish I'd never heard of them."

"Yeah, well, come on," Brand said. "We've got an assignment to do, and I need the money. Besides, the Griffs are just a bunch of kids. Harmless cult. Right?"

"You mean you'd rather cover a peaceful march than a jumper?" Renata asked.

Brand nodded.

"Suicide is better cash," she reminded him.

"Nothing like the thought of someone else's death to perk you up," Brand said.

"If he jumps, we'll get good coverage."

Brand just about ran into Krystal as he turned to go. She took a couple of skipping steps backward to get out of the way.

"Brand," she said. "Everyone is looking for you."

"Why?" he asked. She was still holding her hood up over her lacquered hair, so she had to turn her entire upper body to look down the empty sidewalk. As she did, the light from behind her cut through the rain and shimmered around her cowling like a halo. She turned back to Brand. She bit on her lip and her brow furrowed.

"The jumper wants to talk," Krystal said. She turned and looked down the sidewalk again.

"To me?" Brand asked.

"Don't get cocky," Krystal snipped. She turned back toward Brand again and he tried to hold her eyes with his. The darkness left only a thin edge of blue around her wide, black pupils.

"Why won't he talk to you?" Brand asked.

"Who said he wouldn't?"

"Dunno," Brand said. *Does he know me*, Brand thought. *And how did he know I was here?* He pressed his lips together and tried to slip by, but Krystal's body blocked the way. She was gazing down the walkway again.

"Thinking about Griffs?" Brand asked.

She nodded, almost absently.

"Forget those boys," Brand warned her. "Those guys are way out of your league."

Krystal's head snapped back and she glared at Brand as if he had stepped on her foot. "Don't tell me what's in my league and out of my league," she snapped.

Renata bobbed around behind Brand, trying to get a look around his shoulder.

Brand put his hands up and pulled his chin back. "OK, OK. Sorry." He paused and let Krystal settle down. "What about this jumper. Why aren't you doing the story? You've got the crew and the cameras and the whole schmeal. Take it."

Krystal sighed. "He doesn't want a cop or a mike or a camera. Come on Brand. You're a journalist, aren't you? You gonna pass up an interview with a jumper?"

Brand closed his eyes and pinched the bridge of his nose. "No. I guess not. Rhodes goes with me though."

"Whatever," Krystal said.

Brand followed her. He shot a glance back at Renata, who was grinning like a chimp. Brand narrowed his eyes and Ren stuck out her tongue.

"Do they have a name for this kid," Brand asked.

Krystal turned her hood around a bit so that Brand could see her head move back and forth.

"Uh, uh," she grunted. "Just some punk. But he's got the cops spooked. They won't go near him."

"They think he's serious?"

"Guess so." Krystal glanced over at Renata. "Don't be popping any pictures up there, honey."

Brand spoke up for her. "Ren knows what she's doing."

Krystal backed out of the way and Ren followed Brand over to the main entrance. Devers was guarding the big double doors. He opened the door to let a couple leave. The guy was a suit, and the tight skirt wrapped around a full body looked like his mom. Brand waited for the couple to go by. The skirt watched him with dull eyes, but the suit just ignored all of them, walking out through the mess of cables and strobe lights as if it were just another day at the office. Devers stepped aside and let Krystal pass, but he grabbed Brand by the arm and yanked him close. Devers' body radiated cold from under his dark slicker, and little drops of rain fell from the front of his hood. He smelled like wet rubber.

"Mind your manners up there," Devers hissed. Brand glanced back into the darkness toward the suit and his dame. He wondered if there was a group of raptors out there in the night, waiting for some easy prey. Brand turned his head back toward Devers again. The big cop had him pulled so close, all Brand could see was bushy black eyebrows and shiny, pitted nose. Devers' breath smelled like smoke and garlic, maybe a little grain alcohol to boot. Or maybe Devers had been eating escargot.

"I'm not going to dinner," Brand reminded him.

Devers shook him a bit. "Don't fuck with me tonight," Devers said. "And don't be encouraging any headlines. You're only going up there because I say so, got it?"

"Don't worry about me," Brand said. "I'm not going to be pushy." Brand almost choked on his choice of words.

Brand tried to move on, but Devers pulled him back again. The two of them blocked the door. Krystal paused just inside and carefully released her hood. She stood there dripping water on the marble, while Renata was trapped outside.

"Hey, do you mind?" Renata said.

Devers glanced at her and then turned his attention back to Brand.

"You're a cocky son-of-a-bitch," Devers said. He shoved his face right up to Brand's. "You got a reputation for making stories."

"It's unearned," Brand said. "I just have a knack for being in the right place at the right time."

"Don't be fucking with this jumper," Devers said.

"He a friend of yours?" Brand asked.

Devers pushed Brand away. Renata slipped by the big cop and waited for a moment while Brand readjusted his coat.

"Devers doesn't like you," Renata said.

"Guess lunch with him is out of the question," Brand said. He winked at Krystal as he spoke, but her stare was vacant. The ring of the lift bell echoed through the lobby like a death toll and Brand shivered. "Damn stupid night to be climbing around the top of the Space Needle," he said. The outer doors slid open and an instant later the glass inner door parted as well.

A cop waited for them in the elevator and punched the button for the observatory as if he were a bellman. Brand stood with his hands clasped in front of his body, tapping his thumbs together. The lift popped out of the lower deck and Krystal and Renata stared at the city as if fanned out below them. The cop watched the progress bar above the door. Brand stared at Krystal's dark hair and then shook off his juvenile fantasy. No one said a word, and the car was silent till it hit the top and pinged its arrival. They took the stair up to the outer O-deck.

"I'm gonna stay right back here," the cop said, pausing at the end of the exit corridor. "This guy gets spooked easy."

Krystal stepped out into the night air but stayed under the awning, just outside the door. Her hands were thrust deep inside her coat pockets and her face was serious.

"You got any way to take a shot without flashing all over the place?" Brand whispered to Renata.

She shook her head.

"Well, get ready, just in case I get the chance to talk him back over the fence. But for God's sake don't take a shot before he gets safe on this side."

"Don't worry about me. Just be careful."

"I'm not going over," Brand said.

"I mean, don't do anything stupid," she said. She looked worried.

"Christ," Brand said. He rubbed his hands together and gazed into the darkness. The rain pelted down like ice and a sharp wind blew in off the sound without the buildings and trees to block it. Brand could feel the tower swaying under his feet.

"Crappy night to be camped out up here," Brand said.

"You going to go out there?" Krystal snapped. "Or are you just going to stay here and do a weather report?"

Brand gave her a low, soft growl and then slipped the lanyard for the recorder around his neck. He realized it was still on, still recording, taking everything in.

He stepped into the rain and sensed Renata's cat-like prowl as she followed him, but he stayed focused on the dark night around him. Harsh spotlights cut through the drizzle like knives, and the steel wire that kept O-Deck visitors from leaning too far over the edge glistened black like fresh blood. Locals that remembered the jumpers in the seventies called the wire fence the suicide cage.

"Jule and I used to come up here," Brand whispered as he circled the platform.

Renata's hushed voice rose out of the darkness behind him. "You always talk about her like you guys spent your whole lives together. What was it, a couple of weeks?"

"Ten months, on and off." Brand shut his mouth and touched the fence. He pressed his face up close to the wires, one near his forehead, the next one down near his mouth. Beyond the fence, the light gleamed off wet, black leather. The kid perched right on the edge of the platform, staring at the triple strands of barbed wire that looked as if they were there to give the jumper just a last little bit of punishment. His black leather clothes melted into the night. He was invisible except for his head.

"Hey," Brand said quietly. The wind whipped his voice away, so he said it again, only louder.

"Hey. I'm Brand. Charlie Brand."

The kid turned his head just a bit. "Who's that with you," he said.

"It's my partner," Brand said. "I told her to stay back. I'll send her back inside if you want."

"No, that's okay. Just tell her to stay back."

"No problem."

The kid turned his head away again and stared out over the city. The rain kept visibility low, but they could still see the fringes of towering business district in the distance.

"Someone said you wanted to talk," Brand said.

"You a reporter?"

"Yeah."

"TV?"

"No. I do print."

"For who?"

"For whoever pays. I'm a freelance."

The kid looked back at him and nodded.

"Wish I could do that," he said. "Nobody bossing you around."

"Yeah. That's what people think. You'd be surprised though."

"You just come up here to chat, Mr. Brand? Or are you ready for a story?"

"I'd like to do a story on a kid who decided not to jump."

The kid laughed. "I'm not going to jump, Mr. Brand," he said. "If I was going to jump, I would've done it already. I changed my mind back at about four o'clock."

"Well, great," Brand said. "Maybe we could do this interview back in the lobby then."

The kid shook his head. "As soon as I come back over, they're gonna lock me up. I'd rather jump than be locked up. The cops take me, I'm worse than dead."

"It's not that bad," Brand said. "I've been in lockup before. Sounds worse than it is. TV gives everything a bad rap."

The kid shook his head again. "I'm not talking about lockup," he said. "Lockup doesn't scare me." He was staring off into the distance again.

"So, what does?" Brand asked. "The cops?"

The kid laughed again. A short burst, almost as if he was puking.

"Cops are stupid," he said. His voice almost cracked, and Brand could see his eyes glistening. Not with rain either.

"Just what is it that I can do for you?" Brand asked. He squirmed under his heavy coat as a trickle of cold rain found its way down his back.

"I've been thinking," the kid said. "You know, I've been up here all afternoon, and I keep thinking that I don't want to die. You know what I mean?"

"Uh-huh."

"Well, I got this idea."

"Go on."

The kid tipped his head and squinted at Brand.

"But you gotta come out here," he said.

Brand smiled and shook his head. "There is no way on God's green earth that I am going to climb out on those I-beams."

The kid smiled.

"Oh, I think you will."

"And why do you think that?"

"Cause I'm gonna tell you everything about the Raven. And then you're gonna write it, and we're gonna put him out of business. And then I'll be safe."

Brand stood there waiting. He realized that his right leg was bouncing up and down, but he couldn't stop it. He looked up at the top of the wire fence. A flashlight beam played across his back and he could see the cop back by the entrance to the stairwell, standing next to Krystal with his MagnaLight held up by his shoulder. Renata was squatting down a meter away shaking her head. Rain dripped into her eyes and hung on her lips.

"Don't," she mouthed.

"You just stay right there," Brand whispered. "Don't move no matter what, and don't snap at anything unless I come over this fence with that kid in tow. Got it?"

Renata just nodded.

Brand cleared his throat and hoisted himself up onto the fence. His toes found the top of the concrete wall and the wires dug into the flesh of his hands. The thin cables were hard and tight, and didn't even bend under his weight as he climbed them like a ladder. He swung his legs over the other side and hung for a moment. The wind pushed him back and forth and slipped inside his coat like the cold hand of death reminding him that it was there. He stared down at the framework of beams, looking for a place to put his feet. The spider-like structure of the outer frame looked like toothpicks against the vast blackness of the space beyond. Brand's stomach flopped over as he adjusted to the fact that there was nothing but five hundred feet of salty air between his head and the blacktop.

"Don't just hang there," the kid said. "Have a seat. And welcome to my world."

FOUR

October 13, 1995 — 9:12PM

The kid crouched on a slick metal grating like a monkey in a tree. Brand settled in with his back against the O-Deck wall and made sure that his recorder was outside his jacket. Every gust of wind reminded him that he was outside the security perimeter, and he had to suppress an urge to just step out into the void, wondering if he'd survive a fall like that, wondered how it was for the kid, how he felt, perched up here like a gargoyle.

"What's your name?" Brand asked.

"Kenny."

Kenny tossed his head. His matted hair slapped the back of his black leather coat and his eyes flicked toward the stairwell. Brand turned his head and glanced over the railing, back toward the safety of the main deck and the rectangle frame of light where the cop stood waiting. He was no more than a ghost, obscured by the annoying rain that blew across the tower, catching the light like millions of dreary, black fireflies. Krystal stuck her dark brunette head out the door, paused for a moment, and then disappeared inside again.

"Is that Krystal over there with the cop?" he asked.

"You know her?" Brand asked.

"She's my step mom," Kenny said.

Brand's back suddenly became glued to the wall and he felt a trickle of sweat drip down from his armpit to his waist. Funny thing was, he wasn't hot at all. Cold and clammy was more like it.

"You're Senator Marshall's son?" Brand said. His voice almost stuck in his throat.

"They don't know," Kenny said. "If they did, the whole damn department would be out here. Probably have helicopters, fire trucks, paramedics. The whole city'd be mobile."

"Does Krystal know?" Brand asked.

Kenny nodded. "I asked for the press, the cops sent her up. That's just great, right. Of all the crummy newscasters in the city, I pick my step mom."

Brand felt his skin crawling and his tongue went dry.

"Something's not right here," he said.

"Damn right," Kenny said.

"No, I mean, when things start lining up like this, it's a really bad sign."

The kid's eyes gleamed in the dim light. His lips parted slightly and Brand noticed hard lines around his face. They sat there, staring at each other, letting the rain pelt against their eyes. Brand licked his lips and swallowed the moisture.

"How old are you?" Brand asked. He knew full well that Kenny was a senior in high school. Had been captain of the football team and star quarterback as a junior. Not much in the papers about him last season though.

"Eighteen," Kenny said.

"You took Lakeshore to state two years ago," Brand noted.

Kenny turned his gaze back out toward the city.

"Yeah," he said. "That was a long time ago. Kid stuff."

"What happened?" Brand asked. He shifted his weight a bit and felt his stomach flip as his mind reeled out into the open space around him. He wondered how Kenny could have crouched up here for hours on end without his legs going to sleep. And he couldn't shake the nagging feeling that a bunch of lines were converging around this spot, this time. Krystal Marshall and Devers and Kenny and the Gryphons and Renata skulking around in the shadows and Brand himself somehow getting connected in here, and someone else, or something else. Brand got a sudden urge to just get up and go. Let someone else get this kid's sob story. Brand's internal scanners were off the chart, but he took a deep breath and held his ground.

Kenny stared out into the dark rain for a long time, like a deer waiting for the forest to quiet down after a scare. It was as if time meant nothing for him. Brand's bad gut feeling deepened. *Time means nothing when time is up.* Brand had a lot of questions, and he knew he didn't have much time to ask. He opted to keep his mouth shut and listen. Kenny paid him off.

"I want you to know something right off the bat," the kid said. "I'm not going to jump, okay?"

"Yeah, that's good," Brand said. *I'm a fuckin' reporter, not a psychoanalyst*, he said to himself.

"I mean, I came up here to jump, or maybe I thought I did. I don't know. I mean, I got out here, all ready to jump, and then I lost momentum, it's like I just got real tired." He paused for a moment. "That ever happen to you, Mister Brand?"

"Yeah. Happens to everyone, I suppose. At one time or another."

Kenny nodded. "I still have this urge to jump though. It's like some kind of curiosity thing, or a compulsion. Like some kind of voice that says 'just do it, step off the edge' and then everything will be real quiet and peaceful, no pressure, no strain, just floating free like a balloon."

More like a watermelon, Brand thought. A whole series of splattering special effects ran through his head. He shook them off and concentrated on Kenny's mouth. It was moving, but Brand couldn't hear the words at first, but his ears perked up automatically when Kenny reached into his coat and took a swig out of a flat, brass flask. He held it out toward Brand like a lure.

"Drink?" he asked. Even through the rain and the wind, Brand could feel the sour, dusty taste of Scotch whiskey on his tongue, and his eyes even watered a bit. He shook his head, even though his body ached for it. Kenny slipped the flask back inside his coat.

"So," he said. "Like I said, I got hooked up with these guys, the Griffs. My dad thought it was a rebellious phase. He's got all these criminal psycho theories and all this rational drivel that explains it all, you know? Like I'm just some kind of an idiot, and I got some loose wiring that needs to be fixed. I'm broken. A mistake. Just need to be brainwashed a bit and I'll be right back to normal. Top five percent of my class, letter in three sports, maybe turn out for the debate team and get my picture taken with the nerds and brains. Then he can show me off to his friends again. Me and Krystal. Trophy boy and trophy woman. It really pisses me off."

"The Gryphons," Brand said. The creepy feeling came back. It was as if he had his ear on an invisible train track, and the rusty steel was singing to him, telling him that a train was coming, from somewhere. Maybe fast, maybe slow. His instincts said to run, his dumb persistence made him stay.

Kenny's back suddenly stiffened. Brand saw the kid get about an inch taller, and even in the darkness he could see the tendons in Kenny's neck sticking out. Brand could feel it too. A presence. They sat like that for a long time, frozen, listening, straining into the darkness with whatever senses were available to them. Brand felt the cold rain trickling down his cheeks and under his collar. He could smell the sour stench of pigeons and seagulls, taste the tin-foil acid of fear in his saliva. Darkness kept him from seeing clearly close up, and the rain obscured most of the world beyond, but Brand's inner eyes could still clearly see past the edge of the I-beams and barbed wire, where streets fanned out in angular criss-crosses, the by-product of confused and warring amateur architects that struggled to form a city a hundred years earlier from the forested slopes around Elliot Bay. Denny way cut straight west from above the Interstate down to Elliot along the waterfront, stoplights clicking from red to green, headlights drifting slowly toward the bay, passing a contradictory stream of red taillights going toward the hills. From the freeway, Stewart cut toward the Northwest at an almost perfect forty-five, setting the stage for the lower business district from the needle to Pike Place Market at the base of the giant towers of downtown Seattle, stacked between the freeway and the sound like random stalagmites. At Pike Street, the streets shifted again, following the gradual curve of the bay, until they reached Yessler and the Kingdome, squatting in the distance like a sleeping white turtle. A siren squawked and the blast of a lonely car horn drifted up from the streets below. Yet, in among all this, something else hovered nearby, raising bumps on the back of Brand's neck, and stirring Kenny into a state of anxiety.

"How many people did you bring up here?" Kenny asked. His voice was low and hoarse, but loud enough so that Brand could hear it.

"Just Krystal and the cop in the elevator, and my partner Renata."

"Who's Renata?'

"She's harmless," Brand said. He waited while Kenny sat peering into the night. Brand's heart pounded and his chest felt like a furnace.

"What's spooking you?" Brand whispered. Kenny shook his head.

"If you knew what I knew," he said. "You'd be spooked too." He glanced over at Brand and his eyes narrowed again. "You can feel it too, can't you?"

Brand nodded.

"We're gonna die up here," Kenny said.

"No," Brand replied, but his mouth was still dry and his words lacked conviction. His stomach shuddered and he was suddenly aware of the gentle swaying of the immense tower. *Flow with the wind,* he told himself. *Be the willow and bend.*

"Why don't we get back over the fence now," Brand said. He felt fear, not even sure if he should be afraid. Still wondering if that kind of fall was the ultimate cure. Knowing that, even if it wasn't, it would hurt like hell and be hard to explain.

"I feel safer out here," Kenny replied. He was staring out toward the deep blackness of Elliot Bay again. "You don't look so good."

"Tell me," Brand said.

"Tell you what?"

"Whatever it is that you called me up here for."

Kenny shook his head. "I can't."

"Christ, kid," Brand said. "I'm out here on the ledge with you. Five hundred feet above the ground with no net. You got me here, now tell me what it is."

Kenny took a deep breath and bobbed up and down a bit, chewing on his lower lip. Brand slipped down into more of a sitting position and tried to get his right leg to stop shaking, but it had a mind of its own.

"Having an ex-cop politico task force guy for a dad is tough," Kenny said.

Brand kept his mouth shut and eyes on the kid.

"You know?" Kenny said, shifting his eyes toward Brand for just a second. Brand nodded. The kid turned away again, but kept talking.

"Everything is black and white with him. And anyone that doesn't think like he does is wrong. It's like everyone is either a good guy or a bad guy. So, if I didn't think like he did, I had to keep it shut in, you know? Or I would be a bad guy. He could kill me just with a look. I love that guy, I mean, he's my dad, and he's tough. He's like a hero in this town. Larger than life. I see him on TV, and he's so serious and tough looking. That's how I see him. At home, he's just a guy that eats dinner and then shuts himself in his office. He never even came to any of my games. He

51

probably doesn't even know that I didn't turn out this last season."

Kenny sighed and his body relaxed.

"I was a tough kid in school. A jock. So I figured I could do anything. I was invincible, you know? So, how could a little toke of weed or a few beers hurt me? They didn't. So how about a little cocaine. Hey, I can handle the rush, right? And uppers made me a better ball player. And a little meth helped me calm down afterwards. All the while, these guys, the Griffs, were selling me a little stuff and watching me. Recruiting me. I was like some kind of forbidden fruit. An itch they had to scratch. And funny thing is, with them, I could say anything. Do anything. They'd sell me some stuff, and then I could sit and talk for hours, just spouting off. No one had ever listened to me like that before. I felt like a God."

Brand nodded.

"So I started dressing like them. Just a little at first, you know? A black leather jacket. Then some gloves. I quit summer league baseball so I could hang out more. Traded in Nikes for boots and jeans for leathers. These guys took me in and showed me how to get a tattoo. I let my hair grow, got an earring. Started getting in fights. They taught me how to fight. Not the civilized kind of fighting we do in school like wrestling and boxing, but dirty stuff. Lethal stuff. And we started hanging around the streets at night. One day I was a Griff. I don't even know when it happened. I just became."

Brand licked more rainwater off his lips and touched the recorder on his chest. It was soaking wet.

"And then one night we were prowling, looking for a raid, you know? Someone to mug. We'd started out with old ladies, but I convinced the guys that was kid stuff. Besides, all they ever carried was leftover social security money. Stupid stuff. So we started to go after tougher marks. First ladies, and then guys. Anyone who looked like they had money and who had wandered off the beaten path. Anywhere between here and the market, even as far south as Safeco Field, and up the hill toward Queen Anne. Around the theaters and clubs was best. Late night and early morning."

"So, anyway, we were out prowling this one night, and we hit this couple, and man and a woman, but the woman turned out to be a man, and they fought back pretty good, so this one kid, Leeland, he sticks the fag with a knife, and I mean a good knife, a big hunting blade, and guts this fag. Sliced her right from her pretend cunt to her sternum. But the other guy panics and runs, so I ran after him and tackled him, and I turned him over and just jabbed him in the throat. Hard. And he gurgled and kicked and his eyes got wide, but I just sat there on top of him, and I jabbed him in the throat again and again, just mad, angry, like maybe mad at my dad, and at school, and at myself. I just went crazy, and I pulverized that poor guy's neck. I watched him die. Watched his eyes go all glossy. It was like I crossed some kind of line, and I knew I was never going back."

Kenny turned slowly and glared at Brand.

"I like it. I liked the feeling. I wanted to kill again."

Brand felt the muscles in the back of his neck getting tight and hot. Kenny turned away again.

"When I got up off that guy, I was standing right over him, and suddenly there was this thing in front of me. All black, like one of our guys, but bigger. And his face was covered too. He spooked me, so I jumped back a bit, and then another rush of adrenaline hit me and I rushed the guy. But it was like I was a baby. He just brushed me off. I mean, I jabbed right at him, hit him with everything, I was like a tornado, but he just stepped aside and brushed me off like a piece of lint or something. It was totally crazy. So I rushed him again, and this time he hit me, and I mean hard. Knocked the wind out of me, sent me back on my butt. And now the other guys came up and went after the guy. Five of us against him. Right there, right over that fag's body with the glassy eyes staring up into the sky. But the stranger just wheeled around and flattened my guys. Squashed them like bugs. And he took Leeland by the throat and flipped him around and held him in front of me and snapped his neck. One minute Leeland was staring at me with wide eyes, and the next his head was flopping around and his tongue was sticking out. The dark guy dropped Lee on top of the fag and then stood there and waited."

Kenny shivered.

"Anyway, this guy called himself Raven, said he'd been watching us for a while. He thought we were stupid, but that we had some potential. That's how we met Raven."

Brand leaned forward a bit.

"And who is Raven?"

Kenny shook his head. "We don't know. Never seen his face. He's like some kind of super-hero wannabe. Wears a mask."

"You mean, like a super villain."

Kenny shrugged. "Whatever. He sees himself as a hero. We're all heroes, in our own way. You know? We're just trying to rid the world of mistakes, according to our own code."

"And your code is old women and fags?"

Kenny shrugged again. "The code is…" his voice trailed off as he stared into the night.

"The code is what?" Brand asked.

Kenny shook his head. "It's just hard to explain. What we did, I mean. What we're doing." His head still shook back and forth, slowly.

"Know why we call ourselves the Griffs?" he asked.

Brand shrugged and shook his head. Kenny was staring off into the distance again, so Brand had to voice his ignorance.

"No. Why?"

"At first it was just a name. It sounded kind of cool. But now…"

"Now what?"

"What are gryphons, Mr. Brand?"

"Scavengers," Brand said. "Carrion eaters. The ultimate recyclers."

Kenny chuckled.

"Only the strong should survive," he said. "Science has created a world where the weak and immoral flourish. We're just trying to correct the balance of nature."

"Is that you talking, or Raven?"

Kenny sighed. "I don't know anymore. Doesn't matter though. I'm screwed any way I look at it. As soon as I get off this platform, he's going to find me and kill me."

"More likely you'll go to jail."

"That's what I'm afraid of. At least when I'm out in the open, I can run. The cops put cuffs on me and lock me up, I'm a sitting duck."

"Maybe you'll be safer in a cell."

Kenny let loose a short burst of laughter like a Tommy gun.

"I'll be dead in an hour," he said. "No one..."

He came up out of his squat and stood in a low, crouching stance with his gloved hands held out like claws, his eyes peering into the darkness in front of him. Brand pressed his back against the wall and tried to ignore the sharp pain in the back of his neck.

"What is it?" Brand asked.

"Shut up," Kenny hissed.

They waited. Brand was watching Kenny, so the only way he knew that someone was approaching was by the way Kenny's fighting stance shifted forward.

The thing came slowly, slinking from one beam to the next, gliding like a phantom. It was the shape and size of a human, but all black. A female form, almost like a mannequin, with no distinguishing marks. Solid black, supple, moving like a cloud of ink. She was like an unfinished ebony sculpture, a head with shape but no definition, long arms and legs and a lithe torso that rippled as she moved. It was seductive and sensuous, yet frightening.

"You," Kenny hissed. The thing stopped a few feet from him. Brand could only define her by the silhouette she left against the backdrop of the city. She was a black hole, darker than the night itself. She reached out a hand toward Kenny and he spit at her.

"Fuck you," he said. "If I kill you, Raven will take me back."

"And if you don't?" she asked. The voice was like silk sheets rubbing together, smooth and luxurious. It sent a shiver down Brand's back all the way to his groin, and down his arms to his fingers.

"If I don't, I'm dead anyway," he said. He lunged forward, launching his body toward her as he spun to the left. His right leg lashed forward and up, but his heel stopped in empty space. The thing moved like a ghost toward the far edge of the outer platform, balancing on the very brink as if she were standing on a diving board. Kenny responded in an instant, jabbing with one arm and immediately following with a hook. The thing danced to the right and Kenny teetered on the edge for a moment. The phantom reached out and plucked at his waist, pulling him back just far enough so that he stood stable again. Kenny's eyes were wide, but anger quickly replaced fear.

"That was a mistake," he hissed. He swung again, following with a series of kicks and lunges that drove the thing back but never touched her. As she floated away from the attack, Brand watched the shadows play across her body, first framing hard muscles of one graceful calf and upper thigh, then an arm with a bicep like a body builder, and then across the sleek curves of her chest and neck. As they moved away, Brand followed on his hands and knees, his eyes fixed on the strange fight, his fingers and feet picking their way along the framework of iron. Suddenly, Kenny stopped and bounced up and down on the balls of his feet with his hands held up and ready in a relaxed fighting pose. He smiled at the thing and licked his lips.

"After I kill you," he said. "Or maybe while you are still dying, I'm going to rip that stupid suit off your fucking sweet body and fuck you while the life seeps out of your eyes."

She stood with her palms facing him, her hands held out away from either side of her head, her legs slightly bent, as if she were giving up. They faced each other like that as time stopped. Kenny bounced, swiveling a bit to the left and right, planning his next volley, and yet hesitating.

"Is that the way it's going to be?" she whispered. Brand strained to hear.

"Yeah, that's the way."

They stood there like statues for a moment, and then the thing started to tip her head just a bit. She leaned a bit closer to him, as if she was a snake, thinking about biting him.

She reached out slowly, as if she were going to simply box him in the ear like a naughty child, but her hand just touched his cheek gently. Even in the darkness, Brand could see Kenny frowning. He batted her hand away and took a step backward.

"What the fuck are you?" Kenny's voiced his question like a snarl.

She turned her blank face toward Brand for a moment and then back to Kenny. She was still frozen there, indecisive, as if she had popped a rivet or something.

"You know," she said. She was speaking to Kenny, but her slow, husky voice sent a shiver up Brand's back. "I'd love to be fucked by you. I really would."

Kenny sank a bit lower into his fighter's crouch.

"But," she continued. "I never really liked you that much. Guess that's one fuck I'll just have to miss."

The blow was deceptively quick and it caught Kenny just as he shifted his weight toward the edge of the platform. At the same time, her right leg snaked out and caught the inside of his right knee. He tipped over the edge and his knee cracked against the metal plates. The thing whipped around and landed on her stomach, reaching over the edge. Brand's heart hit the back of his throat and stuck there, and his stomach tightened up like a dead oyster. He slithered forward a few inches until he could see better, and he realized that the thing still had hold of the back of Kenny's long, black overcoat, holding the kid over the city, letting him sway back and forth, even though he weighed half again as much as she did. Brand noticed that her feet were hooked under one of the I-beams. Brand's chest pounded in his ears and he could barely hear.

"Where can I find Raven," the thing asked. Brand couldn't hear the answer, but he could sense the tone of Kenny's voice, panic mixed with fear and hate.

"Give me the Raven," she said.

Brand crept a few inches closer. There was no way that the girl was going to pull the kid back up onto the platform. The kid knew it.

"Kenny," Brand called out. "Hang on kid."

"Stay back," the thing hissed.

"You'll need help pulling him up," Brand said. His mouth was dry again and his stomach was quaking. He pulled with his fingers, but his body refused to budge.

"Stay back," she hissed again. The sexy, sullen voice had turned into stinging venom.

Brand could hear the kid wailing now.

"Oh, God, please don't let me go."

"Tell me where the Raven is, or I'll let you take the fast way down," the thing said. It stopped talking and craned its head back, watching Brand as he posed like a wimp doing a pushup.

"Let me help," Brand insisted.

"I've got this under control," the thing hissed again. Her foot slipped and her body spun sideways, jerked toward the edge. Brand heard her inhale sharply and the kid screamed. From the main deck, the beam of a flashlight cut through the rain in an erratic jumble that meant the cop was running. Brand could hear the man's voice, but the beam was heading south, toward the place they had started. They were on the west side now, looking down over the Food Court and the fountains.

"Brand," the cop shouted. "What the hell is going on?"

"Jesus," the thing said.

"Let me help you," Brand whispered.

There was a sound like air being sucked into a vacuum, and suddenly the thing was laying there sort of calm, relaxed, almost as if she were asleep.

"No," she whispered.

Brand's head wouldn't grasp what had just happened. "Let me help you," he said. His stomach was turning over and over like a dryer full of wet clothes. Suddenly, the thing was standing up, both hands hanging loose at her sides, big black leather overcoat dangling from one hand. She was staring over the edge. Every muscle in Brand's body was rigid.

"Oh, Christ," he said.

The thing spun around and crouched down, grabbing Brand's chin and putting its black face right in his.

"You fuck," she said. "I told you to stay back."

"You let him go," Brand breathed.

She pushed him back and Brand staggered to his feet. Her knee hit him in the chest and drove him back against the wall. She threw the heavy coat to one side and smashed the wind from his body with a sharp blow to his solar plexus, and then the arch of her foot caught him on the jaw. His head snapped back and bounced forward again, and he felt the thing's feet push against his shoulders as she launched herself over the suicide net. Something grabbed his coat and pulled him up over the fence and he came to sprawled out on the concrete deck with Renata hunched over him and the cop running toward them. Brand reached up and grabbed the Ricoh, still strapped around Renata's neck. He rolled over, pulling her with him, and struggled to his knees as he hit the rapid fire button. The flash started strobing as he panned the camera from right to left, filling the night with lightning flashes, but as he turned, something hit him in the side of the head and the camera flipped out of his hand.

"What the hell," Renata said. She was flat on her back. The cop crouched down and hit Brand right in the face with the beam from the Magna-Light.

"What the fuck just happened here?" he said. Brand was staring at the light when he noticed that the cop was holding it above a gun. Renata sat up and blinked.

"Where's the kid?" she asked.

"Where's the Ricoh?" Brand asked.

He took a moment to glance around.

"You're under fucking arrest," the cop hissed. "Anything you say can and will be used against you in a court of law."

"Where's Krystal?" Brand asked.

"You have the right to an attorney," the cop continued.

"Stop it with the bullshit," Brand said.

"If you can't afford one, one will be appointed for you, do you understand?"

The cop circled around and Brand heard the click of steel cuffs.

"Listen to me," Brand said.

"Put your arms behind your back," the cop said.

"Renata, tell him what happened," Brand said.

Renata was shaking her head back and forth. "I don't know what just happened," she said.

"Arms back now Mister Brand," the cop said. His voice was harsh and loud.

"Listen," Brand said. "There's someone else up here."

The cop ran out of patience and Brand's teeth paid the price as the big flashlight capped him right on top of his stubborn head. He staggered toward the stairwell with the cop holding his wrists from behind.

"We've got to find Krystal," Brand said. His tongue felt thick and dry. The cop shoved him through the door and Brand's stomach pressed against the metal railing. He leaned over and threw up. As he came upright again, he saw Renata leaning against the far wall with her eyes closed and her head turned away. The cop swung the door closed and then opened it right up again as someone hammered on it. Krystal stumbled through the door and collapsed on the floor, her clothes in disarray, hair soaking wet and looking like cheap plastic. Everyone stayed like that for a moment. The cop was breathing hard.

"What just happened out there?" he asked.

Krystal exploded like a potato in a microwave.

"That bastard just pushed my son off the edge." Her eyes were red and fierce, and her teeth showed white and sharp.

"There was someone else out there," Brand said. "Some kind of…"

The cop pointed at Renata. "What did you see?" he asked.

She shook her head. "I didn't see anything. Some kind of fight. But it was too dark."

The cop was scanning all three of them with suspicion. He turned up the volume on his radio and Brand winced. The airwaves crackled with panic and horror as the cops cordoned off the patio around the base of the Needle. The cop just stood and listened, shaking his head back and forth.

"Fuck you, Brand," he said. "You are royally fucked."

Krystal raised her head and glared at Brand.

"You're a dead man," she said.

FIVE

Two uniformed cops pushed Brand's head down into the back of a white Ford Police Interceptor. He slumped over on the hard plastic seat and stared at the stripped down inner door. No handles, no locks, no window crank. The car stayed put for a long time before Devers got in and pulled out onto Denny Way, dropping off the curb and wheeling the Ford around like a sports car.

Brand watched the scenery going by and his back came straight.

"Where are we going?" he asked. Every muscle in his body was tense.

"North Precinct. Marshall's orders."

"Does he call the shots down here?" Brand asked. Devers smiled as he peered over his shoulder into the bird cage.

"This is gang related," Devers said. "So, yeah. Senator Marshall calls the shots. He's taking a personal interest in this one. Can ya figure that?"

Brand leaned forward so that his face was close to the grill.

"Listen Devers," he said. "I'm not stupid enough to drop Marshall's kid off the Space Needle while the whole world watches. I'm telling you, there was someone else up there."

Devers' face turned hard as ice. "Shut up and sit back," he said. "You'll get your chance to come clean. Right now, I just don't want to hear it. I just got done watching Marshall's son get smeared all over the pavement. You know? I'm just a little bit pissed off right now."

Brand sat back and watched the low industrial section of Elliot Way blur by. It took a half hour to get to King Detention North, and it went by with only the hum of the tires on the road and the growl of the old black and white's engine. They pulled into a brightly lit parking lot and Devers yanked Brand up a sloping ramp. Inside, a kid guard with a short bristle of blond hair uncuffed him and took his picture and prints on a digital scanner. Devers snapped the cuffs back on, but kept Brand's wrists in front, and tossed him into a harsh white room with a mirror and a table with two chairs. Devers took one chair and Brand took the other. Brand put his hands on the table, clasped together as if he was praying. The clock on the wall read ten after nine. He told Devers everything.

"So," Devers said. "You're telling me that there was you and Krystal Marshall, and Sergeant Barrow, and Renata, and Kenny, and some naked black kung-fu ballerina. Right? Six people? Up there on the roof?"

Brand nodded and rubbed his face with his hands. The cuffs prevented him from rubbing his stiff neck.

"It wasn't a naked ballerina. I'm telling you, it moved like a dancer, fought like a boxer."

"And dressed all in black, like a body suit?"

"Yeah. Only the head too. Everything was covered."

"So, you couldn't see the face."

"No. The face was just like one of those mannequins with no features."

Devers scribbled on his pad.

"What about the recording?" Brand asked.

Devers shrugged. "Couldn't make out much of what Kenny said. And it ran out of tape. Conversation just stopped."

"And the camera?"

We found the Ricoh about a block away. Smashed on the sidewalk. Lucky you didn't kill someone else with that one."

"I didn't throw the camera," Brand said. "Someone snatched it from my hands."

"Your partner says you grabbed it and threw it," Devers said.

"Was there film in it?" Brand asked.

Devers shook his head. "It was empty."

Brand slumped down in his chair and shook his head.

"I'm telling you, Devers. There was someone else up there."

"Barrow says different. He says there was just you and Kenny on the outer edge. Renata on the deck, and him and Krystal at the doorway. No one else came or went."

"Maybe she climbed up from the lower deck," Brand said.

"There is no lower deck. Just the inside observation deck, and we had that closed off. No way out of that one anyway. It's all glass enclosed. Face it, Brand. Your story just doesn't hold water. You are screwed."

Brand slammed his forearms down on the table.

"Why would I do something like that?" Brand asked. "How stupid do you think I am?"

Devers shrugged. "Guess you did it for the story. You've got a reputation for making stories happen when things get boring. Guess you really made one this time." Devers tapped his legal pad with the tip of his pencil, staring at the little dots it made.

"Marshall is on his way," Devers said. "You're in for a shitload when he gets here."

"Christ," Brand said.

Devers stood up and the metal buttons on the bottom of the chair legs raked across the floor, wailing like a banshee. The sound echoed off the hard walls of the ten by ten room.

"You are fucked," Devers said.

"I'm going to need legal counsel," Brand said.

"Yeah, well we got a public defender coming down Monday morning." Devers slid a sheet of paper across the table. "Fill this out."

Brand flipped it around as Devers tossed the pencil on top of the paper.

"Promissory note?" Brand asked.

"You don't qualify as indigent. Just indigent with resources. So state law says you have to pay us back for the cost of your defense."

"Jesus," Brand said.

"You keep calling on him," Devers said as he walked away. "Maybe he'll have mercy on your soul when they fry you."

Brand heard the door open and Devers walked out.

About a half hour later, a militant cop with a crew cut came in and took Brand down the hall and into a basement.

"Here's something you might be familiar with," he said. He tossed Brand into a concrete cell with one big glass window. The floor sloped toward a big drain in the middle, and the place reeked of stale vomit and urine. Brand backed up into the corner and hugged his knees to his chest. Every once in a while, someone would peer in through the window to check on him.

SIX

October 15, 1995 – 2:01AM

Brand dozed a bit, cold floor woke him, he dozed again. Hours passed, but no one else joined him in the drunk tank. No food, no visitors. In a daze, he found his mind back in the Y, in the dance room, of all places, cold again, waiting for Laci Keller to show. He squeezed his eyes shut and tried to think of Ren or Jule or even the kid before he fell, what he said, but Laci would pop up again and again. Eventually, he gave in. Better to linger on a stale memory than to have to face the reality of the concrete around him.

Night melted into day and Brand dozed off and on with no company and no food and no more access to memories, good or bad.

Finally, Devers came and fetched Brand, dragging him to an intake bench, stainless steel and cold. An old clock on the concrete wall read six-fifteen. Brand thought it might be evening.

"We're gonna let you cool down in detention for a few days with some friends of yours. Then Marshall wants to talk to you. He's just too fuckin' pissed right now to even think about your sorry ass."

They stepped into a central foyer and Devers dropped his gun belt on a table. They passed through a metal detector that screamed at Brand's cuffs. A guard waved a wand up and down Brand's arms and legs, tapping him extra hard in the groin as it scanned his inner thighs.

"Have fun tonight," the guard said.

Brand frowned as Devers drug him into an elevator that smelled like a urinal.

"What about my hearing?" he asked.

Devers shrugged. "Always shit luck to get arrested on a Friday or Saturday, 'cause you gotta wait all weekend for you hearing. And funny thing is, on Monday, all of the judges seemed to be busy. Dockets are just full."

"That's bullshit," Brand said. "I've got the right to arraignment first thing Monday morning. First thing."

"Nobody gets an arraignment hearing that fast anymore, Brand," Devers said. He smirked. "You're lucky if maybe three weeks from now you get to go before a judge."

"What about bail?"

"You won't get bail. Quit whining and welcome to the justice system."

"I'm not some stupid con just off the street Devers," Brand said. "I've got rights. I've got due process on my side, and if I don't get a hearing on Monday I'm gonna sue your ass."

"Sue the city's ass," Devers said. "My ass don't have any money or any political power."

"You're full of shit," Brand said.

"Now you're talking like a con," Devers said. He cracked an evil grin. The doors slid open and Devers pushed Brand into a long, green hallway. A steel door slid open with a dull ring like a hammer striking an anvil. Brand stepped in and Devers followed. They stopped at the first guard station and Devers unlatched the handcuffs.

"Strip," the guard said. He was an older guy, round bellied with sagging cheeks and sad eyes. His blue shirt gapped open between each button.

Brand handed over his Nordica and vest and the guard put them in a black plastic lawn bag. Devers waited off to the side with his arms crossed and a smug look on his face.

"You the dropper?" the guard asked. His eyes were as dull as two-cent marbles. Devers chuckled.

Brand unbuttoned his shirt and threw it in the bag.

"What the hell is a dropper?" Brand asked.

The guard shrugged. Brand knelt down and untied his shoes, but kept his eyes on the guard. His name badge read Custody Officer Leonard.

"Just made it up," Leonard said. "Jumper. Dropper. You know?"

"I didn't drop him," Brand said.

Devers jumped in to the conversation as Brand's jeans went in the bag.

"Nice underwear. Those race cars?"

Brand winced at his choice of boxers.

"You just never know where the day's gonna take you, do you Brand?" Devers said.

Brand stood naked listening to a slurred synopsis of the rules. No spitting. No cussing. No fighting. Lights out means lights out. During the monologue, Brand watched Leonard's eyes, saw the suspicion behind them, words unsaid, about how a guy like Brand could look so dead, blue-gray and cold like a stone. He finished murmuring and gave Brand an inmate's handbook on twenty pound paper folded in half, ugly courier type that looked mimeographed, about twenty pages of unruly text that a fourth grader would have been ashamed to author. And a bar of soap and a little rubber thimble with soft spikes on it.

Brand stared at the thimble for a moment.

"What is that?" he asked.

"Toothbrush," Leonard said.

"Only the really tough guys get plastic toothbrushes," Devers said. Brand scowled at him and turned back toward

Leonard just in time to get a stiff orange jumper and a pair of Fruit of the Looms that reeked of bleach but still weren't quite white.

Brand stared at the gauche attire and it finally hit him. His stomach flipped over and his chest heaved.

"Look out," Devers said. "We've got a puker."

Brand hit his knees and threw up on the gray vinyl flooring. Leonard and Devers watched with their arms crossed. They waited for him to finish and then Leonard hauled Brand back to his feet.

"Your new friends are gonna love your sweet breath," Leonard said.

Brand put his foot through one leg hole of his briefs as he hopped toward the cell block on the other.

"I read your series on jail overcrowding in the P.I.," Leonard said. His voice was thick and slow like cold molasses.

Brand grunted and stuck his other leg into the limp underwear.

"Was thinking," Leonard said. "Maybe you'd want to do a follow up. You know? First hand kind of thing. Maybe even get your facts right this time. Like, you said that North was built for four-fifty, but that we had stuffed six hundred in here. The fact is, we're staffed for four hundred, built to house four ten, but holding about seven hundred right now. And the taxpayers voted down matrix release and the new jail bond. Your article about waste and graft just before the November vote couldn't have helped. Did you ever even set foot in here before you wrote about it?"

Brand had pulled the jumpsuit up over his shoulders and was fidgeting with the buttons. Leonard led the way into a large anteroom. Green Block was two stories tall, divided into five big cages on each level, each cage with a dozen cells. All the cell doors were open and the inmates were gathered around the bars, watching the new arrival. The cages faced the middle of the room, where a burly blue shirt sat in a glass-enclosed monitoring booth. Leonard gently prodded Brand in the back with his fingers and shouted into an intercom.

"B Block. Let him in."

"Lock down B," the block guard announced. The voice rang out through the intercom system and echoed off the hard walls. Upstairs, second cage from the right, all the prisoners wandered slowly back into their room. When everyone was in, the monitor flipped a lever and the doors slammed closed. Brand jumped and tried to swallow. Leonard led him up a flight of metal stairs and the cage door popped open as if by magic. Brand glanced down at the monitor, and the man leered at him and gave him a mock salute.

Leonard stepped back and the door slammed closed again. Brand stared at Devers and Leonard through iron bars.

"Have a good time," Leonard said. Devers winked.

"Welcome to B Green," the monitor announced. With a hum and a snap, all the doors on B Block popped open.

SEVEN

Sixty plus inmates in orange jumpers wandered back out into the main area. A few glanced at Brand with curiosity, most just ignored him. Brand turned slowly, taking in the scenery. A wall of black bars looked out over the elevated glass guard booth and across to the double-decker cell blocks on the other side of the anteroom. Behind him, the dozen tiny cubicles stood open and empty. Each had double bunks and a cot, along with a seatless toilet and a small stainless steel sink. Five inmates in each cell, designed for two. The men were a motley crew and hung out in groups. Bikers with wildly tattooed arms and chests; tough, dark men with wiry facial hair, too sparse to be called a beard; one fire-eyed gaunt man that prowled the cage like a trapped tiger. Brand felt his heart pounding in his chest. He backed up and bumped into one of three picnic tables, made of thick fiberglass and bolted into the concrete floor.

"Hey Brand, have a seat."

It took Brand a moment to get his bearings and get focused on the kid. He was playing cards with two buddies.

"Sit," the kid said.

Brand sat down on the very end of the bench seat. The kid ignored him as he played out his hand. Brand recognized the game by the way the cards fell. The kid's buddy played a ten of spades and he dropped the queen.

"Fuck," he said as he pulled the trick toward him. "We need another hand in this game. The kid glanced over at Brand. "How about you? You play Rat Fuck?"

Brand shook his head.

"Remember me?" the kid asked. In standard county orange he didn't look much different than any other monkey, including Brand, but his beaked nose was unmistakable. Brand glanced at the kid across the table and recognized the gargoyle under a Romeo face. Romeo touched his pink tongue to the space where his front teeth used to be and winked at Brand. His frump of blond hair was even worse than it had been the night before. The other player was a stick of a kid with pockmarks all over his face and deep-set eyes. All three of the boys squinted into the harsh lights as if they'd never seen the sun. A little riffle ran across the back of Brand's neck, and he felt a thousand eyes on him, as if every inmate in the block was watching. The kid smiled and Brand recalled an ape-like swagger and the bas-relief raven, defined more by shadow than by light.

Brand nodded. "We met at the center last night."

The kid stuck his hand out toward Brand and smiled like a vampire trying to sell real estate.

"Have you got a name?" Brand asked the beaked Gryphon.

"People call me Pritchert," he said. "And that there's Bobby Reedon, but we all call him Keuek."

Brand frowned a bit. "Keuek?"

"Don't ask," Pritchert said. He flipped out cards with his thumb like a Vegas dealer. A stack piled up in front of Brand. The diamond-backs were greasy and worn. Brand swallowed and tasted bile. Pritchert motioned over at the pock-faced kid.

"The little freak over there is Simon."

Brand glanced at Simon and the boy just stared right through him.

"What did you get picked up for?" Brand asked.

Pritchert shrugged and Keuek smiled big, showing off filed teeth where he had teeth. There were more missing than there were in place.

"Bogus shit, really," Pritchert said. He held out his hands and his face relaxed. "We're just some guys and gals out roaming around, you know? Peaceful like. Then the cops land on us and Keuek and me, we end up in here."

"You acted like you were expecting me," Brand said.

"Well, you know, someone told us you were coming. A celebrity, you know? And so, we just wanted to make you extra welcome."

"I appreciate it."

"In fact, we've got a cot set aside for you in our room. Just you and me and Keuek and Simon here. It'll be cozy. Kind of a special time for us."

"Wow. What can I say?"

Pritchert shrugged. "You know, anything for the guy that dropped Kenny off the Needle. What is that? About four hundred feet?"

"Six," Keuek said.

"Five," Brand corrected.

"Five or six," Pritchert said. "Either way, that's gotta hurt."

"You knew Kenny?" Brand asked.

"Like a brother. You know? We're all family."

Keuek just nodded.

"Did you know that his dad is the gang task force czar?"

"Oh, yeah," Pritchert said. "Real ironic. Bet that was a real bee in his dad's little bonnet."

"Aren't you at all curious about what Kenny was doing up there?"

"Uh-uh," Pritchert said.

Brand took a deep breath. Pritchert picked up the hand in front of him and Keuek followed, smiling into Pritchert's eyes. Simon picked his up slowly, as if he was almost too tired to play.

"I've been reading your stuff on the Griffs in the P.I.," Pritchert said. He glanced over at Brand's cards and nodded once. "Pick 'em up."

"You can read?" Brand asked.

"Fuck you," Pritchert said.

Brand put the cards in his hand and sorted them by suit.

"Let me guess," Brand said. "I got it all wrong."

"It's pretty lame," Pritchert said, glancing at Keuek over the top of his cards. They exchanged smiles.

"Why don't you give me the real skinny," Brand said.

"You got the two of clubs?" Pritchert asked. Simon shook his head. Keuek dropped the two on the table. Simon played a six and Brand hit it with his jack.

"I got an idea," Pritchert said as he played the ace. "We could show you. You know? A picture's worth a thousand words and all. Really feeling it, touching it, should be worth, say, a million words. Can't even buy something like that."

Keuek glanced up at Pritchert.

"Oh, sorry Keuek. I forgot." Pritchert leaned over and confided with Brand.

"Actually, you can buy it. From Keuek. If you know what I mean." He nudged Brand in the ribs and Brand got a flash of Pritchert's power. Under the jumpsuit he was a stick of iron cabled together with steel.

Pritchert scooped up the trick.

"I'm not following you," Brand said. Pritchert played a four of spades. Keuek dropped a two and Simon played a three. Brand took the trick with a five.

"Well," Pritchert said as Brand played the seven of spades. Pritchert took it with a ten. The others dropped an eight and a nine. "We were thinking that tonight, after the lights were out, after lock down, we could show you some of our tricks and stuff. You know? Give you a real taste of the Griff culture. Then you could write all about it. Maybe sell it to some porn sites or something."

"Maybe Hustler," Simon said. His voice drifted across Brand's shoulders like a cold wind.

"Yeah," Pritchert said. He led with a two of diamonds. "Hustler might be good. But you'll have to pretend you're a girl. He glanced over at Brand. "Can you pretend you're a girl?"

Keuek threw away a king of spades and Simon played a five of diamonds. Brand took the trick with a ten, led his queen of clubs and took the eight, ten and four. He took the next trick as well leading with a king of clubs. The king of diamonds took the next trick, and the ace took the rest of the diamonds and the queen of hearts from Keuek. Brand took a chance with the eight of hearts and the bluff paid off. Pritchert played a five, Keuek played a six and Simon played a four. The ten of hearts took the nine and the three and the queen of spades, and Brand took the rest of the tricks with the ace and king of hearts and the ace of spades. The kids turned up their tricks and realized that Brand had taken every counting card.

"Fucking A," Keuek said.

Pritchert chuckled and Simon just sat there.

"You've got some moxy," Pritchert said. He peered at Brand out of the corner of his eyes with a sly smile. "Still, we're gonna have some fun tonight."

EIGHT

October 15, 1995 – 8:07PM

The guards changed at eight and the new security monitor called for lock down and lights out. Pritchert and his buddies escorted Brand into their cube. Simon jumped up on one upper bunk and Pritchert took the other. Keuek stretched out on the lower bunk just below Pritchert. The gargoyle propped his head up on one arm and smiled as Brand sat down on the opposite bunk. He had to duck his head to one side. The lights went out with a bang like a shotgun blast as the big breaker flipped over for the night.

"Christ," Keuek said. "I think my head's gonna split open."

Pritchert's voice floated out of the darkness. "Hey Brand," he said. "How's your night vision?"

Brand sat quietly with his fists clenched and his heart pounding.

"Brand?" Pritchert asked. "You still there? You ready to party?"

"Maybe he's nervous," Keuek said. "He looks a little nervous."

Brand couldn't see a thing. Just darkness.

"Yeah," Pritchert said. "This is kind of like a wedding night, you know? Everyone gets nervous the first time."

"One time, a guy got so nervous, he peed all over me," Keuek said.

"Do you need to pee first?" Pritchert asked.

"Or take a shit?" Keuek added.

Brand pressed his chapped lips together and tried to think of a prayer, but his mind was full of nettles and vetch weed, like an overgrown garden that grabbed at his feet. His neck tightened and his back started to ache with the stress.

"You guys have me all wrong," he said. His voice hitched in his dry throat and his face flushed.

The room was quiet and dark as a tomb for a moment. Brand caught the squeak of metal springs as Pritchert shifted on his bunk.

"Listen," Brand said. "There was someone else on the roof. A woman. Dressed in black. She and Kenny got into it, fighting. It looked like Ali and Foreman. Furious fighting. She knocked Kenny off the edge, grabbed him, shook him up a bit, and then he just kind of slipped out of his coat. She came up empty. She was a strong mother-fucker. You guys gotta believe me. Kenny knew her, knew who she was."

The dead silence was like a pillow over his face. Brand heard a whisper above him, floating in the darkness like a ghost.

"The Dancer."

"Shut up, Simon," Pritchert hissed.

"You know her," Brand said.

"Maybe," Pritchert said. "We've heard of her. Not from anyone reliable. Certainly not you."

"She was after the Raven," Brand said. "I don't think she meant to kill Kenny. I got the impression she was trying to scare him."

"Stupid bitch is a killer," Keuek said.

"Shut up," Pritchert hissed again.

"She meant to kill him," Keuek said slowly. "Sure enough. You drop someone from the Needle, you meant to kill him."

Everyone was quiet for a moment before Keuek went on.

"I've seen her before," he said.

"Bullshit you have," Pritchert said.

"I seen her," Keuek insisted. "One night, we was out scavenging. She came down off the fire escapes and kicked the shit out of Travis and Heather Dee. I ran like a scared sucker and she chased me. I could hear her feet on the pavement. Sounded like I was being chased by some kind of tiger or something. Scared the pee out of me. Then, she just stopped. I kept running, hot piss running down my pants. It fuckin' scared the shit out of me."

"You are so full of shit," Pritchert said. "This Dancer chick is just some kind of wet dream you guys got suckered into. Who's gonna be fuckin' scared of some dancer jumpin' around like a fag in tights?"

Brand ignored Pritchert and focused in on Keuek. "When I saw her on the Needle, she was dressed all in black. Like neoprene or something. It was spongy, soft. But she was agile as a cat and as strong as a gorilla. She picked me up and threw me back over the suicide cage as if I was a baby."

"That's the bitch," Keuek said. He paused for a moment. "So, why'd she save you?"

"She's only after Griffs," Simon said. Brand felt one of the kid's feet swish by his face, so he moved over a bit. His eyes adjusted to the darkness, and he could see Simon's legs hanging down, swinging back and forth as if he was running slowly.

"Simon," Pritchert warned. "You're not even a real Griff yet. So shut up."

"Tell me more about the Dancer," Brand said.

"Why?" Pritchert asked.

"Because," Brand said. "I might be able to help you."

"Help us what?" Pritchert asked.

"Help you find her."

"Why would you do that?" Keuek asked.

"Why do you think?" Brand asked.

"I have no idea," Keuek said.

"To keep you off my back," Brand said. *Literally*, he added to himself. "I help you find the Dancer. In exchange, you leave me alone."

"We'll have to talk it over," Pritchert said.

"With who?" Brand asked.

There was no answer.

"Look," Brand said. "I think I've got a lead on this Dancer. You guys leave me alone, and when I get out, I'll chase down my lead and get back to you. You can take it from there."

Silence.

"Well, you figure it out," he said. He played a bluff. "Maybe Raven doesn't give a rip about this Dancer chick. You tell him you had a lead and you blew it." Brand winced at his choice of words, but he kept going. "Maybe Raven will give you a little pat on the back, you know? Aw, that's OK boys, you were just having a little fun, right? So, we lost a bead on the Dancer, all is forgiven. I'll bet Raven is a forgiving guy like that. Name like Raven, he sounds like he's really nice once you get to know him."

More silence.

Keuek finally spoke up. "I say we just rip you a new asshole anyway."

"Leave him alone," Pritchert said.

"What the fuck?" Keuek replied. His voice almost squeaked.

"You heard me," Pritchert said. "Leave him alone or I'll fuck you up."

Brand could almost feel Pritchert's hot breath and angry eyes burning through the darkness.

"Let's all get some shut eye now," Pritchert said. "I gotta think about this."

Brand eased himself down onto the rancid mattress and pulled a rough woolen blanket over his body. He stared up toward the interlacing wire springs above him, barely discernable in the darkness. His eyes closed for a moment but he came awake again with a start and sucked in a lungful of musty air. The room smelled of Lysol and farts and rotten meat. Brand almost gagged.

A whisper came from above.

"Brand."

"Yeah?" he replied.

"You awake?"

"Yeah."

"You scared?"

"Fuck no."

"You should be."

Brand touched his tongue to his dry lips and waited.

"Brand?" Simon asked again, keeping his voice low and hoarse.

"Yeah?"

"Those guys, Pritchert and Keuek, they're bad guys."

"Yeah? And what about you?"

"I'm one of the old Griffs, before Raven came along. Those guys are new. They've got a different code. They…"

"They what?"

"They scare me. They just do stuff that's, stuff that's kind of unnatural."

"Like what?"

No answer from Simon.

"What about Kenny?" Brand asked. "Was he old Griff or new?"

"He was old, like me. Before Raven. Raven changed everything."

"Like what?"

"Like, who we were. Who we appealed to. You know?"

"No," Brand said. "I don't know. Tell me." From across the room, he heard the deep steady breathing of two sleeping goons. At least, they seemed to be asleep. Brand returned his focus to the disembodied voice above him.

"Raven is recruiting a dangerous crowd. These guys, well they hang out down below, in the underground, you know?"

"The old city?"

Yeah, the old streets. Before the retrograde. There's a whole city down there. Like a town of ghosts. It's the most fuckin' thing you've ever seen."

"I've been on the tour," Brand said.

"So have I," Simon said. "But they don't show you shit. There is way more that you can't see. A whole fuckin' city."

"And that's where Raven is?"

"Yeah, and his Gryphons."

"But not you?"

"No."

There was a long period of silence, and Brand felt himself drifting off to sleep again. Around him, he could hear voices, like throngs of people. The damp smell of packed dirt filled his nostrils. All around him, tourists snapped photos of gray, rotten buildings. Above him the ground shook as cars sped by on some elevated avenue. Dirt trickled down his collar and tendrils of gnarled roots brushed against his shoulders, grabbing at him. He jumped again and a small yelp left his lips.

"You OK?" Simon whispered.

"Yeah," Brand said.

"There's really bad shit going on down in those tunnels, Brand," Simon whispered.

Brand just waited.

"Brand?"

"Yeah?"

"Don't make a deal with these guys."

"I have to," Brand said.

Simon sighed. He was silent for a long time.

"You'd be better off letting them fuck you now," he said. Brand's eyes just wouldn't stay open. He drifted off and woke up with a start again as the doors popped open with a crash that sounded like two cars hitting head on.

NINE

First thing Monday morning brought group showers for B Block Green and then breakfast of a rubber substance that might have been oatmeal. A crew-cut custody officer escorted Brand from the stainless steel table with his mush still in the bowl, the spoon stuck in the glue on its own at a forty-five degree angle. The officer led Brand to another white cubicle and left him there, alone, for at least an hour. Brand's left leg was bounding up and down by the time a young man dropped a briefcase on the table.

"I'm Cooper," he said. "I'm your appointed counsel." He popped his case open and scowled at Brand.

"Thank God," Brand said. "Listen, I have to pee. Can you get a guard for me?"

"Uh-uh," Cooper said. "This won't take long. And we can dispense with the small talk." He sat down and reached into the briefcase. Brand noticed that the cuffs of his white shirt were worn and threadbare, and there was a dark shadow around the back of his collar. Frat tie in green and red, but polyester, like a

JC Penny brand, and his suit was a wool-poly blend, gray pin-stripe, too big around the shoulders and the sleeves were too short. Cooper pulled out a note pad and took a deep breath.

"Let's get one thing straight, Mister Brand," he said. "My job is to protect your rights, and I'm going to do that to the best of my ability, no matter what kind of scumbag you are."

"I'm not a scumbag," Brand said. "I didn't kill that kid."

"Maybe, maybe not. That's not for me to decide. The courts decide the truth."

Bullshit," Brand snapped. "The truth is not a decision someone makes. The truth is just what really happened."

Cooper leaned forward and glared into Brand's eyes.

"The truth is, Mister Brand." He paused. "Can I call you Charlie? That's what you go by, right? Charlie?"

Brand nodded. "Sometimes."

"Well, Charlie. The truth is that when your name came up down at the PD, it was like a dream come true. We were all flipping coins to see who would get your case."

"Really?" Brand asked. One of those cold drops of sweat ran down his side.

"Yeah. You know, that expose you did on our office last year was really a slammer, wasn't it? I mean, a lot of people read that. Didn't you win some kind of award for that?"

Brand nodded. "Just a local award. No big deal."

"Yeah," Cooper said, leaning back. "No big deal. You know, our budget got cut after that. I even had to take a pay cut. You know what a PD makes in Seattle?"

"About twenty grand," Brand said.

"Yeah. Of course, that was before your series. Now we make about eighteen. Know what my law school cost me?"

"A hundred grand?" Brand asked.

Cooper nodded. "A hundred and twenty, actually. I graduated near the top of my class from the University of Washington. Got a wife and two kids. Another on the way. I'm a public servant, and a darn good one. I protect the innocent, and the constitution, and the rights of every human being on the planet. And I obey the law. I don't even jaywalk."

Brand suppressed his applause.

"You think whatever you like, Charlie," Cooper said. "Point is that I'm better than you, and I don't go around killing kids for fun. You're a sleazebag to me, Charlie, so if you burn in hell or rot in prison, I'm going to feel pretty good about it."

"Can I get a different attorney?" Brand asked.

Cooper relaxed into his chair and hooked his right arm around the back.

"Nope. I'm it."

Cooper grinned at him for a moment and then stood up. "Know what, Mr. Brand?"

Brand shook his head.

Cooper leaned forward with his hands on the table and his face over Brand. "Today is Monday. I've got court appointments all day. And tonight I'm going to go home to my wife and kids and watch the Sonics cream the Blazers. Tomorrow is the same for me, except the ball game is different. That's how my life goes. It's kind of boring, but nice. And I won't even think about you for a while. Not until something comes across my desk in a couple of weeks announcing your hearing. And then, you know what? I'm probably going to file for a continuance. You know? Just not enough time to get ready. So, maybe I'll see you in three weeks or so. Maybe not. Meanwhile, you have a nice time, OK?"

Cooper turned and left and Brand just blinked. Despite Cooper's negative attitude and Devers' threats, Brand got a morning pre-trial hearing and Cooper had to drag his sorry ass into court to stand beside Brand as a Deputy P.A. asked for no bail. The judge looked tired and bored and set bail at three hundred thousand. By the time Brand got back to his block, lunch was over and his stomach was tight. Acid bubbled up and he felt as if he'd swallowed boiling mud. He dropped onto one of the benches and closed his eyes for a moment, but Simon and Keuek sat down next to Brand and stared at him.

"Where's Pritchert?" Brand asked.

"He's pouting in the cell," Keuek said.

"No one ever got a pre-trial hearing that fast in his whole life," Simon muttered.

"You're some lucky son-of-a-bitch," Keuek agreed. "Word is that Raven wants to make a deal."

Brand's stomach churned and he glanced over toward the wall of bars that held him in. Two guards came up to the cage door. One stood to the side while the other waited for it to slide open. Brand recognized the one at the door as Sergeant Leonard.

"Brand," he called out. Brand stepped forward, glad to be away from his new friends. The rest of Green Block watched Brand and the guards with a listless enthusiasm that comes from long days of doing nothing.

"You've got a visitor," Leonard said. Brand came up to the door and Leonard took him by the arm. "Your lucky day," he said. "Senator John Marshall is here."

"Great," Brand said. The big iron door slammed shut behind him as Leonard led him down the hall.

"How was your night?" Leonard asked.

"Best night's sleep I've had in a long time," Brand said. "My apartment is so noisy, you know? Bad part of town. Fights every night."

Leonard pursed his lips and frowned.

"And my cellmates were real swell," Brand said. "Made me feel right at home."

"Yeah," Leonard said. "I'll bet they did."

"I was wondering who set that up for me," Brand said. "I sure would like to send a thank you note."

Leonard unlocked a white door and sat Brand down in a little white room with a single table and two chairs; a twin to the one he had sat in two days ago. Leonard left him there with no cuffs. Brand sat patiently with his back to the door. His stomach rumbled and he felt a bit dizzy from lack of food. After a while, the door opened. Brand stared at the far wall and waited.

"You guys go on," a voice said. "I can deal with this on my own."

The door clicked shut and John Marshall came around the table, staring at the prisoner. Brand cleared his throat but said nothing. Marshall sat down and put his hands in his lap, out of sight below the table. He looked down as if he was praying, giving Brand a good look at the top of his crew-cut head and broad shoulders. On most days, Marshall's military background still showed in they way he walked and in his confident attitude. But today, his head was down and his shoulders slumped forward just a bit.

"Senator," Brand said. "I didn't kill your son."

"I know," Marshall responded. He took a deep breath and set his jaw forward as he stared Brand right in the eyes. Brand looked back with some misgivings.

"Everyone else is sure I did," Brand said.

Marshall nodded. "Yesterday I took comfort blaming you for his death. But the closer I got to the jail, the more I realized that you weren't that stupid or impulsive. I've read your work. You're a bit left wing, but fair. Bordering on sensational but mostly objective. And you make some good points. You're a decent writer, I guess. And I've seen my share of killers. Done my share of killing too. You don't have it. It's not in your eyes or your talk or your attitude."

"Thank you," Brand said, knowing that Marshall was dead wrong on at least one important point.

"But you were there the night Kenny died," Marshall said.

Brand nodded.

"What happened?"

Brand tried to moisten his lower lip and swallow, but he was dry as an old wheat biscuit. He gave up and shook his head.

"Did they let you listen to the recording?" Brand asked.

"Not much to hear," Marshall replied. He paused for a moment before he went on. "Tell me everything."

"Kenny was distressed," Brand said. "That was for sure. I'm not sure that he ever gave me the real reason, but it definitely had something to do with the Gryphons." Brand consciously omitted Kenny's confessions about the killings.

Marshall sighed and his eyes dropped toward the table. "Maybe I was gone too much. Maybe I was too tough. You know, I remember when he was just a kid, maybe one and a half, just a toddler, and we were on a trip somewhere, back east I think. Anyway, we stopped at this little park and he held onto my finger with his tiny hand as we walked to the playground, and I was thinking how great it was, what a miracle it was to have this little man, so young, so full of energy, with his baby babbling and chattering, and wondering what kind of man he would grow up to be. Back then, I always imagined he'd be some kind of athlete, maybe a military hero. Save his battalion or something with an act of selfless bravery."

Marshall shook his head.

"Never thought he'd become what I despised most."

Marshall looked back into Brand's eyes.

"I've spent most of my waking hours over the last five years trying to make some headway against gang violence in the inner cities, all over the United States. Cleveland, Milwaukee, New York, Chicago, D.C., Atlanta, even L.A. And yet I lost my son to one of the most violent, despicable gangs imaginable. Right here in my home town."

Brand cleared his throat again, but there was nothing to say. Marshall looked like a beaten man.

"We're gonna find that bastard Raven," Marshall said. "You and me. And we're gonna bust his bawls all over the place."

"I'll do whatever I can," Brand said.

"This is personal now," Marshall said. "I quit the task force this morning. Quit the Senate too. To hell with due process and the justice system. I'm taking this fight to the streets. Just Raven and me."

Marshall was leaning forward, his fingers gripping the edge of the table as if he was trying to break it.

"And you're gonna tell me how to find him."

Brand raised his eyebrows a bit.

"How am I going to do that?" Brand asked.

"Because," Marshall said. "Kenny was a disciple, and the story is that you killed Kenny. So Raven will be after you. And when he comes for you, I'm gonna be there. Waiting."

"You're using me for bait?"

Marshall nodded.

"Do I have any say in this?" Brand asked.

Marshall shook his head slowly.

"Well," Brand said. "I'm kind of locked up right now."

"Someone made your bail this morning," Marshall said.

"Already?"

"Do you know who might have done that?" he asked.

"You?" Brand ventured.

Marshall shook his head. "No, really. I'm asking you if you know who posted bail for you."

Brand shook his head. "I don't even know who pulled what strings to get a hearing so fast. Someone wants me out."

"Well, whoever it is got their wish. You're out of here. For now." Marshall stood up. "I'll be in touch."

"Senator," Brand said, stopping Marshall for a moment. "Who set me up with the Griffs in jail last night? Was that you?"

Marshall shook his head.

"Not me. I'm just about as far in the dark about all this as you are. All I know is that I'm gonna find a way to kill the Raven and your Dancer friend. That's all that matters to me now."

Marshall turned around and Brand stood up he left. Leonard met Brand at the door and escorted him down the hall and down the elevator. They walked out into another unidentifiable hallway and into a locker room. Leonard unloaded a small locker and laid Brand's clothes out on the counter, along with his wallet and the keys to the van.

"Where is my recorder?" Brand asked.

"Evidence," Leonard said. "Here's the receipt."

"Did you listen to it?" Brand asked.

Leonard just glared at him and pushed a clipboard toward him. The sergeant tapped the clipped on papers with a pencil.

"Sign here," he said.

Brand scanned the document. "Says here if I sign this that I'm agreeing that I got everything back."

"If you don't sign, you don't get anything," Leonard said.

"You guys deserve your bad rep," Brand said, scribbling his signature on the receipt.

Leonard held out his hands and waited while Brand stripped off the county orange and his day old underwear. He put his own clothes on and waited.

"You're free to go," Leonard said. "We don't have bell hops. Just take a left and then go straight out the door with the red exit sign. Even the drunks can do that."

"Thanks," Brand said. "You've been really great."

"Fuck you, Brand," Leonard said.

Brand took a step back and then strained to walk out as casually as he could. When he hit the steps, he let his breath out. The day was overcast and warmer than it had been, maybe mid-fifties. Brand looked out across an empty swamp filled with cattails and skunk cabbage toward an old Frito Lay plant. He walked around to the front of the building. There was a pay phone by the double glass doors. It looked as if someone had puked on it. Brand found thirty-five cents in his pocket and dialed Ren's number. No answer. No machine. He stuck his hands in his pockets and took a look around. As he stood there, a big guy with skin like a panther stepped out of a very plain late model Chevy sedan. Five strides and the man was face to face with Brand.

"Charles Brand?" The big guy stuck out a hand the size of a deli ham and his smile got bigger.

Brand nodded.

"My name is Joshua. Joshua Ray Breakman." The smile got even bigger. "And I own your ass."

TEN

Brand's throat got tight again and a little ball of fire burned along one side of his empty stomach. A gull landed on the metal railing a few feet away and screamed at Joshua and Brand as they stood there looking at each other. Brand glanced at the gull and then looked back at Joshua. The big guy was still smiling. Brand shook his head and rubbed his temples. It sounded like there was an ocean inside his head.

"Get in line," Brand said. "Seems like everyone wants my ass these days."

"Yeah," Joshua said. His voice reverberated off the concrete walls as if he was speaking into a microphone with extra bass dialed in. "I expect you're right. I saw Senator Marshall go in there a few minutes ago."

"Longer than that," Brand said. "How long you been waiting out here?" It was getting hard to talk.

"A while."

"Why?"

Joshua pulled a few sheets of paper out of his coat pocket and showed them to Brand, along with a black business card with white lettering. The card had a nice black and white photo of Breakman along with just his name, profession and phone number.

"I'm the guy that got you out," Joshua said. Brand glanced at the bond and then handed it back to Joshua.

"Who posted the bond?" Brand asked.

Joshua shook his head. "Confidential," he said. "Just wanted to say hi and let you know that you're an expensive piece of property. You aren't planning on going anywhere in the next few weeks are you?"

Brand shook his head.

"Yeah, well that's good. 'Cause I don't want to have to come chasing after you." Josh paused for a moment before he went on. "That's what I'm good at, you know? Getting people back. The person that posted this for you, that person most likely picked me on purpose, you know? Like maybe that person thought you might be a runner."

"Why would 'that person' bother then?" Brand asked. "Why not just leave me in the joint?"

Joshua shrugged. "Damned if I know. But I will tell you this, Mr. Brand." Joshua shook the papers in his face. "You run, and I'll catch you. I played defensive linebacker for the SeaHawks, and when I catch you, I'll break something. Got it? Cause, see, I'm good at catching folks that run, but I don't like it. I like to sit in my office and sip coffee, and I like to go home at night, and when my wife asks me how my day was, I like to say, oh just boring. What I don't like," he took a step closer to Brand and shook the papers again. "What I don't like is having to call my sweet wife and tell her that I'm gonna be late because I have to chase down some scumbag who's jumped their bond. I really don't like that. And since you're such a big liability for me, I'm gonna be watching you extra careful."

"I didn't do it," Brand said. He rubbed his temples again. The surf was really pounding now.

"Don't matter to me if you did or didn't," Joshua said. "All that matters to me is that you show up for your hearing. Got it?"

Brand nodded. Joshua pulled a big, ugly black plastic sports watch out of his pocket.

"I'm gonna give you this tracker," Joshua said. "Hold out your left arm."

Brand just stood there, staring at the strange watch.

"You gotta take it," Joshua said. "Or it's right back in there you go. Condition of bail."

Brand held out his arm and Joshua clamped the thing on. The strap ratcheted closed and Brand pulled his arm away. It looked like a watch, but there was no face. Just a black box.

"That's a GPS tracking device," Joshua said. "I can tell where you are in near-real time. Got a portable receiver in my car, and I can log onto the web and find you anytime I want. If you cut it off, alarm goes off and pages me with your longitude and latitude and I come find you myself. I'm my own bounty hunter too. See? So I own your ass. You try to lose me, you go back into jail. You wander too far off, you go back to jail. You forget to check in with me every two hours, I come find you and you go back to jail. Got it?"

Brand just kept staring at the GPS transmitter on his arm. "This is military technology," he said.

"Not any more," Joshua replied.

Joshua watched Brand for a moment and then slowly backed away. He turned and headed toward his car. Brand shook his left arm so that the sleeve of his coat covered the transmitter and called after Joshua.

"Since I'm such an expensive piece of real estate, can you at least give me a lift home?"

Joshua turned and looked at Brand over the top of his open door.

"No such luck," Joshua said. "I give you a ride, then I have to give every hard luck case in town a ride." He pointed down the long access road that led past a series of office buildings and industrial lots. "You walk to the end of that road, there's a bus station there. Busses go to the transit station, from the station you can go wherever you want. Just stay close, and keep in touch. Got it?"

"Yeah, I got it."

Breakman ducked into his car and drove away slowly. Brand started walking down the road, following Joshua's taillights, hoping that they would slow down and stop. Joshua hit the end of the road about a quarter of a mile further from where Brand was walking. His turn signal flashed. One moment he was there, the next moment he was gone. Brand kept trudging forward with his hands in his pockets and the misty air piercing his sleeves. He looked up at the sound of crunching gravel. An almost classic Mercedes 550SE pulled up along side him and Renata rolled down the window. Her eyes held a look of anxiety, fear and concern.

"Jesus," she said. "Look at you."

"That bad?" Brand asked.

"Worse," she said. "What'd they do in there? Torture you and starve you?"

"Pretty much," he said.

"You should never have written that scathing piece on the County jails," she said.

Brand rubbed his forehead and tried to keep his eyes open. He felt as is he was falling asleep on his feet. His eyes kept crossing and he felt his knees go weak. Somehow, Renata got her door open and caught Brand just as he fell. She pushed his limp body toward the open door of the car and pushed him in like a bag of old laundry. She had to tip his feet upward and jam them the rest of the way in with her shoulders, but she finally got him over the driver's seat and into the passenger side. Brand's head lolled backward and his eyes barely opened.

"What are you doing here?" he asked. His voice was thick and slurred, and he sat like a dead man.

"Nice to see you too, Brand," she said as she buckled her seat belt. He slept all the way to the island.

ELEVEN

Brand woke with a start as the big car lurched up onto a sloped driveway.

"Laci?" he asked. The little bit of sleep made him feel worse instead of better. He'd felt the name come out of his mouth, knew he'd been dreaming about her, but couldn't remember what. Too hazy.

"Jesus, Brand," Renata said.

Brand rubbed his forehead and looked around. They were pulling slowly along a narrow driveway of white pavement. Just beyond a wide expanse of green grass bordered by some short azaleas, already bursting with red blossoms, and a healthy crop of snow-on-the-mountains, the glimmering blue water of Lake Washington stretched out toward the west hills of Seattle. The sun had come out, and Brand could see all the way over to the floating bridge that led to Mercer Island. He touched the dashboard in front of him to get himself grounded in reality again. He felt a thin film of gritty dust under his fingers, and noticed that the metallic blue paint on the hood of the car was chipped in several places. His head felt as if it was too big for his shoulders, and his eyes hurt when he moved them. Tiny details, like the grit and the paint chips, seemed as large as the lake and the far hills. He took a breath and closed his eyes again for a moment.

"Sorry," he said.

"Nice dream?" she asked. She wasn't smiling. Her crisp white tee shirt and blue jeans looked almost out of place against the brown leather of the German tank. They stopped in front of an older Tudor-style home surrounded by scaffolding and empty paint cans. Renata flipped the sun visor down and punched a garage opener.

"I don't know," Brand said. "I'm just...confused."

"I'll say."

"Thanks for picking me up," Brand said.

Renata pulled the car into the garage and parked next to a red Jeep Wrangler. Brand opened the door and stood up, but his legs buckled and he ended up back in the seat at an odd angle. Renata stood by with her hands on her hips.

"I'm not going to carry you," she said.

"I need some food," Brand said. "My blood sugar is all out of whack."

She leaned over and slipped a slender arm under his shoulder. Together, they managed to stagger through the kitchen. Renata helped him ease into a hard-backed chair in the dining room and then she went back into the kitchen and started rattling around in the fridge. She came back after a few minutes with an orange and a can of Slim Fast.

"This should help stabilize your blood sugar," she said. "You eat this and drink this and I'm going to go get something that I think you ought to see. I'll be right back."

Brand nodded and Renata stalked off into some other part of the house. Brand sniffed the thick shake and would have thrown up again if there had been anything in his stomach. He dumped the shake down the sink and ran some water. Ran some more into the cup, rinsed it out, then drank as much as he could stand. He put the orange in the fridge and found a small rib eye steak. Ate that instead. He was drinking another glass of water when

Renata came back with a manila folder in her hands. She sat down across from him and stared.

"Thank you," he said. "And really, I'm sorry about what I blurted out in the car, I have no idea what was going through my head."

"I do," Renata said. She waited for a moment. "Laci Keller. You don't even know her."

Brand stared at the manila folder that sat on the table between them. "She's involved somehow."

Ren frowned.

Brand tried to get his mind around Laci, the griffs, the boy on the needle, the fall. Traced his memory back, trying to find the thread that started the sequence of coincidence, not believing in coincidence at all, trying to find the *sequitor*, the cause and effect.

"Laci," Brand said. He lost whatever loose train of thought existed there, wanted to get it back, but Ren sat, staring at him, waiting, and then she sighed, opened the manila folder and spun it around so that it was facing Brand. He looked long and hard at the black and white photo on the top of the stack. He tipped his head one way and then the other, trying to make it out.

"It looks like some kind of low-contrast art-deco shot of a concrete pillar, taken at an extreme angle. Not one of your best photos."

Brand took a look around the dining room. Framed photos hung on every wall, a testament to Renata's skills. Her gift showed in the wizened faces of old men, shot in a harsh light that revealed every nook and cranny, every pore, and in the aura around the faces of young girls, shot with a diffuser and over-exposed, so they looked like angels. Her photography was often more art than real.

"This is a beautiful place," Brand said. It was old, lathe and plaster walls, coved ceiling, arches between each room, light oak flooring, tidy and well-kept, but showing signs of wear and tear like a patina. The dining table was polished cherry, and the chairs were delicate and dark. Everything was a staged like a scene, with a practiced eye for contrast and a revulsion for clutter. The pastel rugs and curtains told of a woman's touch and tastes. The house was devoid of hard lines and metal and the occasional element of male presence that dominated Brand's own apartment up on First Hill.

Renata waited patiently while Brand settled in.

"Photography must pay a lot better than writing," he said.

"I've had my good days," Renata said. "And my bad ones."

"Yeah," Brand said.

Renata tapped the photo, bringing Brand's attention back to task.

"Do you know what this is?" she asked.

Brand shook his head.

"It's a shot of the upper o-deck of the Needle, right where the wall meets the floor."

Brand frowned and took a closer look. He pushed it aside and glanced at the next one. It was nothing but a blur.

"I don't get it," he said.

"Synchro-flash," she said. There was a wicked gleam in her eye, and suddenly Brand realized that she was toying with him.

"I set the Canon on synchro-flash with the Ricoh that night," she said. "That way, I can sometimes get black and white shots at the same time I get color. It's a bummer trying to handle both cameras but sometimes it pays off. And film is cheap."

Brand's eyes were on the stack of photos now, and so were his hands. He fanned them out across the table and examined them one by one.

"The one you want is here," she said, tapping a muddled eight by ten.

Brand got his nose right on it and peered closely. The film was grainy, sensitive to light, but not to detail. Great for night shots, but only if everything held completely still, and only if the flash was in range. Brand could make out a running figure of a man, the cop, and something like a shadow crouched just beyond. The shadow was lithe, dangerous even in 2D, sleek like a snake, one leg stretched out in a sweeping motion. It was like looking at a ghost.

"That's your missing link," Renata said. "The other person on the roof."

Brand tapped the photo with his finger and nodded.

"Don't touch," Renata said. "You're getting grease all over it. Why are your fingers greasy?"

"This is the proof," Brand said. "We have to show this to Devers."

"This is proof of nothing," Renata said. "They'll just accuse you of faking it."

"But you'll testify that you took this that night, right?"

"Of course I will, but it still won't prove anything. Believe me, my ex was, is, a lawyer. I spent enough nights digging through case files at this table to know what's going to fly and what's not."

Brand rubbed his face and then his temples, resting his elbows on the table.

"But now at least you believe me," Brand said. "Right?"

Renata rubbed her chin. "I know you're not a killer," she said. "When you're you."

Brand shot her a quick look of warning and then he picked up the photo and peered at it for a moment.

"We have to find this woman," he said.

TWELVE

Renata put Brand in her spare room. It was almost as big as his whole apartment, but he preferred the stiff sheets and flat foam of his prison cot to the puffy quilt and spongy pillows of Renata's guest bed. He tossed and turned, too tired to sleep, thinking about Ren and then Laci, and getting them somehow confused together. He drifted into a light sleep, found himself somewhere else, sometime else, with the rain falling outside and Laci stretching out in the front, watching her body in the mirror, watching the class, watching Brand, her eyes covered with dark glasses even in the dim light.

He wiped a thin layer of sweat from his upper lip and noticed that his gut churned as if he had just had a brush with danger, and now, laying there in that soft bed, in Renata's house, where he should feel safe and warm, he felt naked, cold and unprotected, and that churning feeling was still there, but somehow he drifted off into a dreamless sleep.

Sun god. Raven. Gryphons. Dancer on the deck.

He slept all afternoon and into the next morning. It was the smell of coffee that got him out of bed and into the shower, still thinking about Laci and Renata and confused about them both. His clothes, washed and folded, waited for him on the bed when he came out of the bathroom. He came downstairs and sat at the counter while Ren fixed him an egg and ham scramble with wheat toast.

"I never knew you were this domestic," Brand said.

"What's that supposed to mean?" she asked.

Brand shrugged. "I've only ever seen you on the street, snapping photos like you were still in the trenches. And you usually drive that old jeep. This is a side of you I never would have guessed." .

Renata set the plate in front of him and he savored the steam for a moment as she refilled his cup.

"Are you going to eat too?" he asked.

"No, go ahead. I ate earlier."

Brand picked at the eggs. His stomach gurgled and racked a bit, but what he managed to get down, he held down.

"You don't look good," Renata said. She leaned against the counter as he ate. Her white tee shirt hung down a bit, and he couldn't help but notice her straight collarbone and the first few ribs, pressing against her tight skin. She supported her body with her forearms, and one hip jutted up a little higher than the other. She watched Brand eat as if she was studying him.

"My stomach bothers me a bit," he said.

"You should probably lay off the coffee," she said. She reached out to pull the cup away, but Brand put his hand over it.

"Just let me finish this one cup. It's just so decadent, and for some reason, life seems especially sweet to me right now."

"It's just plain old Starbucks," she said.

"Hey, for all I know, this may be the last cup I ever get."

"Don't they serve coffee in prison?" Renata asked.

"Don't even joke about that," Brand said.

Renata glanced at her watch. "Day's a wasting," she said.

"What time is it?"

"Nearly noon."

"Geeze."

"Yeah."

"What day is it?" Brand asked.

"Tuesday," Renata said. "You really are confused."

"I never know what day it is anymore," he said.

Behind Ren, hanging on the wall, an old-fashioned Farmer's Almanac calendar, with the phases of the moon mapped out. Of course Ren would have that. Would watch for that.

She thinks she knows more about me than I do, he realized.

"So, what's your plan?" Ren asked.

Brand used the last of his toast to wipe his plate clean. The eggs and the meat had gone down fine, but the toast tasted like cardboard and felt like paste in his mouth. He washed it all down with the last of the coffee, now tepid and bitter.

"Got a piece of paper?" he asked. Renata fetched a clean piece of twenty-four pound bond and a pencil. Brand drew a rough sketch of Laci's tattoo. Renata watched from over his shoulder.

"Wow, you can draw too," she said.

"Recognize this?" Brand asked. Renata shook her head.

"This was the emblem on the back of Pritchert's coat."

"Who's Pritchert?" she asked.

"Pritchert is the name of the kid we saw at the Center that night, the point man for the Gryphons."

"I thought you said his name was Riff," Renata said. She was frowning as she peered at the drawing.

"Jesus, you have a good memory. No, I just called him Riff because he acted tough and I thought he was the leader. You know? Riff?" Brand snapped his fingers to the beat in his head. Renata just stared at him as if he were speaking in an alien tongue.

"Never mind," he said. "Look, the kid that we ran into Saturday night at the Center was in jail yesterday, or whenever it was, Sunday. Anyway, his name is Pritchert and his friend, the baby-faced guy, his name is Keuek."

"You are making no sense right now," Renata said.

"I do sound like I'm having some kind of seizure, don't I?"

"Uh-huh," Renata said, nodding.

"OK, look, here's my plan. You take this down to the library, or get on the web, or something, and you track down the meaning of this symbol. Try Tsimshian Sun God." He spelled it for her.

"You're like a walking encyclopedia of weird and obscure information, aren't you?" Renata said.

"More like just the index. I remember a lot of stuff, but no details. That's why I need your help. You're like the detail genius."

"And what are you going to do?"

"Well," Brand said. "There's a pair of these things out there. We know that Pritchert and the Gryphons have one. I'm going to go take a closer look at the other one."

"That's right," Renata said. "You said you'd seen it twice that same day." Her eyes narrowed. "Where did you see it the first time?"

"On Laci Keller's chest," he said.

Renata looked at him as if he was a dead fish. She wrinkled her nose and pursed her lips.

"You saw her chest?"

Brand nodded. "I went back after my shower, and she was changing in the back room there. I caught her with her shirt up over her head. She's got this tattoo running from shoulder to shoulder and from her neck to her belly. Black as night, big as life."

"You walked in on her with her shirt off?" Renata said. Her eyes said horrible.

"I didn't know she was going to strip in the back room," he said. "Anyway, it's the same design. Exact same."

"What else did you see?" Renata asked.

"Just the tattoo," he said. On a better day, he would have teased her a bit, but his instincts said no, and he wasn't really in the mood for fun and games anyway. He looked away from her.

Renata's eyes narrowed, but she shut her mouth and then almost laughed.

"You are really a piece of work," she said. She looked at the paper again and sighed. "OK. So, I get to socialize with my computer while you go out and hit on our aerobics instructor."

"Well," Brand said. "That's one way to look at it." He paused for a moment. "I'll call you when I have more."

Renata grunted. "What about Clayton Dash?" she asked.

"He's not here till Friday, right? We've got plenty of time to figure that out. Besides, I'm kind of preoccupied right now."

"Yeah, well you need money too. Don't forget that. Even if you are innocent, a good defense is expensive."

Brand's face relaxed a bit and his stomach got a hot knot right in the bottom, almost like a cramp.

"I didn't push him," Brand said.

Renata's eyes got wide. "No, that's not it," she said. "I meant that even innocent people need a good defense to prove their innocence. You won't get that from a public defender."

Brand took a deep breath and decided to give Ren the benefit of the doubt. Cooper's face flashed into his head and he smiled.

"I've got an attorney," Brand said. "A public defender. Protector of truth and justice. And a big fan of mine."

Renata shrugged and stepped by Brand. Her white shirt brushed against his arm and she left a wafting smell of watermelons and citrus in her wake.

"Come on then Romeo," she said. "I'll drive you home."

Brand followed her to the garage. "I can bus it," he said. Renata turned and gave him a short laugh.

"There's no good bus service to Mercer Island," she said. Her face went serious all of a sudden. "I'll take you to your place, then you're on your own."

"You're a sweetheart," Brand said.

They stared at each other, Ren holding the driver door halfway open, Brand holding the passenger door.

"Thank you," he said. "For taking me in."

Ren nodded, and Brand couldn't help but ask the question that seemed to fill his mind.

"Were you scared?"

Ren gave him a thin, tight smile and then slipped into the Wrangler.

THIRTEEN

October 17, 1995 – 6:15PM

Ren dropped Brand off at the front door to his apartment and then drove off. Brand checked his watch as he climbed the stairs. His key still worked in the lock, so the landlord hadn't kicked him out yet. He checked his e-mail, scanning through quickly before he logged on to the Y's web page to check the schedule. Laci was listed as the six o'clock instructor. Brand walked to the studio, missed the class but hit the crowd coming out. He waited on the street for Laci, feeling like he was still wearing the orange jumper and a number across his chest, but no one even gave him more than a glance. He gave up a dollar and fifty cents and grabbed a Tuesday Post Intelligencer out of box. Before he closed it, he checked the bottom for a Sunday paper, but they had been dutifully cleared out. He flipped through the front section of evening daily but found nothing on Kenny's death. Old news. As he fumbled with the limp sheets of newsprint, Laci came out and turned toward the monorail station. Brand threw the paper in a nearby trash bin and followed her, trying to catch up, but her long strides kept him about thirty seconds back.

"What're you going to do, Brand," he asked himself. His stomach was tight again, and he was almost ready to give up the chase when Kenny's dark eyes came back to him and he tasted the metallic air of the county jail. He pressed his lips together and pushed his legs harder. A drop of rain hit him on the cheek, and within a block there was a steady drizzle coming straight down.

Laci took a seat near the front of the elevated train. Brand slipped in the back. He followed her out at the Seattle Center station, glancing at the Space Needle and the peace garden just beyond. One large area was still cordoned off with yellow tape. He felt like a criminal returning to the scene of the crime. Laci huddled under her hooded cape and jogged down the concrete steps toward the needle. She skirted around the base of the tower and headed north up Harrison toward Queen Anne Hill. Brand kept a good distance back, noted the old brick apartment building she went into, and then waited. He paced back and forth, stewing, with his hands thrust deep into his pockets. Twice he almost left, circled around the back of the building instead, and then paced the sidewalk on the opposite side of the street again. After thirty minutes, Laci came out again and walked to a bus stop at the bottom of the hill. Brand cleared his throat as he came close, ready to say something, but just then six co-eds that looked like U of W Husky fans sat near Laci, chatting about nothing and laughing at everything. Brand stayed at the edge and followed them onto the number thirty-nine heading for Tukwila. Laci sat front again so Brand stayed back with the co-eds. He sat by an old man who was snoring and smelled of urine. It was almost an hour, most of it freeway, before Laci got off. Brand dropped a buck fifty in the meter and jumped off at the last minute. The rain was colder and heavier, forcing Brand deeper into his pockets. Laci walked seven blocks and then took a seat on top of a picnic table in a little neighborhood park. She just sat there, huddled under her coat, doused in orange light from a single sodium vapor lamp. Brand could see an occasional wisp of steamy breath coming from under the dark hood. Even though it was still supposed to be autumn, the dark, penetrating cold was like a prelude to the coming winter. Brand watched for a while, and then finally walked. He stopped next to her.

"Mr. Brand," she said.

"Hello."

He took a seat on the table by her, adopting her pose and attitude.

Laci turned and stared at him with her big, black eyes. "May I ask what you are doing here?"

"Following you." Brand didn't know what else to say.

"For what reason?" He could feel her hackles going up.

Brand sat down next to her. She glared at him. He pointed at the house across the street.

"What're you watching for?" he asked.

"None of your business," she said. "Why are you following me?"

Brand turned and looked at her. Under her hood, her face was stern, but there was an underlying current of worry, almost a frantic tremor, like a mouse in an exposed field, not knowing if there was a hawk above or not.

"I need to know what you were doing last Friday night, after class."

"Friday. The thirteenth. Why?"

"Research," he said.

"For a story?"

He nodded.

"Seems like you're the big story this week, Mr. Brand. Dropping a kid off the Space Needle. You've got guts, but no brains." She turned her head so that her eyes were on the house again.

"There was someone else up there," Brand said.

"Yeah, I read the story in the P.I."

Brand fixed his eyes on hers. His stomach flipped, but not with fear.

"You don't seem to be too nervous about me following you," he said.

"I've been watching you since the Y," she said. "You're not that great at holding a tail."

"Well," he said. "In my defense, I held it. Just because you made me, doesn't mean I didn't hold it."

"Whatever."

They both watched the ranch rambler across the street as it just sat there, an identical twin to its neighbors. A faceless, uninteresting testament to the homogeneity of the fifties. A single-storey rectangular space-saver, the genesis of mass produced homes. The windows were mostly dark, except for one large, single pane of glass that flickered with the reflected light of a television.

"Why are you following me?" she asked again.

"I told you," he said. "I'm trying to find out where you were the night Kenny died."

"Why?"

"Because, I am in possession of some evidence that places you at the scene."

"Bullshit," Laci said. "What kind of evidence?"

"I can't say," Brand replied.

Laci glared at him again. "There is no evidence placing me at the scene, Mr. Brand. I can tell you that for sure, because I wasn't there."

"Then who was?" Brand asked.

"You tell me."

Brand waited for a moment, trying to regroup his thoughts as the cold soaked through his pants.

"I ran into a group of the Gryphons just before I went up to see Kenny," he said. "One of the kids was wearing an emblem just like your tattoo."

"So?"

Something in Laci's eyes shifted. It was as if the light had suddenly changed, and her face receded into the darkness.

"Just before he was killed, Kenny was telling me about someone called the Raven. Kenny was in good, or bad I guess you'd say, with the Gryphons. And these Gryphons are in good with the Raven. Then this thing, this black dancing fighter, came up and beat the shit out of Kenny and dropped him over the side."

Her eyes glistened in the dim light, but her face was very cool.

"You still haven't told me what this has to do with me," she said.

"Yes, I did. I told you that I saw one of the Gryphons wearing an emblem on his coat, just like the tattoo on your chest."

"So what? That doesn't mean squat. Why the hell are you trying to pin something on me?"

"Because, you're a fighter and a dancer, and you have a tattoo that is identical to one that appeared just before Kenny's death. Too much coincidence."

"So," she said. "If I am your dancer, what would stop me from killing you right now?"

"What stopped you up there on the needle?"

"You just don't get it Mr. Brand. I'm not your girl. I didn't not kill you on the needle because I wasn't there. Wasn't even close."

"Where were you?"

"Probably here. Not that it's any of your business. Now, if you don't mind, I'd like to be alone."

"I have to find that girl," Brand said.

"Let it go," Laci replied.

"If she would just come forward, we could both attest that it was just an accident. We tried to save him, but he just gave up. Slipped out of his coat, on his own, before we could pull him up. That's what happened as I remember it. Wasn't it?"

Laci smiled and shook her head.

"Brand, I wasn't there. Much as you want it to be me, it wasn't."

She stood up and stomped her feet and shook her shoulders as she exhaled a big breath of air. She stared at Brand for a long time. He felt a chill run down his spine, as if he was being assessed for an invitation to dinner by a wild animal. Laci's nostrils flared a bit as her eyes delved into his. Brand's hands wrapped around the edge of the table and he felt his knuckles going white. They stayed like that, blinking away the persistent rain, until Laci finally relented.

"Come on," she said. "I need to get out of here."

"First," Brand said. "You have to tell me the truth. What is your connection with the Raven, and was it you up on the needle that night."

"No," she said. "It wasn't me. I swear. But I will tell you what I know about Raven. Now come on. You wanted me to go out with you, remember? Well, maybe we'll go out with a bang."

Brand just stared at her. She reached out and took his hand.

"I know you didn't kill Kenny Marshall," she said. "And neither did I. Now come on or we'll miss the next bus. I'll give you my story on the way back." She paused as Brand slid off the table and stretched himself back into a standing position. "And then you can tell me yours too. Quid pro quo. "

She paused for just a moment and then added, "I especially want to know about the colloidal silver. What the hell are you thinking?"

FOURTEEN

October 17, 1995 – 8:08PM

They walked back down the hill slowly, side by side, staring straight ahead at the glistening sidewalk.

"This whole thing is like some weird, avante-guard hell," Brand said.

"Dante went into hell and made it out again," Laci said. "So did Herakles."

"Then maybe you're Virgil," Brand said.

"Maybe I'm Beatrice," she responded.

Brand cocked his head to the side and watched her eyes for a moment. He pursed his lips and then recited a little piece from Dante's fifth Canto.

"Always there is a crowd that stands before him. Each soul in turn advances toward that judgment; they speak and hear, then they are cast below."

She picked it up without a hitch.

"Arresting his extraordinary task, Minos, as soon as he had seen me, said, 'O you, who reach this house of suffering, be careful how you enter, whom you trust. The gate is wide, but do not be deceived.'"

"You're well read," Brand said.

"Well enough, on things that deal with hell and death. Kind of a hobby of mine."

"Then you must have seen Bartolomeo's painting down at the L'Beurge?"

She nodded. "It's a copy. Not the real thing. Anyway, it's gross. All those naked bodies stacked one on top of another. He was a pervert."

"The dead were eating each other," Brand noted.

"Yeah. Like I said. Masterpiece or not, it was gross."

"We're kind of avoiding the real subject," Brand said.

The hit the bus stop at the same time the big Grunner transit pulled up. Laci flashed a pass, Brand dropped another buck fifty in the fare box, and they skirted by the up front customers, choosing a seat in the far back corner. Laci sat by the window and Brand sat next to her.

"Where do you want me to start?" she asked. She was staring out the window.

"Tell me about Raven," he said.

"He's crazy," she said. "I maybe I did that to him. I don't know. My therapist says I take too much responsibility for stuff."

She paused for a moment, still staring out into the darkness.

"I was a student of his, way back. Long time ago. Or, at least it seems that way now. It was really only eight or nine years ago. Just seems like a long time."

"Yeah," Brand said. "I know how that feels."

She glanced at him, checking him out as if she was seeing him for the first time. She nodded and then turned back to her reflection in the dingy glass.

"Anyway, he was this brilliant guy. Like, he could do anything. Wealthy, arrogant, smart, connected, and on top of everything else, he was a champion fighter. It was like he could do anything, be anything. And I was this timid little girl, just out of college. I got raped once, in college, and I was really scared. It was like everything I ever believed in had just been stripped from me. All my confidence, all my dreams, all my naivety. So I signed up for this self-defense for women class, and this guy was the teacher. Jack Raevyn. Big, muscular, tan. The kind of guy I would have drooled over when I was younger. But then he just scared me. But a friend convinced me to sign up anyway. She'd been fighting for about a year and was really into it. A star pupil. Moving up the ranks very fast. So I came in and started fighting, and this guy, Jack Raevyn, he took a personal interest in me. Said I was a natural. But it wasn't all talent. When I got in there and started punching and kicking, I started feeling like I was in control again. And every time I hit that bag or went through a kata, it was like I was taking revenge on the guy that raped me. And on me too. You know? I kind of blamed myself. I blamed myself for being scared. I blamed myself for not being stronger. I guess I really hated myself, and I could look in that mirror and hook and jab right at my own reflection, and I could beat the shit out of myself, day after day."

She paused and caught her breath. As badly as Brand wanted to check his watch, he kept his eyes on Laci instead. She checked on him with her eyes, noted that he was listening, and then turned away again.

"Raevyn paid a lot of attention to me. He was a fighter, but he was always gentle and kind and patient with me. And good looking and rich."

She shook her head and looked down at her hands.

"I never really fell in love with him. I just married him because I thought that maybe it would make my life normal."

She stopped for a moment and then blew air out through her nose, almost as if she was laughing. She shook her head and stared out into the darkness again, taking a deep breath.

"Anyway, this friend of mine, the one that introduced me to fighting, she and I were, well, we were close. Know what I mean?"

115

She shot a glance toward Brand and he nodded.

"So, Jack turns out to be a bit of a drinker, and a hard man. He had me fooled. As soon as we were married, this whole other side of him comes out. He was like Jekyll and Hyde. I never knew which Jack Raevyn was coming home at night. But my fighting was good, almost as good as his, so our fights were doozies. We destroyed our house more than once. Broken windows, broken furniture, broken arms, broken noses. It was horrible, but there was this perverse part of me that liked it. I mean, I actually started to look forward to it. It was like a contest, and I knew one day that he'd win and he'd kill me, and I thought, go for it buddy, 'cause then I won't have any more worries."

She cleared her throat and pulled her legs up against her chest, hooking her heels on the edge of the seat.

"The whole time, my other friend and I were having an affair. She was always so tender and caring and sweet, and she just hated Jack. I think she would have tried to kill him if I hadn't stopped her. But she wasn't half the fighter he was. Even so, we planned all kinds of ways to kill him. Guns, knives, poison, fire. It was kind of our after-sex pillow talk. How to kill Jack. But it was all talk. I never had the guts to really kill anyone. But something told me that K.O. did. She always did have this strange look in her eyes."

"So, I was living this lie, the whole time. And K.O. and I got more and more bold, almost like we didn't care if we got caught. She even started coming over to my house, sleeping with me in Jack's bed during the day. He was a workaholic, so we never really worried about him coming home. But one day he did. And it was a bad day too. Something bad had happened at work, he was a geneticist, a scientist. Working up at Longview Hospital in the R&D department. Government funding. Some big project got pulled. Anyway, he was pissed, and he came home, and K.O. and I were in that kind of groggy half sleep you get after some really good sex, so we didn't hear the front door. But we heard something, 'cause I'll never forget that feeling. It's like one minute you're so relaxed and peaceful, like you're in God's arms, and then boom, all of a sudden your heart is down in your stomach and your whole body is shaking with adrenalin 'cause you know you're about to die."

She stopped talking and just stared out the window for a long time.

"So," Brand said. "He caught you. What happened next?"

Laci shrugged, as if it was no big deal.

"A fight. A big one. I just pulled the covers up over my body like one of those mousy ladies in the movies. K.O. just stood up and said 'hi Jack,' like it was no big deal. His eyes were like fire, and he just stood there, with his fists clenched and his jaw tight, and that's when I got scared. Really scared. I was petrified. I mean, really petrified. You know, together, K.O. and I might have stood a chance, but I just cowered there, under the covers, like a mouse."

She shook her head, and Brand saw the reflection of a tear drift down her cheek.

"Jack came right across the bed and hit K.O. in the back with both feet as she was trying to pick up her clothes. She rolled over and came up like a tiger, and my God they hammered each other."

Laci shuddered.

"But Jack was big, and a mass of muscle. Plus he knew all the techniques. Fourth degree black belt, ju jitsu, jeet kun do, aikido, wu shu karate, and any kind of street fighting. KO was tough though. A lot of fire and guts. But he nailed her. Crossed her, kicked her, threw her right out the window. I never saw her again. She ran. Or probably crawled. Can't blame her. Then he came after me. We fought, but I was nowhere near the fighter that KO was. Jack played with me. Taunted me. Chased me over the whole house and finally outside. I was running down the street, naked, screaming for help. He just trotted after me, calling out to me like a loving husband, pleading with me to come home. It was raining that night. Like this. All the neighbors must have thought I had a nut loose."

She sucked in a breath as if it was painful.

"A police cruiser finally picked me up and then they stopped and got Jack and he told them this story, all calm like, about how I was having a seizure and I really needed to get home. They put me in the back and Jack rode in the front as if I was the criminal. Then these two big cops drug me back into the house and Jack shot me up with some kind of stuff from his lab while they held me. It was like I knew everything that was going on, but I couldn't do anything about it. They laid me out on the pool table, in the rec room, and Jack offered them a beer and they all agreed that it wasn't worth reporting, and all they while they're staring at me as I'm laying there with my arms and legs all spread out, and Jack's just watching them watch me, and pretty soon, after they have a couple more beers, they start talking guy talk, about pool and balls and pockets and all that crap, laugh, laugh, haw, haw."

Laci shook her head and stared at her knees.

"They took turns with me, and I couldn't do a damn thing about it. They shoved pool balls up inside me and raped me with a pool cue and a beer bottle and then they took turns fucking me with their little, pitiful cocks. And then afterwards Jack showed them out as if they were dinner guests. I could hear them laughing at the front door. And then Jack went upstairs. Just left me there on the pool table. I have no idea what he was thinking. Maybe he thought I was dead. Maybe he thought that I'd be out all night. I don't know. I managed to get off the table and into the kitchen, and I was going to slash my wrists but I couldn't reach the knives. I just laid there for a while, like a rag doll. But my willpower started to come back to me, and pretty soon I was sitting up, and then I made it out to the garage, and I was just going to get in the car and drive, which would have been really stupid, but instead I saw that can of gas sitting there by the mower and so I picked it up and it was like all my strength came back to me. I was the angel of death, the angel of mercy. I laughed out loud as I carried the can upstairs and I doused my loving husband with it. He woke up right when I threw the match. I was in total control. I saw his eyes go wide as the flames lit him up. They were almost clear, you know? Hot and blue, racing like lizard's tongues. It was amazing. And hot too. Insanely hot. But he didn't even scream at first. He just sat up and stared at me, as if he couldn't believe what I was doing. You know? Mr. perfect, like, 'what did I ever do to you?' I just walked away. He started screaming and I then I ran. I ran out to the garage and I got in the Buick and ran into the door before it opened. I was shaking and trembling and I threw up as I went down the drive. I crashed into the gate and just sat there, naked, in the car, until the police came and the ambulance and the fire trucks. They hauled me away as our house burned to the ground."

"So," Brand said. "You're ex-husband can't be the Raven."

"I'm not finished yet," Laci said. "They locked me up in the psych ward. No one believed anything that I had to say. I sounded like a nut case, and really, I was. I mean, I was crazy. I'm not even sure what was real and what wasn't. Maybe I did dream the whole thing. Maybe I really was just this fabulously lucky housewife with the gentleman catch of the century, the envy of all the socialite women of Seattle, recipient of the silver spoon award, and I was just crazy, imagining all the other stuff. "

She shrugged.

"I don't know. It all seemed real enough to me at the time."

"So," Brand said. "What happened to Jack?"

She shook her head.

"No one knows. He just disappeared. No one found his body. He never turned up in any hospital. That's why I didn't get murder one. That and the fact that I was pregnant."

"How pregnant?" Brand said. He kept his voice low and quiet.

"It happened that night. Had to have. I don't even think that Jack is the father."

"You think Jack is still alive?" Brand asked.

"I know he is," she said. "He came to me in the night. Last year. Right after I got out of the institution. I'm not allowed to leave Seattle, or I would have. But I got this little place up in Magnolia. I was waiting tables, trying to get something going again so that I could someday get Alicia back."

"That's your daughter?"

Laci nodded.

"And she lives there, in Tukwila?"

Laci nodded again.

"Do you ever get to see her? I mean, be with her?"

She shook her head.

"She doesn't even know who I am," Laci said. "She's never seen me. And I'm not allowed to see her. She's a ward of the state. They don't even consider me her parent. They put her in foster homes. But she's trouble. Got a lot of fire in her, you know? Like, maybe some of my anger and pain got put insider her little body."

"How old is she now?"

"Four, going on eighteen."

Brand smiled and Laci beamed.

"You know, I watch her all the time. And sometimes she even comes over to me and says hi. One time, she was so proud, because she's been to a tag sale and she was wearing this little dress, almost like a nightshirt, and she had a metal lunch pail with cartoon dragons on it she was using for a purse to protect her stuffed dolphin. She was so proud because she'd bought all this stuff herself at the sale for a dollar. And then I look over at the foster parents and God bless 'em, they're trying to do their best, but they've got three other kids of their own and the dad just lost his job."

"But they take good care of her," Brand said.

Laci nodded. "She's been in over a dozen foster homes. That's like three or four homes a year. They try, they really do, but she can be a pistol. She just needs a mom."

Laci looked Brand in the face for the first time in almost an hour. Her eyes glistened with tears.

"How can a little girl live like that, Brand?" she said. "She doesn't have any friends and doesn't have any parents. Doesn't even know that she has a mom somewhere that loves her and just wants to hold her. When I saw her with those clothes and toys that she bought all on her own, my heart just about exploded. Oh, God, what I wouldn't give just to be her mommy."

All the hardness fell off her shoulders and she slipped into Brand's arms. He held her and she sobbed. Brand left her there until the bus hit Fifth and Denny, just north of the Seattle Center.

"Laci," he said. "We have to get off now."

Laci's head was still buried in his chest, but he felt her nod. He helped her stand up and they got off like two drunks supporting each other. The rain had stopped, so they stood on the sidewalk and Brand waited while Laci caught her breath.

"Can I walk you home?" Brand asked

Laci shook her head. "Actually, I was thinking that maybe I could stay with you."

Brand stared at her for a moment.

"You seem harmless enough," she said. She gazed off toward the rain clouds that hung over Elliot Bay. "I'm lonely," she whispered.

He took her hand and they walked up Denny toward the freeway overpass that led to First Hill. Laci's hand was cold and hard in his, and for some reason the thought of dead man walking drifted through his mind for a moment. He shook it off. Behind him, Brand could sense the watchful eye of the Space Needle as it towered above them. Laci looked down at their clasped hands, but did not let go.

FIFTEEN

The streets shined like silver as they walked up the hill toward Brand's apartment.

"What about you?" Laci asked. "What's your story?"

"Mine seems pretty lame compared to yours."

"Doesn't matter," she said. "Quid pro quo, remember?"

"I'm just a writer. Not much exciting about that."

"You were on the best seller list once, I remember you."

"Yeah. People always think that there is some money in writing. It's a myth. I had a little bit once. Blew it all on drugs and booze. Couple of bad habits that I couldn't seem to lick."

"But you did?"

Brand shrugged. "Every day is a chore. I lost it all. My house, my car, my... Everything."

"So, what keeps you from drinking now?"

Brand shook his head. "Lots of things."

They walked right by the 1911 Tavern as she said it, and Brand glanced in the window at the clusters of late-night after-business cocktail cliques standing around the bar, suits hustling on skirts with highlighted hair, guys drinking beer and laughing about how stupid their boss was, three gals with spiked heels sipping cheap Chablis and pretending they were in LA instead of grimy Seattle. Brand licked his lips.

"All the time," he said.

From the 1911, they walked up over the freeway and across a short stretch of Bellevue Avenue to The Capital Arms without saying a word. Brand fumbled with his keys a bit before he got the door open. His eyes went for the stacked rows of gunmetal gray mailboxes, and he paused for a moment before he realized the futility of checking his mail right now. He checked his watch instead. Just past six and pitch black already. He led Laci up the stairs and down a short hall. His apartment smelled closed and musty.

"I'm hungry," Laci said. She was staring at Brand as if he was a rack of lamb.

"I have to check in with my probation officer," he said. "Then maybe we can find someplace to get a bite."

"I'll use the bathroom," Laci said.

Brand nodded and pointed down a short, narrow hallway.

"Watch out for my cat," he said. "She sleeps in there. And she gets jealous when I bring girls home."

"I'll be careful," Laci said. She walked away, but glanced at Brand over her shoulder. He look gave him a chill up and down his spine. But it was a good chill. He suddenly thought about the 1911 again, and how good it felt to take that first sip of cold, sour beer. He gulped and took a deep breath. Laci disappeared down the hall and Brand shook his head and tried to get his knees to work again. He stepped into the bedroom and picked up the phone. As he listened for the dial tone, he bumped the mouse on his computer. The slight jar brought the screen out of power-saver. The desktop showed fifty-seven e-mails and his PAT live account showed twenty-eight voice mails as well.

Brand turned away from the computer and called Renata her cell. While it was ringing he dropped his wet blue jeans and picked a dry pair of wool slacks. She picked up and he thanked God.

"Ren, it's Brand." He held the phone on his shoulder as he unbuttoned his shirt.

"Hey," she said. "Where you been all afternoon. I left you a couple of messages. You know, most people have cell phones nowadays."

"Yeah, well, I don't. I've only got a moment. What did you find out?" Brand tossed his worn shirt onto the bed and grabbed a heavy woolen work shirt with quilted lining. He shifted the phone from shoulder to shoulder as he stuck his arms in the sleeves.

"About the sun god? Not much. But it is a Gryphon. So your hunch was right on there. Lots of legends about it. Mostly about creation of the world. He's a trickster god. Kind of naughty, even mean sometimes. Likes to take human form now and then. Sometimes even eats his own people, the humans. Is any of this making sense?"

"No, not really. But thanks." Brand heard the toilet flushing. "I gotta go, but first, do just a bit more research for me, would you?"

Ren's response sounded like a sigh. Brand pulled on wool socks and a pair of slip on Danners.

"Laci Keller or Laci Raevyn. Also, Jack Raevyn. Go back about four or five years."

"Keller is a pretty common name," she said.

Brand shut the door to his bedroom and put his back against it.

"Raevyn isn't. Try that one first. He was a player at one time. A mover and a shaker. Scientist. Wealthy. There was a big family blow-out."

"Is this guy *the* Raven?"

"Yeah, I think so. Either the Raven or the Phoenix."

"Huh?"

"You'll see what I mean when you find the right guy. I really gotta go. I've got an appointment."

"You mean a date."

Laci knocked on the door. "Brand, you got anything to drink here?"

Brand covered up the mouthpiece and tipped his head back.

"Sorry, no," he said. "I'll be right out." He put the phone back up to his ear. There was dead silence on the other end of the line.

"Hello?" Brand said. "You still there?"

"You come back dead, after I do all this research for you, and I'll be really pissed."

"If the Raven wanted me dead..."

There was silence again.

"I gotta go," Brand said.

"Yeah, I know."

Brand hung up wishing he didn't have to. He dialed the number on his wristband and got a real person.

"Where you been?"

"Joshua?" Brand asked.

"Yeah. You get directed right to me."

"Well, here I am, checking in."

"So, where you been?"

"Out and about."

"Downtown, Tukwila, now home."

"I'm glad you're tracking me so closely."

Joshua was silent.

"Well, been nice chatting with you," Brand said.

"Call me again in the morning," Joshua said.

"No problem," Brand replied. He hung up and stared at the GPS band on his left wrist. Laci knocked on the door and then cracked it open. Brand turned toward her.

"You okay in here?" she said.

He nodded. She was still wearing her jacket, and water dripped on the hardwood floor. The rest of the apartment behind her was dark.

"Do you want some dry clothes?" Brand asked. "Some of my stuff should fit you. She shook her head.

"No, I'm fine."

They stood there, staring at each other for a moment, and then Laci flipped off the bedroom lights and dropped her coat to the floor. The only illumination came from a dozen small lights on Brand's computer. Laci walked up to Brand and concentrated on each white button as she pressed them through their slits. She pushed his shirt off his shoulders and pushed on his chest. The backs of his legs hit the bed and he toppled slowly backward. Laci landed on top of him and then pushed herself up to her hands and knees, straddling Brand. He thrust his hands into her wet hair and pulled her face down against his. Her lips were cold and firm. Brand opened his eyes and found her staring at him. She pulled back and ripped his shirt off and then pulled her own sweatshirt over her head, revealing her sculpted, tattooed chest and muscular abdomen. She stood up and pulled off her jeans and Brand's heart raced. He kicked off his shoes and she stripped his jeans off his legs, and then slowly crawled back up his body, running her lips and tongue across his legs, up around his groin and his pelvis to his chest and then his neck. Brand waited as long as he could before he forced her over onto her back and pressed himself against her. As he penetrated, she arched her back, nearly throwing him off, like a bucking bronco. She grabbed his back and pulled him against her hard, nearly taking his breath away. He felt her fingernails digging into his back, and even felt a warm trickle something warm and thick, like blood, dripping down along his ribs. He rammed his hips against hers and she brought her head up. Their foreheads cracked together and Brand's eyes went white for a moment. When his vision cleared, he found Laci's wide, black eyes locked in his. She wrapped her legs around Brand's waist and her arms around his back and started rocking him in and out, slowly at first, then faster and faster, arching her back and tossing her head back and forth. Brand clenched his teeth and grabbed Laci's hair, pulling her head back against the bed. She shook him loose and he could hear her gasping, moaning, almost crying. He body started to shake, and her trembling coursed through his own body. Laci drove Brand back onto his back and held his arms down as she slammed her body against his, her eyes wild and blind, her breath hot and sweet against his face. Her body glistened with sweat, and her dark eyes filled with tears as Brand exploded inside her. She gasped quietly, her chest heaving, and Brand felt the world suspended in time as she pulled her lips back and plunged her face against his shoulder. He felt every muscle in his body go hard as she bit into his flesh, tearing deep into the flesh and muscle. But instead of pain, he felt a desperate ecstasy as she held her mouth against him, biting harder and harder.

"Oh my God," he whispered. He felt as if someone was dumping sweet, hot, licorice flavored Ouzo down his throat. His whole body was suddenly heavy and hot. Brand grabbed the back of Laci's head and pressed her harder against his shoulder, pushing her teeth even further into his neck as he rammed his hips against her and came again. He pushed again and again, wanting more and more, wanting her to bite deeper and deeper, but Laci suddenly shot up straight, screaming and throwing her arms out wide. Blood covered her mouth and chin and dripped down along her chest, coursing in and out of the black lines of the bird figure that perched there with its piercing eyes and gaping maw. Brand felt his heart stop for a moment and his lungs stopped working as if they were frozen. Right then, at that moment, he wanted nothing more than to tear Laci apart, piece by piece, bite by bite.

SIXTEEN

October 18, 1995 – 1:08AM

Brand jumped and sat straight up. A fine film of sweat covered his body and his shoulder ached, but there was no bite mark and no blood. He shuddered and ran his hand across the rumpled sheets next to him. The room came into focus slowly as his mind came awake, but the dream stayed with him, still vivid and immediate, as if it had really happened. He wrapped the blanket around his body and wandered out into the apartment. He found Laci sitting in the dark kitchen, wearing a thick cotton bathrobe that Jule had given to Brand as a wedding present. Laci was staring out the window toward the building across the street.

How long did I sleep?" Brand asked. He realized that he had no idea where reality had ended and the dream began.

"Maybe an hour," Laci said.

"I'm glad you waited for me," Brand said. His heart still pounded in his chest. He pulled out a chair and sat down next to her, put his hand on his shoulder and rotated it a bit. Laci turned her head away and stared out the window again. Brand reached out and touched her hair.

"Laci," he said. She turned toward him with tears in her eyes.

"Walk me home, Charlie Brand," she said.

"Sure," he said.

Brand put his warm clothes back on and dug some more out of his drawers for Laci. She put her wet tank top and cotton panties on under Brand's loaner clothes. The pants were a bit loose, so she grabbed a belt and cinched it up tight. She looked like a female logger in Brand's red plaid shirt and dark green pants. She borrowed his best cork boots and a corduroy hunting jacket. While she was getting her clothing adjusted, Brand stuck his spare digital recorder into his pocket. The phone rang and Brand picked it up. He expected Ren's voice on the other end but it wasn't.

"Brand, this is Jule."

Brand stood still, staring into the hallway where Laci stood with her hands in her pockets, watching him. Brand stepped back into the bedroom so that he was out of her sight, and so that she was out of his.

"Jule," he said. "Hi."

"Sorry it's been so long," she said. "I kept meaning to return your calls, but..."

Brand just stood there, listening. The sound of her voice was like a hot needle piercing his heart, and yet his mind kept drifting toward Laci. He still couldn't shake the dream, or even sort it out from what had really happened.

"Brand," Jule said.

"Yes?"

"Jesus, Brand," she said. "I thought you'd hung up."

"No."

Jule cleared her throat.

"I need to see you," she said.

Brand's mind was reeling.

"Can we get together for coffee or something?" she asked.

"Tonight?" Brand asked. He glanced at the clock on the wall. It was well after one in the morning.

"Do you have time?"

"Uh, no. I'm sorry."

Jule pressed him. "How about tomorrow?"

"Yeah," he said. "That would be better." He felt groggy and off balance. Two days ago he wanted nothing more than to see her again, even if only for a moment – to look into her blue eyes, to watch her lips move, to hear the sound of her voice. But now, he just wanted to walk Laci home. He squeezed his eyes shut and tried to concentrate on Jule's voice, realizing that today was already tomorrow, and wondering if she meant later, after sleeping, or tomorrow. Brand tried to figure out what day of the week it was, what day tomorrow would be. Nothing made sense to him.

"You OK?" she asked.

"Yeah," he said. "I mean, no. I'm kind of tired tonight I think. I'm sorry. I'll be better tomorrow. I promise. How about the Starbucks down on Fourth Avenue. The one we always used to meet at."

"Morning?" she asked.

"Sure. Can you make it ten?"

"Yeah," she said. "Ten will be fine. And Brand…"

"Yes?"

"Thanks."

"No problem," he said. He set the phone down gently, not wanting to end the conversation, but not able to go on. Laci poked her head into the bedroom and Brand pinched the bridge of his nose trying to get rid of a deep, pounding headache that threatened to surface. He picked up a baseball cap off the dresser and on a whim he pulled the digital out of his pocket and dropped into his hat. He stared at it for a moment and then grabbed a piece of duct tape from a roll he kept in his desk drawer. He slapped the tape across the recorder and tested to see how well it stuck by turning it over and shaking it before he snugged it onto his head. He touched Laci on the shoulder, gently guiding her to the door. They zipped up their coats as they walked down the hall.

They walked down to the street in silence. The fresh night air cleared Brand's head a little and the dull ache behind his eyes dissipated.

"Are you still hungry?" he asked.

"Ravenous," she said.

"Me too," Brand said. "I know a place down on Pike Street. Stays open late."

Laci turned and looked at him, and he suddenly knew that he didn't want to leave her alone tonight. They took the pedestrian bridge over the freeway and headed downtown.

"Tell me about Raevyn," Brand said.

Laci touched her chest and her hand drifted up toward her neck.

"That night that he came to me, he beat me and tied me down. He was covered in black, from head to toe. Kind of a thick, almost rubbery black material. It smelled rancid. Even his eyes were covered. And he was wearing a big black cape, like he thought he was some kind of superhero."

"But you knew it was him."

"Oh yeah. It was him. He beat me but good too. It was as if he was stronger. I would have thought that the fire would have made him weaker. He must have lost most of his skin and some muscle, and been totally covered in scar tissue, but he seemed faster, stronger, more sure of himself. I was like a toy. But I fought back, I'm telling you, I fought for my life. He knocked me down, tied my wrists to the bed, and my ankles and gagged me, but this time he didn't drug me, didn't rape me. He just pulled out this black bag and started needling me."

She glanced at Brand. "Ever had a tattoo?"

He shook his head.

"Hurts like hell. Even a little one. I bled all over."

"Then he left?"

Laci nodded. "Yep. He just left."

"Did he say anything?"

She nodded again. "Yeah. He said that I was still his. I still belonged to him. And my little bastard girl too. And he said that he'd be back for me."

"Back when?" Brand asked.

Laci clammed up. They turned down Stewart and crossed the freeway again. The cars below sent up sprays of water and the tires hummed on the pavement. Stewart was busy too, and Brand wondered where these people went, where they came from, why anyone would be out at this ungodly hour, and yet here he was, with Laci.

They took a left and ended up on Third Avenue behind the old Bon Marche, walking along the loading docks. Most of the businesses along this stretch were either boarded up or closed, not just for the night. Laci froze, her smile gone in an instant.

"What is it?" Brand asked. Her eyes were wide open and her nostrils flared slightly, like a tiger about to pounce.

"Shut up," she whispered. A single car passed by, throwing a sheet of water across the sidewalk in front of them. Brand shivered and held his breath, listening. He thought he heard a low growl coming from deep within Laci's throat as a black cloaked figure sauntered slowly across the street near the far end of the block, maybe a hundred yards away, followed by another dark figure that approached with the same slow, sulking gait from across the street. He turned his head and glanced back. Two more punks took up positions at each corner behind them. Laci glanced back as well, and then glared at Brand.

"Gryphons," she hissed.

Brand's heart was hammering on his sternum. The two kids behind them leaned against lampposts. The one approaching from the south stopped about twenty yards away and crossed his arms. Brand recognized the cherubic face of his buddy Keuek. Brand watched Keuek as Pritchert came up right up and stared at Brand, ignoring Laci's harsh glare.

"Hey, Brand. Long time no see."

"How did you get out so quick?" Brand asked.

"Question is, my friend, how did you get out so quick. Most guys arrested for a stunt like yours would be in for three weeks before they ever got a bail hearing. Even then, they'd probably get no bail and spend another year cooling their heels till trial. You get out in a day. Must have some friends somewhere."

"Yeah, maybe I do. What are you doing here, Pritchert?"

"Just checking up on you, you know? Kind of watching over you." Pritchert tipped his head back, pointing at Laci with his chin.

"You should watch the company you keep," he said.

Laci's teeth were clamped together and her upper lip was pulled back just a bit. Brand could sense the energy radiating from her body. He knew her fists were clenched without even having to look.

"Couldn't find my friends from jail," Brand said.

"Just out having a little romantic stroll?" Pritchert asked.

Brand nodded. Pritchert glanced around.

"Nice," he said. "Where ya heading?"

"Nowhere," Brand said. "Like I said, we're just trying to get some time alone. Ya know?"

"Yeah," he said. He took one more look across the street. Laci's eyes drilled him as he stood thinking. He finally shrugged and shook some of the water off his sleeves.

"Well, anyway," he said. "I wouldn't have bothered you, except that the day's getting along, and the Raven wants to see you."

"Raven," Brand said. He could hear Laci's breath, slow and steady, but there was a trace of an energy change in it, almost as if she was breathing fire, and the temperature went up a hundred degrees.

"Yeah," Pritchert said. "He wants to meet you. Tonight." Pritchert glanced at Laci then back at Brand. "You know where the underground tour starts?"

Brand nodded. "First and Yessler."

"Yeah, that's right. So, you go down there and wait till the last tour of the day is gone, then go in. The gatekeeper will let you pass. You come alone. Go down to Doc Maynard's and wait on the front porch. Someone will meet you there. Got it?"

"Yeah," Brand said. "I got it."

Pritchert nodded and took a few steps backward. He tipped his head toward Laci and smiled.

"You're a pretty lady," he said. "Maybe you shouldn't hang out with this deadbeat."

"You're the deadbeat," Laci said.

Pritchert's smiled melted. He took a good, hard look at Laci.

"You're a pretty gutsy little broad," he said.

"Tell Raevyn I'm coming too," she said. "I'm sure he'll be glad to see me again."

"Yeah," Pritchert said. "He's expecting you. Both of you. Should be a fun time."

Pritchert took a few steps back and then turned around suddenly and walked quickly, picking up Keuek as he passed. Keuek nodded at Brand and then followed Pritchert across the street and down Pike toward the market. Brand glanced back. The other two Gryphons were gone.

"He knows you're coming," Brand said. Laci's eyes were fixed on the street ahead.

They hustled down to Yessler but it took them ten more minutes negotiate through the labyrinth of the empty Farmer's Market and then down the steps to First Street. A few big trucks on the Alaskan viaduct above them whined and growled on their way north as they bypassed the city. Driving on the elevated freeway always gave Brand a queasy stomach, so he avoided it. Walking under it now was almost as bad. Structurally, any way you looked at it, the hundred-foot high, four-lane highway seemed like a bad idea. But it had been around since fifty-three, and even though it was tipping three inches after the last earthquake, there was no money to replace it. Now, over fifty years old, it made a grimy, ugly barrier between the city proper and the waterfront. Most urban planners agreed that it was a major contributor to the seedy quality of the streets below. Brand and Laci dropped into the darkness of the lower waterfront and jogged to the opening of the underground, where Bill Seidel and his students had created a cash cow out of the old streets of Seattle. After the fire of 1889, the city had been rebuilt with bricks and mortar, and the streets were raised up by a couple of stories in some places, to cure some really gross drainage problems. Now, from the lower levels of the waterfront, gawking tourists could walk under Seattle, along concrete paths that led through the abandoned lower stories of Seattle long past. The tour always started at Doc Maynard's speakeasy and wound under the streets for an hour and a half. The last tour of the day would have been at eight o'clock, so the place should have been completely closed up, but Brand and Laci found it lit up and the door unlocked.

Brand and Laci stopped just inside the Rogue's Gallery gift shop. Laci picked up a six inch Space Needle souvenir and looked at the bottom for the Made in China sticker. She set it down gently and followed Brand over to the counter.

The old guy smacked his gums and shook his head. "Last tour of the day's long gone."

"We have a special pass," Brand said.

The old man peered at Brand and nodded.

"So you have," he said. He glanced at Laci. "There's only room for one."

"She's just a ghost," Brand said. "No need to worry."

The old man glared at Laci for a full minute before he got a phone call. He nodded as he held the receiver to his ear.

"Yeah, all right," he said. "You can both go on it. Just follow the path. Someone'll meet you."

He flicked a switch and the door popped open. A gust of musty air wafted out, jingling the cheap wind chimes and riffling a stack of papers. Brand led the way. The inner hallway was lit with dangling incandescent bulbs. They walked down a triple flight of wooden stairs and stepped onto the concrete path. Brand leaned his face close to Laci's ear and whispered.

"What makes you think you can take Raevyn now, if he beat you before."

"He caught me at a bad moment last time," she said. Her voice floated in the dank air like oil on water.

"But we're on his turf, surrounded by his people."

"Don't worry about me," Laci said. "When the action starts, just high-tail it outta here. Get out and don't look back."

"I can't do that," Brand said.

Laci shrugged. "Your choice."

"I tell you what," he said. "If we make it out of here in one piece, I'll take you up on that drink."

Laci nodded. Brand felt his stomach tighten and he let a smile sneak across his face. Fear left a taste like tin foil in his mouth, but it fired up his insides and he suddenly felt a little bit alive.

"This is really stupid, isn't it?" Brand said.

"Yeah. It is for you. I'm on a suicide mission anyway."

"Great," Brand said. "That makes me feel better."

"Look at it this way," Laci said as they stopped in front of the old speakeasy. "You'll get a great story."

"I just want my life back," he said.

Laci's mobile phone rang like an air raid siren going off in the darkness. She fished it out of her coat pocket and put it up to her ear.

"Yes?"

In the silence Doc Maynard's front porch, Brand could hear the tinny voice on the other end of the line.

"Laci Keller?" The timbre was feminine.

"Yes?" Laci replied.

There was silence on the other end.

"Who is this?" Laci asked. She was all business.

"This is Judy Stayberg. Alicia's social worker."

Brand's heart jumped and he could tell that Laci's had done the same. She stood there, holding the phone against her ear, but her eyes stared into space, empty, vacant like the dirty windows of the abandoned buildings around them.

Laci spoke slowly, carefully. "Why are you calling me." It was not a question.

"Where are you?" Stayberg asked. Laci's face flushed and her fingers went white against the phone, as if she was trying to crush it with her hand.

"Where is Alicia," Laci said. Again, it was an imperative, not a question.

"There was an incident at the house tonight," Stayberg said. Even though her voice was far away and thin, Brand could hear the tension in it.

"Just give me what the fuck is going on," Laci growled.

"That's why I'm calling you," Stayberg said. Laci stood there, oblivious to Brand. Her shoulders hunched forward and her eyes looked like they could burn through iron.

Laci shook the phone and stared at it. Brand could see her hand shaking. She looked up at Brand with tears in her eyes. Her voice was barely a whisper.

"Fucking phone," she said. "The Raven has her."

SEVENTEEN

October 18, 1995 – 2:29AM

A voice came out of the darkness and echoed off the walls around them.

"What took you so long?"

"We're here," Brand said. "That's what counts." He could feel Laci next to him, compressed like a steel spring, ready to explode.

Pritchert came forward, sauntering like a cocky ape. His thumbs were jabbed into his hip pockets and his overcoat slapped softly at his boots. He put his arms out in a welcoming gesture.

"Welcome to our world," he said.

"Nice," Brand responded.

Pritchert smiled and turned.

"Follow me," he said. "Raevyn is waiting."

Brand glanced at Laci. She poised on the balls of her feet with her knees bent just a tiny bit. Brand felt his heart step up a few beats as he followed Pritchert along the path. There was no sign of the five o'clock tour as they ducked under the ropes that ran along the path. Pritchert stepped through a crooked doorway into darkness. Brand hesitated, but Laci just slipped around him and disappeared into the opening. Brand took off his cap and punched the record button on the digital, readjusted the cap on his head, and then held his breath and followed.

They had to stoop over to get through the first tunnel, and it was dark. As he hobbled along, Brand pulled out his knife and cut the band on his GPS tracker and stuck the black box in his coat pocket. He tried to swallow, but his throat was dry. He folded the knife and stuck it back in its pouch just as they came into a large opening that looked as if it had once been a stockroom. Dirty water splashed up their legs as they walked into the middle of the room. Forty feet above them, a series of purple glass blocks, embedded in the sidewalks of Seattle, let a bit of filtered light fall through from the sodium vapor lamps of the real world.

Pritchert stopped in the center of the room and Laci and Brand followed suit. Simon and Keuek emerged from the darkness around the edges of the room and converged on the threesome in the middle. Keuek did the ordering. "Search them," he said.

Simon frisked Brand. Pritchert stepped up to Laci with a wary look in his eyes, but she stood her ground with a tense snarl on her face as Pritchert ran his hands up and down her body several times. He stepped away frowning.

"She's got a body like a damn man," he said. "It's like feeling up my high school gym teacher."

"Tough little bird," Keuek said. "Raevyn said she'd be like that."

Simon nodded at Keuek and held out Brand's knife and flashlight in one hand and the tracker in the other.

"This one's soft enough," Simon said. Keuek's grinned and Brand caught it out of the corner of his eye. Simon showed the tracker to Keuek. "This is all he has."

Keuek walked over and turned the GPS over and over in his hands.

"What is this?" he asked.

"Just a piece of junk off one of my cameras," Brand said.

Keuek tossed it away and Brand heard a splash.

"I need that," Brand said.

"I thought you said it was junk."

Keuek put the knife and the flashlight into his pocket.

"Where is Raevyn," Laci demanded.

"He's not here," Pritchert said.

"Well, shithead," she said. "We're here to see Raevyn, not his toy soldiers."

Pritchert leaned closer and sneered at her, baring his pointed teeth. Brand could smell the kid's sour breath, and his teeth glistened in the purple light. Something dark and black, like dried blood, crusted along the edges of his mouth. Brand pulled his head back a bit and wrinkled up his nose. He felt his eyes change, adjusting to the darkness and the smell of fresh blood, and he could see the griffs perched around the edges of the stockroom, a dozen or so of them. Their bodies were black, and only their occasional movement gave them away.

He tried to get an idea of how many gryphons they were up against, but they crept in the shadows, flicking back and forth. Brand guessed ten, plus or minus a half dozen.

"Quit fucking around and tell Raevyn we're here," Laci said.

Pritchert leered at her and tipped his head to the side. Keuek crept a few steps closer. Simon glanced at Brand and took two steps back. Laci waited, balanced on the balls of her feet. She let her jacket fall back off her shoulders and then she jerked on the front of her borrowed shirt. The buttons popped off like bullets and her arms glistened in the soft light as she pulled the shirt back and off. Her tank top clung to her hard body, barely more than another layer of skin. Pritchert grinned.

"Oh yeah," he said. The words were barely out of his mouth when the laces from Laci's left boot hit him in the side of the face. He spun halfway around, staggering, and then turned back toward her with a roar. Laci brought her leg around again in a wide arc, this time dropping her heel right on top of his head. Brand saw Pritchert's eyes roll up into their sockets as he dropped to his knees. Keuek swung at Laci with a vicious right hook that looked as if it was coming right at the back of her head, but she bobbed forward, turned a bit, rammed her left knee into Pritchert's face and then spun all the way around to deliver a round house kick to the back of Keuek's head. He lurched forward a few steps and then stopped, shaking his head for a moment as Laci regained her own balance. The other Gryphons moved forward slowly, almost casually, as if they were unconcerned for their comrades. Laci bobbed from foot to foot, waiting, and then stopped and gaped as Pritchert rolled over to his stomach and came to his feet. He touched his bleeding nose and smiled.

"Oh, shit," Brand said. Laci's mouth opened for a split second, and then her lips went tight and grim.

"We are gonna have some fun tonight," Pritchert said. Keuek stood next to him and nodded.

"This is not good," Laci said. Brand's eyes flicked toward her and then he rotated so that his back was to hers. Three Gryphons approached from his direction, sauntering forward, letting their long coats float open like wings. They stalked like nosferateu, the undead. Brand's stomach knotted into a ball and his butt bumped against Laci's as they backed into each other.

"This is not good," Laci said again.

Brand looked over his shoulder. A dozen man-sized vultures surrounded them. At least a dozen more lurked in the darkness beyond. Laci turned to face Pritchert, rotating Brand toward two female predators with pale skin and dark eyes. The two girls glanced at each other, grinned, and then leapt forward. Brand brought his fists up in front of his face and took a foot in the solar plexus. As he doubled forward, one of the girls grabbed his hat and threw it behind her. Brand looked backward with one squinting eye and saw Laci parry a kick from Pritchert and a hook from Keuek. He lost sight of her as someone pulled him forward and spun him around. He came up face to face with a demon co-ed from the Rocky Horror Picture Show and launched an uppercut into her chin. Her head snapped back and she took a step back. Brand brought his left elbow back into the other girl's chest and took a rack of pain up through his forearm. Rocky Horror came right back at him with a leering grin and he kicked her low on the inside of her knee as she swung at his face. A bright red ring glanced off Brand's face, leaving a hot trail of blood. Brand planted his leg between hers, spun around and cracked her jawbone with his elbow. Another shaft of pain ran up his arm but he crossed it forward right into the left eye of Rocky's evil twin. Someone grabbed him from behind, pinned his arms back and held him while the evil twin recovered and swaggered forward. She smiled, took his face in her hands, and stuck her lips against his. Brand gagged as she forced her hot tongue into his mouth, and he tasted copper and tin foil. He bit down and she screamed and pummeled him in the stomach before she crashed her knee into his groin. Brand slid to the ground, his knees resting in a pool of cold water. Evil twin kicked him in the side of the head with a roundhouse and Brand landed prone next to Laci. She blinked, started to push herself up, and then splashed back down, throwing a small wave over Brand that filled his nose and mouth. Brand coughed and spit black oil. The foot that had pressed Laci back to the ground disappeared and Brand waited. The air was dead and heavy, as if a tornado had just passed by. Brand pushed himself up and came to hands and knees before he rose to his feet. The underground lurched a bit and he reeled to compensate. Laci stood up. Brand offered her his hand, but she ignored it. The chamber was empty. The only sound was a ringing in Brand's ears and a steady drip of water from somewhere in the dark.

"They're gone," Laci said. She spit blood at the floor.

Brand glanced around the room. She was right, but even so, the hackles on the back of his neck went up. The steady drip became footsteps in shallow water, moving like a tiger, heavy and mean and lithe. Brand and Laci turned as one, breathing hard and painful, as the steps came closer and a dark figure emerged from the shadows. He stopped a few paces away and stood with his arms at his sides. His black cape swung forward once and then settled. His entire body showed only as a deeper black against the darkness behind him. Even his face was covered.

"Laci," he said. His voice was hoarse and deep.

"Jack," she replied.

"Welcome," he said.

"Fuck you," she said. She wiped her lower lip with the back of her hand.

"You're looking good," he said. "As if time has not touched you."

"Wish I could say the same for you," she said. She stood up straight and pulled her shoulders back. "Black looks good on you, Jack. Kind of slimming. And a good funeral color too."

Raevyn brushed her off like a loose hair.

"Mr. Brand," he said. The voice sent a chill down Brand's back and twisted his already sore stomach.

"You must be Raevyn," Brand said. "The Raven."

"Mmm. They call me that."

"Thanks for the welcoming party," Brand said. "You must be pretty pansy-assed to have to rely on a bunch of kids to do your fighting for you."

"My gryphons could have easily killed you," he said. "I simply allowed them to toy with you, as a kitten toys with a vole."

"So you're the big, bad mother kitten," Brand said.

Raevyn stepped around Brand, using him as a pick against Laci.

"I've read your work," Raevyn said. "Your novels were literary trash. Poorly plotted and the characters were flat. And your articles reek of cynicism. Did you finish high school?"

Brand felt heat rising in his face. He crossed his arms and kept his mouth shut. Raevyn circled around, forcing Brand to swivel a bit to keep his face toward the absence of light that addressed him. Laci turned as well, her fists clenched and her jaw set.

"My criticism hurts you," Raevyn noted.

"I've got a thin skin," Brand said.

"Perhaps the truth simply hurts," he said. "Everyone has within them the sense of some greater purpose, Mr. Brand. What is it that you seek? Certainly it is something more than chasing after the next big story."

"You didn't ask me here to give me career advice," Brand reminded him.

"No," he said. He paused for a moment. "I've got this silly little itch, Mr. Brand. And I really need you to help me scratch it."

"Can't say that sounds very appealing to me," Brand said.

Raevyn ignored his sarcasm. "Pritchert tells me that you saw the Dancer up on the Needle that night. That she was the one that threw Kenny off the edge."

"She didn't throw him," Brand said. "She dangled him. He slipped free on his own."

"Why would she do such a thing?" Raevyn asked.

"She was pressing him for information on you."

"And did she get it?"

"No."

Raevyn kept circling, and Brand noticed that Laci swiveled on the balls of her feet so that she kept her shoulders toward him.

"And you, Laci," Raevyn said. Why are you meddling in my affairs again?"

Laci's arms hovered a few inches from her body. Brand sensed that she was poised to attack.

"I came for Alicia," she said.

Raevyn froze and the threesome stood there as if time had halted.

"I don't have her," Raevyn said. Laci responded quickly.

"Liar."

Raevyn shook his head.

"I don't have her," he said.

"Then your goons the Griffs have her," Laci snarled.

Raevyn's head shook again.

"They would never touch her," he said. "They wouldn't dare."

Laci's crouch deepened. Raevyn put his hand up to halt her attack.

"You're poised to pounce, my love. But please don't forget who is the stronger. You do not want to engage me. I have learned much since we last fought, and do not think that my burns have limited me. In a way, they have set me free."

Laci stayed in her crouch, but did not spring.

"I did not take Alicia," Raevyn said. "But even if you don't believe me, attacking me will not help you." He started circling again, moving slowly, like a black cloud.

"The Dancer," he said.

"Why would she take the girl?" Brand asked.

"To get to me," Raevyn said. He stopped again. "We must work together, Laci," he said.

"Never," she said. She spit the words out as if she had swallowed kerosene.

"We have a common enemy now," Raevyn said, shaking his finger. Brand could hear the smile in his voice. Suddenly, he stopped, his finger poised in mid air. "She plays us against each other," he said. His head tipped back and moved from side to side as he surveyed the rafters and girders above him. "And she is here, now." He took two steps backward. Laci kept her eyes on him, still crouching in a fighter's stance. Brand's head started spinning and he realized that he was not breathing.

Just as he finally took a breath, lightning struck.

EIGHTEEN

October 18, 1995 – 3:42AM

Brand heard the heavy smack of metal against packed dirt just before the flash, but even so, it blinded him completely. The sharp staccato crack of a short-barreled two-twenty-three followed the flash, and then at least two more joined in. Brand felt a spray of dirt hit his face as a row of bullets punctured the ground around him.

With his vision nothing more than a bright, white dot, he dropped into a crouch and reached out to his right as the gunfire raged on. His hand touched something hard and cold, slick with sweat and mud. The thing grabbed his hand and pulled him back. He scrambled to his feet and felt Laci's arms wrap around him, pushing him further and further back. He hit the wall and grunted, still trying to blink away the searing flash.

Someone screamed and one gun went silent. Chunks of Teflon hit the wall just above Brand's head and shards of mortar and brick rained down on him. He dropped into a crouch again and pulled Laci against his body. She tucked her head into his chest and they stayed there, rooted like a tree. Brand shut his eyes tight and held them that way, praying for his sight to return. He opened them, saw nothing but black and white, and then closed them again. Only one gun was still firing, and the sound was more distant, as if it had traveled down a hallway. The steady popping turned to silence but Brand stayed put. He opened his eyes again and blinked rapidly. Two shafts of soft light penetrated from above, and three ropes hung down from the broken purple glass blocks.

"What happened?" Laci asked.

"Intervention," Brand said. "Someone's joined us."

"How?"

"Dropped in from the street. They've got rappelling ropes and machine guns. Pros. And I think they're pissed."

"Marshall," Laci said.

Brand nodded. "Could be."

"How did he find us?"

"That I don't know. But I do think it's time to get out of here." Brand pulled Laci toward the far end of the room.

"We have to find Alicia," she said. She pulled her arm away.

"We're gonna need help," Brand said. His foot got tangled in something soft and he tried to shake it off. It was his hat. He picked it up and ripped the recorder out of the top. He stuck the digital into his pocket and threw the hat back on the ground.

"Which way?" Laci asked. Her hands were out and her eyes were wild. Brand grabbed her and headed for the exit. "That's not right," she said. "We came in over there."

"Uh-uh," Brand said. "This way out."

Laci pulled her arm away from his grip again and stared him down. "You're turned around," she said.

"And you're not thinking straight," Brand said. One of the ropes snapped like a whip and Brand jumped. It hopped around just long enough for Laci to notice.

"What was that?" she asked.

Brand squinted into the darkness and shook his head.

"We've got to get out of here," he said.

"I have to find my daughter," Laci said.

Brand nodded. "I understand." He took a step away from her. Her eyes begged him.

"Stay with me," she whispered.

Brand stared at her, torn. He shook his head. Laci's face changed from pleading to nothing to a scowl.

"She's only four years old," Laci said.

"She's not here," Brand insisted.

"How do you know that?"

"Raevyn didn't take her."

"He's a liar."

Brand shook his head. "I don't think so."

They stood in the middle of the cavern, staring at each other, indecisive. The place had gone silent as a tomb, but a deep voice echoed off the walls, drifting down from above. Laci and Brand both looked up at the same time.

"Brand? Is that you down there?"

Far above, framed in the silver light from the streets of Seattle, a silhouette of a man leaned over the broken glass sidewalk.

"Joshua?" Brand shouted.

"What the hell are you doing down there?" Joshua called back. "And what the hell is going on?"

"Took you long enough," Brand said. His voice bounced around the cavern as it traveled upward.

"Get your ass up here now," Joshua said.

Brand glanced at Laci. "Can't," he shouted. "Why don't you get your ass down here. We could use some help."

"Don't make me come down there after you," Joshua warned. Brand saw one of the ropes snake around as Joshua tested it.

"Who is he?" Laci whispered.

"He's my probation officer, bail bondsman and friendly bounty hunter," Brand said.

"How did he find us?" Laci asked.

"Just before the Griffs found us, I got spooked and cut my EHC band."

Laci shook her head and glanced around.

"I can't stand around here and chat," she said. "I have to find Alicia." She turned and started to walk away.

"Wait," Brand said. "These Griffs. They're not..."

"Normal?" Laci finished his sentence.

"Not quite human."

Neither am I, Laci's eyes seemed to say, and at that same moment, her eyes read the same words in Brand's.

Joshua slipped over the edge of the hole and slid down the rope like he knew what he was doing. His feet landed in the water and he crouched for a moment as he looked around.

"Welcome to the party," Brand said.

"What party?" Joshua asked.

Laci was staring at the ground.

"There are no bodies," she said.

"What bodies?" Joshua asked. "And who are you?"

Brand stepped in. "Joshua Breakman, this is Laci Keller. Long story."

Joshua put his hands on his hips and shook his head. He craned his neck back and looked up at the three ropes that still dangled from the skylights above. Brand followed his gaze and Joshua hit him like a sledge hammer. Laci jumped back and stood in a fighting stance with her hands up. Joshua whipped out a nylon strap and cinched it around Brand's wrists like a practiced magician. He shoved Brand forward and away from Laci. Brand tripped and landed on his face in the rancid water. He shook his head and spit.

"Damn," he said.

Joshua had his hands up. He faced Laci and tried to calm her down.

"Now, I don't know who you are," he said. "Or what you two are doing down here, but I'm taking this guy out. Understand? Nothing personal. Just doing my job."

Laci glanced at Brand. She took a deep breath and let her guard down. Joshua's shoulders relaxed and he smiled, but Laci wiped it off his face with kick to the side of his head followed by a strike to his chest. Joshua reeled backward but came up snarling. He swung at Laci but only found damp air. She landed a punch to his belly that left him wide-eyed and followed with a hook that split the side of his cheek. She swept his legs and landed next to him with her elbow poised above the bridge of his nose.

"Wait," Brand hissed. "Stop it. Both of you."

Laci glared at him and he could see the hate and fear in her eyes. Joshua rolled away and Laci stood up slowly. She took the same relaxed, easy stance she'd had just before she'd pummeled him to the ground. Joshua stood up and wobbled sideways, touching his bloody cheek.

"Who the fuck are you?" he asked.

"Untie him," Laci said. "Or I'll take you down for good."

Brand struggled to a sitting position and Joshua looked over at him.

"You really hang out with some bad ass women," Joshua said. "This the same one you met on top of the Needle?"

Brand took a look at Laci.

"I don't think so," he said.

"Untie him," Laci said.

"I can't do that," Joshua said.

"Listen," Brand said. He rose to his knees and then to his feet. "Joshua, she'll probably beat the shit out of you if you cross her, but listen. There's a little girl's life in the balance here. Help us find her. I cut the band because I thought we could use some help."

"I don't need his help," Laci said.

"We need all the help we can get," Brand said.

Joshua touched his cheek again and his eyes narrowed.

"All I want is this guy," he said. "You seem like you can take care of yourself."

"Joshua," Brand said. "There are some real bad asses down here that make Laci look like a butterfly. We hit 'em with everything and they just laughed at us."

"Gryphons," Laci said. "Only, they're fired up on PCP or something. And they have my daughter."

"This is completely screwed up," Joshua said. He jerked his thumb at the ropes. "And what about those?"

"Some kind of paramilitary intervention," Brand said. "We were blinded by a flash grenade."

Joshua looked around and shook his head.

"You really do earn your reputation, don't you Brand."

"No. But listen, let me go and help us find this little girl. Then you can throw me back in the slammer. No fight from me."

Joshua snorted. "I'm not worried about a fight from you, pussy-cat. But your girlfriend here, the tiger, she's got me worried."

"Let him go and I won't be any trouble," Laci said.

Joshua's jaw tightened. Brand and Laci stared at him.

"I'm gonna kill you," Laci said.

Joshua put his hands up and smiled. He took a step back.

"Hold on there," he said. He pulled a knife from a sheath behind his back. The eight-inch blade flashed in the dim light. Laci hunkered down and Brand barely even felt the adrenaline pump on top of his already overloaded system. Joshua moved slowly toward Brand, keeping his eyes on Laci. She watched him like a patient cat. Joshua held the knife out toward Brand, and Brand turned his back and held his wrists away from his body. The nylon snapped and Brand took three quick steps away from Joshua. The three of them stood in an uneasy triangle. Brand rubbed his wrists, Joshua held the blade lightly in front of his body, and Laci crouched like an angry puma.

"Are we all gonna kill each other?" Brand asked. "Or are we gonna find a little girl?"

"First," Joshua said. "I've gotta know what the hell is going on here."

NINTEEN

October 18, 1995 — 4:03AM

"We don't have time to bullshit," Laci said. "We've got to move."

"Move where?" Joshua asked. He took a look around the ancient underground plaza. Dark tunnels led off in all directions. Silence surrounded them.

Laci stepped right up to Joshua and stuck her nose in his face. He held his ground, but Brand could see Joshua's toes lift out of the water a bit as his weight shifted back to his heels.

"Buddy, I don't know you from hell's housecat, and after what I've been through down here so far, I'm not about to trust you or confide in you or put up with you in any way. Got it?"

Joshua put his hands up but didn't touch Laci.

"Hey, I'm on your side lady," he said.

Brand stepped up and touched Laci on the shoulder. She jerked away from his hand and snarled at him.

"Joshua," Brand said as Laci backed away and started prowling the plaza like a caged cat. "What we've got here is a shit name of Jack Raevyn who's hanging out down here in the underground recruiting gang members for his club of Gryphons."

"And what's this got to do with her?" Joshua asked.

"She's Raevyn's ex, and he's got good reason to be pissed at her. She's got good reason to be pissed at him too. And their little girl, Alicia, is right in the middle of all this."

"And you think the little girl is down here?"

Brand glanced over at Laci. She was still prowling.

"Laci does," Brand said. He shook his head and lowered his voice. "I'm afraid there's not much chance of finding her down here. And I'm worried about what kind of condition she might be in if we do find her."

"This is a pretty far out story," Joshua said. He brushed his hand against one of the nylon ropes that hung limp from the street above. "And what about this?"

"My guess is that it's John Marshall. He's after Raevyn too. For recruiting his kid. For killing him."

"So now you're saying that this guy Raevyn killed Kenny Marshall?"

Brand shook his head, still keeping watch on Laci out of the corner of his eye.

"No. Raevyn didn't kill Kenny directly. The thing that got Kenny was smaller, lithe, female. This guy Raevyn is big and definitely not female."

"Maybe she took Kenny down," Joshua said, nodding toward Laci. She turned her head toward him and stared for a moment, and then went back to her prowl.

"I don't think so," Brand said.

"She fights like a wild animal," Joshua said. He touched his cheek and looked at his fingers. The blood was black in the dim light, light a layer of dark oil against his chocolate brown skin.

"It wasn't her," Brand said. A scream cut through the silence. It came from far away, drifting like a vesper across the cavern.

"This way," Laci said. She was already running toward a brick archway that looked like a big, black eye in the wall. Brand turned and ran after her with Joshua trailing at an easy gait. Pitch black welcomed them into the hallway beyond the arch. Brand followed the sound of Laci's feet as they pounded against packed dirt and splashed in thin lakes of ice water.

"Shit," she said. Her movement stopped and Brand ran into her. Joshua ran into Brand and Laci pushed them back hard.

"Steps," she hissed. "Going down."

Another scream, this one more like a moan. It was definitely coming from below.

"Go," Brand said. Laci took the steps at a run. Brand followed more slowly, placing his feet carefully in the darkness, feeling the walls like a blind man.

"Joshua," he whispered.

"Right behind you." Joshua's voice was quiet but intense.

"Who sprung me?" Brand asked.

"Not now," Joshua hissed.

"Shut up," Laci growled from somewhere below.

Brand ran into her again. He ducked his head down and peered into another cavern, larger, rougher, but better lit than the plaza above. Rows and rows of cathedral-style arches reached up to a roof of broken tiles. The marble floor was covered with fragments of the fallen ceiling, and Brand could see that the near edges of the giant cavern sloped inward in a strange sort of talus slope of tattered rags and debris. Laci's breath was coming in short gasps. Joshua tried to peer around the two of them, but Laci pushed him back. Brand wrinkled up his nose as the pungent smell of dead animals filled his head. The stifling aroma took him back to a time as a child when he'd climbed under his parent's single level house to help his dad work on the plumbing. All summer long, his father had been poisoning possums, and the dying animals crept under the house to rest. The smell was horrible, and as Brand had crawled along, he had accidentally put his hand in a rotting corpse, festering with maggots. He'd screamed and torn his way out from under the house, and never went back again. The smell here in the underground was almost the same. Reeking, stinking, suffocating.

"Smells like something died down here," Joshua whispered.

"A lot of something," Laci said. She pointed at the wall just outside the doorway. "Look."

Brand took a harder look. Clothes. A purse. A boot and a nice shoe, a wing-tip, maybe a cheap one like Bass or Dexter. A coat. And bones. Not white, like bones stripped by weather, but gray and dirty with the fiber of muscle and tendon still attached, like a spare-rib, chewed to the bone and left on the plate. The entire talus slope was a collection of human remains. The smell hit Brand again, and he sensed maggots and decay all around him. He hit his knees and heaved, spilling nothing but a stream of thin hot liquid on the ground. Laci and Joshua grabbed him at the same time and pulled him back deeper into the darkness of the stairwell.

"What the hell is that?" Joshua asked.

In the complete blackness, Brand could only sense their presence. He felt the change coming over his body, lurking beneath the surface like a snake under an old skin.

"We have to get out of here," Brand said.

"Get him out," Laci said.

"Uh-uh," Joshua said. "I'm sticking with you, lady. You may be a hell of a fighter, but you're gonna need some help down here."

"You two don't look like you'll be much help," Laci said.

Brand came to his feet and reached out in the darkness, grabbing a big, hard shoulder with one hand and a mass of wet hair with the other.

"I'm gonna be all right," Brand said.

"Yeah," Laci replied. "Right."

Just outside, they heard a flutter of wings and the scrape of a boot against stone. A ghostly voice brought them all to a rigid stand.

"Come out, come out, wherever you are."

"Don't move," Laci whispered.

Laci and Joshua pushed Brand back against the rough bricks and all three held their breath as a dim figure passed by the opening to the grisly cathedral. After a moment, a wraith in black leather came whirling into view, dancing a macabre Viennese waltz with an imaginary partner. He carried a long bone in each hand, and as he passed one of the dingy white columns, he hit it with the bones as if he were fighting with the immovable stone. He threw his head back and laughed, and for just a moment his face came into view, crazed eyes, bloody lips and chin. He twirled the bones above his head and laughed again, spinning out of view.

"Come out, come out, wherever you are," he called into the space above him. His feet made shuffling sounds on the dusty, stone-littered floor, and then the sound stopped with a grunt and a popping snap that sounded like a wet towel hitting concrete. Brand took a deep breath and then held it again, listening. Laci moved away from him, toward the opening. She stuck her head around the corner and then pulled it back.

"Our little friend has broken his neck," she said.

TWENTY

October 18, 1995 – 4:47AM

Laci slipped out the door and ran low and fast over to the fallen Gryphon. Joshua followed, crouched down like a commando, and then Brand.

Brand knelt down next to the kid and tipped his head a bit. He took a deep breath, felt himself savoring the freshness of the body, and then shook it off. "I know this one," he said, looking at the baby face, now peaceful in death. Keuek's neck was clearly broken. His shoulders faced the outer wall, but his nose was pointed toward the center of the cavern. "We spent some time in county."

"I fought him in the upper chamber," Laci said. "Couldn't even knock him down."

Joshua glanced at her with a frown.

"You're telling me that there's someone down here tougher than you are?" he asked. Laci glared at him.

"Buddy," she said. "There are a whole hell of a lot of things down here tougher than I am." She glanced around, surveying slowly. "And whoever did this is not someone we want to get messed up with."

The three of them spent a moment pondering Keuek's fate before the crunch of a boot on stone and the rapid slap-snick of a magazine getting jammed into an empty socket followed by a slide shoving a fresh round into the breach of a gun brought their heads up. A big, bloody guy in army fatigues and a flak jacket stood staring back at them.

"Marshall," Brand said. "Glad to see you're still alive."

"This the lady that killed my kid?" he asked.

Brand shook his head slowly and started to stand up. Marshall shoved the barrel of his gun toward Brand, freezing him in a half-crouch.

"You all should get the hell out of here," Marshall said.

"Where are your men?" Brand asked.

"Dead," he said. "These thugs down here aren't even human. We shot them and they just kept coming. Pinned Ned down and tore his arm off. Ned kept fighting, and Navajo jumped on top of them, cutting and hacking like a madman. They just threw him off. Never seen so much blood. Never seen creeps dismember a man before either."

Marshall had a far away look in his eyes, as if he was recounting a scene from a book or a movie that he might have seen a long time ago.

"Those guys've been with me since forever."

He paused again.

"These underground creeps tore them apart. I fired into them. Gave them a whole clip of nine millimeters and everything out of my forty-five. Killed maybe two of them. But the rest hauled my guys down here. I followed. Too late."

He crouched down and his eyes flicked back and forth.

"They eat the dead," he said. "They started chewing the flesh off the bones of my men. Started eating Ned while he was still alive. I saw them chewing on his arm as they held him down."

His voice got even quieter.

"Ned was one of the bravest, toughest men I ever saw," Marshall said. "But I saw his eyes as those demons ate the flesh off his arm, right there in front of him. I was shooting, Ned was screaming and the monsters laughed and yelled and fought and I..."

His voice trailed off.

"How did you survive?" Joshua asked. His question was gentle, his voice low and soft.

"I ran," Marshall said. "I ran. And then I hid."

His head fell forward and he shook it. Joshua made a small move and Marshall brought his head up quick and swung the barrel of the compact little automatic like it was a finger, pointing it right at Joshua's head.

"This lady thinks her little girl might be down here somewhere," Joshua said. "We're just gonna find the girl and then get the hell out of here."

Marshall's laugh was more like a snort of disgust.

"If her little girl is down here," he said. "May God have mercy on her soul."

"How did you find us?" Brand asked.

"Your GPS tracker. I hacked the signal."

Joshua's eyes narrowed.

"How did you know I had a tracker on him?" Joshua asked.

Marshall shook his head. "Doesn't matter. Nothing matters except finding Raevyn and killing him."

"Leave him to me," Laci said.

"No," Brand said. "When we find Alicia, if she's down here, you're gonna take her out."

Laci shook her head.

"I'm on a one-way trip, Brand. I find Raevyn, I kill him or he kills me. Either way, I'm dead. If he doesn't get me, his goons will."

She brought her head up, ignoring Marshall and Joshua. She stared into Brand's eyes.

"Promise me, that if we find her, no matter what, you'll get her out of here and take care of her."

Brand's mouth hung open.

"I can't..." he said.

"Promise me," she growled. She reached out and grabbed the front of his coat with her hands. Joshua leaned back, trying to stay out of the way. Marshall watched with dead eyes.

"Promise me," she said again. "Get her out and take care of her."

Brand shook his head.

"I can't," he said. "I can't take care of a little girl. There are things about me that you don't know."

Laci pushed him back and he fell on his butt, catching himself with his hands.

"Then you really are a piece of shit," she said. She stood up. Marshall rose to full height and trained his gun on her stomach.

"Are you serious about killing Raevyn?" Laci asked.

Marshall nodded.

"Then come on," Laci said. She turned her back on Marshall and started walking with her head held high. She headed for the far side of the cathedral. Marshall followed, swiveling his gun left and right as he trailed behind. Joshua looked at Brand. Brand looked away. Joshua stood up and grabbed Brand by the shoulder, pulling him to his feet. He jerked Brand after Marshall, and the four of them made a ragged line across the vast chamber. They walked about halfway before Laci ran into two mangy Gryphons. As Brand took a breath of the reeking air and tried to get his heart to stop racing, he recognized the two girls that had roughed him up earlier. They swaggered away from each other a bit, making a wider target for Marshall's rattle-gun. The one on the right winked at Brand and licked her lips like a bit player in a bad porno movie. She smiled, showing her pointed teeth. Her lips and the corners of her mouth were caked with something black. Blood, drying, coagulating, rotting in her mouth. Brand swallowed hard. Joshua turned toward the left with his hands up, guarding his face, ready to fight. Two more Gryphons joined the girls, and then two more. Pritchert came out of the darkness, and now Laci and the three men were surrounded by seven Gryphons.

"Welcome to the bone yard," Pritchert said. "Won't you join us for dinner?"

Marshall raised his gun, but Laci put her hand on the barrel and forced it back down.

"We don't want you," she said. "We just came here for Raevyn."

Pritchert threw his head back and laughed, and then snapped it forward again. His face was suddenly dead serious.

"Are you fucking kidding?" he said. "You think we give a shit what you are here for? Lady, we're just gonna kill you, and then maybe we'll go out for some real entertainment."

Marshall's gun came up and showered a spray of bullets toward Pritchert, but the kid moved like a snake, diving out of the way and rolling into a ball. One of the girls came flying toward Marshall's back, but he ducked and turned and gave her an appendectomy as she flew by him. She toppled over and rolled up to a sitting position with wide eyes. Another Gryphon dove in and swung hard at Brand, sending him crashing against a nearby pillar. The impact smashed the wind out of his body and sent a shooting pain up his spine. His Gryphon buddy grabbed him and pinned him against the column. All he could do was watch the rest.

Joshua threw a flurry of fists and kicks at the other girl, but she flicked them off as if she was sparring with a child. Two Gryphons grabbed Marshall and held his arms, forcing him to drop his gun. Laci kicked one kid in the face and then took a hard kick to the midsection that sent her reeling backward. Another Gryphon hit her in the back and Brand could hear her ribs snap and she fell forward into the dirt and grit. For just a moment, everything seemed to stop, as the Gryphons made it clear that they were in charge. Pritchert kicked Laci in the side and she rolled over, wincing and groaning. He stood over her with his hands on his hips and glee in his eyes.

"You see? When the Raven gives us our medicine, we are Gods."

"You're insane," Marshall growled.

The glee went out of Pritchert's eyes and he took a step toward Marshall. He pulled out a long-bladed hunting knife and held it between his own body and Marshall's.

"Know what Haggis is?" Pritchert asked.

Marshall kept his eyes on the kid and said nothing. Two Gryphons still held his arms. He struggled a bit, but they held him like a vice.

"Haggis is the intestines of sheep, stuffed and served up hot. But, what I would like tonight, it your intestines, stuffed with whatever you have for dinner, and served warm. Body temperature."

Pritchert licked his lips and shuddered.

"It just sounds so," he paused for effect, as if he was searching for just the right culinary term. "So juicy," he said. "Are you juicy, Senator Marshall?"

Marshall's chest was barely moving. Pritchert waved the knife back and forth with wickedness in his eyes.

"Do you know why we eat people?" Pritchert asked.

Marshall nodded and Pritchert took on a thoughtful, pensive look.

"Of course you do," Pritchert said. "Of course you do." His knife flicked out like a serpent's tongue and Brand winced as Pritchert buried the blade into Marshall's stomach to the hilt. Marshall bent forward a bit, still held upright by the two Griffs who smiled with satisfaction and hunger in their eyes. Pritchert turned the blade a bit and Marshall arched his back, groaning. Pritchert slid the blade along from hip to hip and then pulled it out again. Marshall's shirt bulged open and something wet and gray began to spill out. Brand turned his head, but the Gryphon holding him forced his face toward Pritchert again. Brand's eyes seemed to watch against his own will, as Pritchert reached into the bubbling mass of steaming ropes that poured slowly out of

Marshall's abdomen. The kid pulled a long, thin piece of Marshall outward and upward, staring into Marshall's ashen face. Marshall groaned and his legs dangled loose beneath his body. Joshua came to his hands and knees and took a kick to the ribs that sent the big man rolling. Laci pushed up so that she could see Pritchert and groaned as the kid stuck Marshall's living entrails between pointed teeth and bit down, chewing and pulling as Marshall wept like a baby. The senator's head rolled back and he wailed an incoherent prayer toward the ceiling. Pritchert looked up, bloody intestines still hanging from his lips, still connected to Marshall's body, still chewing thoughtfully, as if he was enjoying a Sunday dinner at home. Suddenly, the arm that held Brand was gone.

Brand stepped away from the pillar, still staring at Pritchert and Marshall, but Pritchert spit out Marshall's guts and stared at something just past Brand. Brand turned and looked as well, groggy, disoriented. The Gryphon that had been holding Brand was standing a few feet away from the pillar with his arms above his head and his face toward the floor, as if he were about to fall down and atone for his sins. All eyes turned toward him as he stood transfixed by some unseen force. His head bent further forward and then snapped and his body fell to the ground. Where he had stood, only a shadow remained. Something darker, denser than the gloom beyond.

"You," Pritchert said.

"Let's dance," she whispered.

The voice sent a chill down Brand's spine and he glanced at Laci. She was staring as well. Marshall fell to the floor as his supporters left him, and as Joshua's Gryphon attacker stepped toward Brand and the Dancer, the big black man came to his feet and planted a kick right in the small of the Gryphon's back, sending the black demon staggering forward toward the end of his misery. The Dancer was quick and strong, stepping right by Pritchert with a kick to the kid's messy face that sent him spinning. She launched herself up and over Joshua's Gryphon, raking his throat with something sharp that cut his neck from ear to ear. He grabbed the wound and ran forward. Brand ducked sideways and used both arms to propel the bloody Gryphon straight into the pillar. The bird's head sounded like a ripe watermelon as it hit. He slumped to the ground and Brand turned back toward the group. Pritchert had jumped into a fighting crouch with his arms out and his eyes angry and wide. The one remaining girl was sitting on the ground, holding her Gryphon sister in her lap. The one that Marshall had shot was clutching her friend with her head buried against her shoulder. The other two males were going toe to toe with the Dancer, but they were outclassed and outmaneuvered. It was over in a matter of seconds. One guy fell next to Laci, and she grabbed his head and face with both her arms and flipped her legs into the air, spinning his head almost one full revolution from his body. Brand tasted bile in his mouth as the spinal joints popped apart. The Dancer took an opening in the last Gryphon's defenses and slipped her hand upward, through his jacket. His eyes went wide and he just stopped moving, as if someone had removed his battery. The Dancer's arm was up his shirt all the way to her elbow. She pulled it out with a gush of blood and a sound like someone plunging a toilet, and then she stepped back and watched him fall to the ground in almost slow motion. Even in the semi-darkness, Brand could see the blood dripping from the Dancer's jet black arm. She spun around and crouched down, facing Pritchert. His eyes were wide and his mouth was open. Brand read it as disbelief at first, and then recognized that Pritchert was experiencing a sort of fearful awe.

"Who the hell are you?" Pritchert asked.

"Don't kill him," Laci begged. She held her hand out toward the Dancer. The Dancer glanced at her for only a moment, but Pritchert seized the opportunity and lunged with his knife. Dancer deflected the stab but it threw her off balance just enough for Pritchert to land a lightning fast hammer kick to her head. She reeled sideways but came back into a fighting stance quickly.

Pritchert scampered backward, kicking his heels up a bit and tossing his knife from hand to hand.

"This isn't over yet," he yelled. He turned and ran into the darkness. The Dancer stayed. Laci started to run after Pritchert, but after a few steps she collapsed. Brand ran over to her and helped her back to her feet. She put her hand against her side and winced. Marshall had dropped to his knees and was somehow clinging to life with his arms crossed over his bloody stomach. Joshua picked up Marshall's gun and pointed it at the two girls.

"Don't kill them," Laci said. He words came out with the force of pain and anguish.

"They don't know anything," the Dancer said. All eyes turned toward the black apparition. She stood there, lithe, alluring, and deadly, glistening with blood and sweat and God knows what else.

"They may know where the girl is," Joshua said.

The sitting girl shook her head. There was no more glee or fun in her eyes. Whatever magic she'd had was worn off. Her friend's arms hung limp and dead eyes stared toward the citadel above.

"We don't know nothin'," the live one said.

"Kill her," the Dancer said.

Joshua brought the gun up, but Laci lunged forward and pushed it skyward.

"We still have to find my girl," Laci said. Her breath came hard and hoarse, and she could barely push Joshua's arm. He could have swatted her away like a fly.

"They don't know where your girl is," the Dancer said.

Laci glared at her.

"What the hell do you know about it?" Laci growled.

The Dancer crouched down next to the Gryphon and her fallen sister, facing them, ignoring Joshua and Laci, who were standing like some kind of strange statue.

"Tell Raevyn that I have the girl," the Dancer said. The black, featureless face turned toward Laci. "If he wants her, he'll have to come to me," she said. Laci let go of Joshua and took a step forward. The Dancer backhanded her and Laci staggered backward, tripping over the body of a fallen Griff. She landed hard and groaned. Joshua swung the gun around toward the Dancer.

"Where?" Laci whispered.

The Dancer turned back toward the girl Gryphon. "Tell him to keep his eyes on the news," the Dancer said. She turned toward Marshall and stepped over to him. His eyes followed her legs up to her torso and head. He looked tired and beaten.

"You've played your part, old man," she said. She stepped back and then forward, planting a hard kick to his lower body. A gush of blood followed an avalanche of entrails as he doubled over. Joshua fired at her but missed wide and ran out of ammo after only a short burst. Laci tried to move toward them but fell to her knees. Brand stood frozen. The Dancer grabbed Marshall's head and twisted it hard to the right. She opened her arms wide, like Mary-mother-of-God and Marshall's head plopped onto the hard-packed dirt. She skipped away, as if she was a little girl heading for the playground, leaving Marshall on the ground stretched out like a gutted fish.

Brand and Joshua and Laci stood in the middle of five dead Gryphons. Only the one girl remained alive, and she was rooted to the ground, arms hanging limp by her sides.

Brand and Joshua each took one of Laci's arms and pulled her to her feet. As they half-carried, half-drug her away, Brand took one last look back at the girl and she stared into Brand's eyes as if she were begging to be taken home. There was a tear in her eye as she watched them go.

TWENTY-ONE

October 18, 1995 – 5:09AM

Joshua slapped the end of one of the ropes around Laci's torso in a makeshift rescue harness, did it quickly, as if he'd done it every day. He climbed up forty feet of nylon rope, hand over hand, his legs swinging free. Brand stood with Laci, waiting, but didn't have to wait long. She stood up, looking like a surprised marionette, and then her body floated upward as Joshua hauled. Brand grabbed a free rope and climbed quickly, a strange strength in his arms that scared him. He joined Joshua and together they pulled Laci onto the sidewalk. The three of them sat down and stared at the broken hole in front of them.

"Where are we?" Brand asked.

"Second Avenue extension," Joshua said.

"Why aren't there any cars?"

"Marshall's men blocked it off before they went in. Made it look like street work."

Brand noticed that the ropes were tied off to the bumper of a white city public works truck with no license plate. Somewhere off in the distance, he heard the thump of a heavy bass from a nightclub, and the sweet, tangy air of Elliot Bay started clearing his head.

"No cops, no back up. What was Marshall thinking?"

"Unauthorized action," Joshua said. "Marshall is ex-military. Must have called in some favors. Vets'll do that. Especially for a guy like Marshall."

Laci groaned and spit blood onto the wet pavement.

"We have to get her to some help," Brand said. "You got a car nearby?"

Joshua nodded and stood up. Brand slipped an arm under Laci's and together, he and Joshua helped get her to a blocky-looking SUV that was probably blood-red but looked black in the silver light of night. They put Laci in the back seat and she lay down with her knees up.

"Where to?" Joshua asked.

"Memorial," Brand said.

"No hospital," Laci said. Her voice was barely more than a hoarse whisper. "Just take me home."

"Uh-uh," Brand said. He sat for a moment, thinking.

"Not your place either," Joshua said.

"I have a friend on Mercer Island," Brand said.

Joshua grunted and put the rig into drive. He punched it, sliding the back end around a bit before the tires bit into the wet concrete. Once the big rig was on Stewart and headed toward the floating bridge, Brand put his head on the dash and closed his eyes. The steady rocking of the SUV and the whine of the tires on the road lulled him a bit, but his shoulders stayed tight and he couldn't get the gritty taste of dirt and blood out of his mouth. Joshua slowed down suddenly and pulled up a long drive, and Brand looked up.

"We there already?" he asked.

"You dozed off," Joshua said.

The question formed in Brand's mind, but he didn't ask it. *How did you know where to go?* Instead, he turned around and glanced down at Laci, still stretched out in the back seat. A wash of light from an overhead sodium-vapor played across Laci's face and Brand felt his heart jump. She looked like a ghost.

"We need to get you to a hospital," Brand said.

"No," Laci croaked. "I just want to go home. Just let me die. That's all I want now. Just to die."

Brand glanced at Joshua. His face was a stone as he brought the SUV to a stop. He tapped the horn three times, and a light came on upstairs. Brand got out and opened the back door, and together, he and Joshua carried Laci up to the front porch. Brand slammed the knocker and the light came on. Ren opened the door and glared at the three of them for a moment before she realized that Laci was hurt.

"Get in here," she said. Ren pulled the sash tight on her floral robe, closing it over a long satin nightgown.

They settled Laci onto an overstuffed couch in the formal living room and Ren lit a gas fire. She kept the lights low. Brand tucked a heavy polar fleece blanket over Laci and turned to Joshua.

"The girl," Brand whispered.

Joshua nodded and shot a glance at Ren. She ignored him, but Brand didn't miss the interchange.

Joshua came over to Brand and held out his hand. Brand shook it. Joshua gripped tight and slapped a GPS over Brand's wrist and locked it on with one hand.

"Sorry, buddy," he said. "But you gotta wear this still."

Brand pulled his hand away and stared at the wristband.

"I'll go back," Joshua said. "With help. You all stay here until you hear from me."

Joshua left and Ren locked the front door after him. The lights of the SUV washed across the walls like twin searchlights as Joshua turned it around. As he pulled down the drive, they could see the taillights through Ren's thin curtains, and they could hear the deep rumble of the engine and the snap of gravel being spit from under the tires. Ren's house smelled of vanilla and cinnamon. Brand dropped into an overstuffed chair and closed his eyes. His whole body felt numb, as if the life had been sucked out of it.

"Charlie," Ren said.

Brand glanced up at her.

"What happened to you?"

"Long story," Brand said.

"I mean, your skin."

Brand looked at his hand. His fingers gripped the arm of the chair. Skin the color of leather, roughened by years in the sun. The blue-gray cast was gone. He held his palm out in the light and frowned.

"Impossible," he said.

"What does it mean?" Ren asked.

Brand shook his head.

"You need to protect yourself," Brand said.

Laci curled up under her blanket and turned her back on the room, burying her face into the back of the couch. Ren stood and waited for a moment and then retreated into the kitchen. Brand heard a soft noise, like metal touching glass, and a few minutes later, the steady rattle of a teakettle boiling. He followed Ren's movements with his ears until she came out carrying two cups on a tray. She put the tray in front of Brand and he took a cup.

"This will help you sleep," Ren said.

"I can't sleep," Brand said.

"You need to. So does she."

"Let me die," Laci mumbled into the dark fabric that covered her face. Brand took a cup and stared at it. The tea was strong but green, with powder floating around the edges. Ren took the tray over to the couch and sat down, pressing her back against Laci's body.

"You need to get some sleep right now," Ren said. "Now sit up and drink this. I think it will help."

Laci burrowed deeper into the couch. Ren put the tray on the coffee table and leaned closer to Laci's head.

"Laci," Ren said softly. "Your body needs to heal. I don't know what you've been through tonight, but I do know that right now, right here, you have a chance to rest. Take it. Take the chance. You may find that tomorrow things will be different than they seem tonight. And you'll want all your strength."

Ren touched Laci's shoulder and rubbed it gently.

"I've got some herbal tea here that will help you sleep," Ren said. "When you feel like it, sit up and drink some. Charlie and I will be right in the next room. Okay?"

"Leave the light on," Laci said. Her words were muffled by the blanket, but her voice was clear. Ren patted Laci's shoulder and stood up.

"Come on," Ren said to Brand. "I have something to show you, and you have a hell of a lot of explaining to do to me."

TWENTY-TWO

October 18, 1995 – 6:22AM

Brand stood up and followed Ren into the dining room. Ren sat at the computer terminal but didn't log on. Instead, she swiveled to face Brand as he took a seat at the table.

"You start," she said.

"How much do you know?" Brand asked.

"Assume I know nothing."

Brand stared into his tea for a moment and then took a sip, more to delay the conversation than for its healing properties. It was not good, but it gave his mouth something to do other than talk.

"When we were on the Needle, Kenny told me that the Griffs had met a man named Raevyn, who was leading them in some fashion, and I kind of inferred that Raevyn had taken the Gryphons in some direction that disturbed the hell out of Kenny. He talked about the Gryphons killing folk downtown, but I was pretty sure that wasn't the root of the problem. Anyway, before we could finish our conversation, that thing they call the dancer showed up and tossed him over."

Brand took another sip of tea and made a face.

"Go on," Ren said.

"I thought that Laci was the Dancer," Brand said. "Because I had seen the mark of the Raven on her chest. The same mark that I'd seen on Pritchert's coat when we me the Gryphons in the food court."

Ren nodded. Her eyes were locked on Brand's.

"So, when I got out of jail, I followed Laci from the Y to her house, and then from her house to a little neighborhood in Tukwila. Turns out that four or five years ago, she and Raevyn were married. Raevyn beat her, she retaliated by setting him on fire. He escaped, she went into treatment, and her kid became a ward of the state."

Ren kept staring, prompting Brand along with her intense gaze. Brand stared into his cup again and swirled the tea around.

"Laci parked herself on a picnic table and I confronted her. She swore she wasn't the dancer, but agreed to help me. Told me her whole story. We went back downtown and Pritchert found us."

"How?"

Brand frowned. "I'm not sure. Funny thing about him and his friends. They turned up in jail at the same time I did. Even ended up in the same cell block, same cell. And they were out again as soon as I was."

"There's no such thing as coincidence," Ren said.

It was Brand's turn to nod.

"So, anyway, when I was in jail, I made a deal with these kids. If they would leave me alone, I would lead them to the Dancer. Of course, I was pretty sure that the Dancer was Laci."

"Why?"

"Because of the shape of her body, the way she moved, the way she fought. It seemed like a slam dunk. I was sure of it."

"But?"

Brand shook his head.

"We were invited to meet with Raevyn in the Underground. He's lurking around down there with his Gryphons."

Brand shuddered. "These kids are superhuman. I mean strong, almost indestructible. And vicious. And they're down there eating the dead."

Ren just stared at him.

"All hell broke loose down there. Marshall dropped in with some buddies and the Gryphons slaughtered them. Not that Marshall didn't get some licks in. But he never got to Raevyn."

"Why was Marshall after Raevyn?"

"He figured that Raevyn was responsible for Kenny's death."

"How did he know about Raevyn?"

Brand frowned again and shook his head. He sipped on his tea.

"I don't know," he said. "Seems like everyone knows way more than I do."

"So," Ren said. "Marshall drops in. And Joshua."

A bell went off in Brand's head, but he was getting groggy.

"Yeah," Brand said. "Joshua had me wired up with a GPS device. A tracker. I cut the circuit just as we went into the Gryphon's lair. Joshua came in to get me, because he thought I was on the run. Anyway, while we're down in the pits, Laci gets a call from Social Services accusing her of abducting her daughter. The little girl's gone missing, Ren. She's only four years old."

"Did you find her?"

Brand shook his head.

"No. But we found a deeper cavern. Bone yard. Nasty place, where the Griffs must be dragging their late-night victims and eating them. Right down to the bone. Had to be a hundred rotting corpses down there. Maybe more. The Gryphons surrounded us and would have killed us, but then the Dancer shows up and takes them out as if they were children."

Brand leaned forward and lowered his voice.

"Ren, these Gryphons are like wild animals. There was nothing we could do to stop them. And Laci took out Joshua as if he was a rank amateur. But she couldn't hardly knock a Gryphon down. So the Dancer shows up and snaps Gryphon necks like toothpicks."

Brand finished his tea and felt his eyes getting heavy.

"What's in here?" he asked.

"Just herbs," Ren said. "Nothing to be afraid of. Are you getting sleepy?"

Brand nodded.

"Why don't you go crawl into bed. I'll check on your friend."

"Ren," Brand said.

"Yes?"

"We have to find that little girl."

Ren smiled and touched Brand's hand as she took his cup away.

"We won't be able to find her tonight," Ren said. "Besides, I thought this was about clearing your name."

Brand shook his head. It felt thick and slow.

"That doesn't matter anymore," he said.

Ren leaned closer and looked into Brand's eyes.

"I'm afraid," Brand said.

"You're going to be okay."

Brand shook his head again. "I'm afraid for you."

Ren sighed and stood up.

"I can take care of myself," she said. "You know that. Besides, I trust you."

Brand let out a breath he'd been holding.

"I don't trust me," he said as he stood up.

She took his hand and led him upstairs. Brand curled up on the bed and Ren tucked a blanket around his shoulders. She whispered into his ear, "Brand, if anyone can help, it's you. You know that." She slipped under the covers with him and the last thing Brand remembered was her hands on his shoulders and her warm body pressed against his back.

TWENTY-THREE

October 18, 1995 – 10:17AM

Brand wandered downstairs to the smell of coffee. He poked his head into the living room. Laci was slumped on the corner of the couch. The TV was on to the news, but Laci's eyes were closed. KING 5 was showing a view from the far end of the Second Avenue extension where it cut behind Pioneer Square Garden. A dozen police cruisers blocked the complex intersection where Yessler and James and Second Avenue converged. The extension came off Second Avenue proper at a forty-five degree angle, an anomaly even among the confused spider web of Seattle streets. As northbound Second Avenue jogged thirty degrees to the west, the extension headed almost due south, cutting across Third and finally petering out at Fourth, just past the King Street Station, four blocks from its beginning. Krystal Marshall held a mike and her lips were moving, but Laci had the sound turned down too low for Brand to hear. He headed into the kitchen and almost ran into Ren. She jabbed a coffee cup toward his chest.

"Good morning," she said.

"I thought Mormons didn't drink coffee," Brand said.

"I don't," she said. Brand took the cup from her and sipped it. "I just keep it around for couch surfers like you."

Brand followed her into the living room. Ren pulled the blanket up around Laci's shoulders. Laci groaned and stirred a bit, but her eyes stayed closed and her breathing was heavy and slow. Brand turned toward the TV and watched Krystal jabber into her mike. She looked serious, but her eyes were hidden behind dark glasses.

"Krystal doesn't know," Brand said.

"Know what?" Ren asked.

"That her husband is down there somewhere with his guts torn out."

Ren clenched her jaw and stared at the screen.

"First her boy," Ren said. "And now her husband."

"Bad luck," Brand said.

Ren nodded.

"Can I turn it up?" Brand asked.

Ren nodded. Brand dug the remote out from under Laci's blanket and clicked the volume five times. Krystal's nasal broadcaster voice came up slowly.

"...scene of grisly violence. The police still aren't letting us go in, but we suspect that whatever they are finding down there is not good. Already we've seen dozens of body bags, and at least that many officers come out from the Underground unable to return. The police are going in wearing full riot gear, armed with shotguns and M-16s. But all we have right now are rumors."

Krystal stopped and the anchor jumped in.

"Thank you Krystal Marshall on location at Second and Yessler. We're taking you live now to the entrance to Seattle's Underground Tours, where Jim Martin is standing watch."

Ren tugged on Brand's arm and he backed out of the living room with his eyes still glued to the screen. Martin was reporting on the police barricades around the tour opening, also admitting in a hundred words or more that he knew nothing.

"We have to watch the news," Brand reminded her.

"The Dancer's just playing with you," Ren said. "Laci watched NWCN all night and started flipping between KOMO and KING 5 this morning as soon as they came on the air. How long are you supposed to watch? What are you watching for?"

Brand shook his head.

"I don't know. I don't know."

"I think the key is to find out who the Dancer is, and what she wants. Her message is going to be for Raevyn, right? Not you. So, you have to know what Raevyn knows. Think like he thinks. That means that you need to know who he is."

Ren hit the space bar and a background of stars became a web browser.

"Where are we?" Brand asked.

"MIT archives," she said. "Can I summarize for you?"

"Go."

"Jack Raevyn is a star athlete and whiz kid from some Podunk town in the Midwest. Lamar, Colorado. Lettered in four sports. Four point. His dad died when he was a kid. Raised by his mom, but according to the Lamar papers, she had a bit of history. Died just after or maybe just before Raevyn left for college. She was old. Maybe forty when Raevyn was born, so she must have been almost seventy when he graduated from high school. Gets a full ride scholarship to Baylor where he majors in molecular biology."

"How'd you get all this?" Brand asked.

"Research, my dear, research."

"Go on."

"Well, so Brand studies molecular biology, then medicine at Johns Hopkins, and then he goes to MIT, where he's doing a second PhD in bioengineering. His dissertation and research project is anti-aging."

Brand nodded. "He loved his mom. She got old and died. He wants to find a cure for aging. Nice goal."

"Yeah, so here's the interesting part. This was kind of the first thing I hit. The rest was just ancillary research."

Ren scrolled down through an archived copy of an old print article.

"This is from an underground student paper called the Anarchist. Apparently there was an incident in the biomedical lab. Raevyn took the blame, but there were at least two other students involved, neither one named."

Ren pointed at the screen.

"See here? Dr. Hank Blankenship, director of the lab, came in one Sunday morning and found the lab destroyed. The rats appeared to have eaten each other, and the Rhesus monkeys had broken out of their cages, killing, maiming and also eating each other. It was a terrible disaster, covered up by the Dean's office and dismissed as just a rumor. But Jack Raevyn was expelled nonetheless. His accomplices seem to have gotten away scott free."

"How trustworthy is that publication?" Brand asked.

"Not very," Ren said. "But it would answer some questions."

"Like what? Like Raevyn developed some kind of anti-aging drug that turns animals into raving psychos?"

"Or people into supercharged cannibals," Ren said.

"But why?" Brand asked. "Why would Raevyn start feeding his rat poison to street punks?"

Ren shook her head.

"I don't know." She pulled down her list of favorites and opened a folder named CB. She clicked on a link and started scrolling through on-line PI articles.

"I picked up the trail again here in Seattle about five years ago. This guy Raevyn pops up out of nowhere operating a lab over on Bainbridge Island. Longview Research Corp. Privately held, government funded. He and his wife are social butterflies, but every once in a while there's a row at home and the cops get called in. About once every two or three months. Domestic dispute. His name keeps popping up in the little neighborhood crime section, but nothing ever seems to come of it.

"Then, one day, about five years ago, all hell breaks loose. Big fire on Bainbridge. LRC is completely destroyed. There's a

WalMart there now. And a day later the Raevyn estate in Lakewood burns to the ground. Laci Keller gets arrested for arson and admits that she torched her husband, but his body never shows up. They put her in a mental ward. End of story. She must have been paroled just recently."

"No mention of a kid?" Brand asked.

"Uh-uh," Ren said. "But it probably just wasn't newsworthy. By then she would have been old news."

"How does this help us?" Brand asked.

Ren shook her head.

"I'm not sure yet. It's just data. Like a box of puzzle pieces dumped on the table. We have to put it together."

"With most of the pieces missing and no big picture," Brand reminded her.

"We're missing something," Ren said.

"We're missing a lot of things."

"No," Ren said. "We're missing something obvious."

Brand slumped back in his chair and stared at the screen. He took a sip of coffee and closed his eyes.

"What if," Brand began. "What if this isn't about revenge."

"What do you mean?" Ren asked.

"Money," Brand said. "What if it's about money?"

"Why would it be about money?"

"Government funding. That's big money. And anti-aging. What if Raevyn actually succeeded? Wouldn't the patent on an anti-aging compound be worth more than Microsoft Windows? I mean, what if he found a way to suspend or even reverse the aging process?"

"Aging is simply disease," Ren mused. "Anti-aging would be anti-disease."

"We'd be talking a trillion dollar market," Brand said.

"Still doesn't make sense," Ren said.

"I'm just thinking out loud," Brand said. He paused for a moment. "I'd be interested in finding out who Raevyn's chums were at MIT."

"I put in a call this morning already," Ren said. "Dr. Blankenship retired and moved to Arizona. I left a message, asking the college to forward it to him so he could call me back."

Brand's thought swirled, but nothing would coalesce.

"What day is it?" Brand asked.

"Why don't you get a calendar," Ren suggested.

"I'm all disoriented," Brand said. "This whole week's been just one long nightmare."

"It's Wednesday," Ren said. She frowned. "Don't you have a lunch date with Krystal Marshall?"

"Jesus," Brand said. "I almost forgot." Something else was nagging at him, but he couldn't quite place it.

"Well," Ren said. "Given her situation, I'm sure she's not thinking about lunch."

"I should call her and see how she's doing," Brand said.

Ren twisted her mouth up but said nothing. Brand leaned back in his chair and peered into the living room. He couldn't see Laci, but he could see the TV. The news was preempting whatever other show might have been on, but the studio was showing stock footage of the barricades in a window above the anchor. Brand dug out his wallet and found Krystal's card.

"Can I borrow your phone?" he asked.

Ren sighed and nodded.

Brand dialed Krystal's cell number and got her live.

"Hello?" she asked.

"Krystal," Brand said. "This is Charlie Brand."

"Oh, hi. I was hoping you'd call."

"How're you doing?"

"I'm OK. I just keep working to keep my mind off Kenny." Her voice choked up a bit as she mentioned his name.

"Yeah," Brand said. He heard her take a deep breath, and in his mind he could see her straightening her back and shaking her head a bit. He got a strong vision of her perfect hair, loaded with spray, barely moving as she tossed her head.

"Can you still come over for lunch today?" she asked.

Brand frowned, glanced at Renata, and then nodded.

"Sure, but..."

"I could really use some company," Krystal said. "You know? Just some normal company. All my friends and all John's friends just want to hug me and pat me on the back and stare into my eyes to see if I'm okay, and with John out of town, I gotta tell you, I'm not OK. I just need someone normal, you know? Just like a normal, ordinary lunch."

"Sure," Brand said. "I can do that. Where do you want to meet?"

Ren shot him an acid glance.

"My place," she said. "I'll fix us something and we can sit out in the cabana by the pool and watch the rain churn up the lake. I don't want to go out where there are lots of people. Too stressful."

Okay," Brand said. "Noon?"

"Or eleven thirty. Any time around there."

"You live out by Lake Sammamish, right?"

"Yeah, just drive out Lake Road till you get to the sign that says Guylands Manor. That's us. I'll leave the gate open."

Okay," Brand said. "Lake Road. Guylands Manor. I'll see you then."

"Brand," she said.

"Yes?"

"Thank you."

"Sure." He hung up and stared at the phone.

"You're actually going to go have lunch with her?"

Brand nodded.

"I take it she doesn't know about her husband yet," Ren said.

Brand took a deep breath.

"No."

"Are you going to tell her?" Ren asked.

"I don't know. Maybe she'll know by then. I don't know."

"Why are you doing this?" Ren asked.

Brand pursed his lips.

"Just seems like the right thing to do. Maybe she knows something that can help us."

"Well, be careful," Ren said. "She's in a delicate spot. Just lost her son. And her husband, even though she doesn't know it yet. Don't go pressing her for a bunch of information."

"I won't."

Brand glanced at the clock. Ten thirty already.

"I'd better get home so I can get ready," he said.

"You can shower here," Ren said. "And I still have some clothes here that my ex left. Don't know why I keep them. But you can borrow some. They should fit okay."

"How about wheels?" Brand asked.

"Take the Mercedes," she said.

Brand leaned over and kissed her on the forehead.

"Thanks," he said. "You're a dear."

He poked his head around the corner and checked on Laci before he went upstairs. She was still sleeping, but the remote hung from her limp hand, resting on the edge of the couch. As he stood there, her eyes opened. She blinked a couple of times and then stared at Brand. He nodded toward her, but she just stared at him. He stepped away with a queasy feeling in his stomach. Ren came up behind him and looked over his shoulder. Laci turned her attention back to the TV.

"She needs medical attention," Ren said.

"She won't go to the hospital," Brand said.

"I called your buddy Fletcher. He's coming over."

Brand turned and glared at her. She shrugged. Brand went upstairs and took a long, hot shower. Ren left a black turtleneck and black slacks on the bed along with clean underwear and socks and a pair of black leather loafers. Brand put it all on and looked in the mirror. It fit well enough, but he felt like a rube. He fished a black sports coat out of the closet. It smelled like cherry pipe tobacco.

"I look like I'm going to a funeral," he muttered. He heard voices downstairs.

Fletcher stood in the middle of the living room with his arms crossed. Ren sat on the couch next to Laci, who had receded into her blanket like a hermit crab.

"Hey, doc," Brand said. Fletcher turned around and smiled. He pushed his glasses up his nose with a long, slim finger. Light glinted off the top of his head where his scalp showed through the fine stubble of salt-and-pepper. Even though he was well over sixty, he stood like a gangly teen-ager.

"Charles," he said. He stuck out his hand and Brand grabbed it. Fletcher pulled him close and gave him a one-armed hug without letting go of his hand. Brand patted Fletcher on the back and they pulled away.

"How are you feeling?" Fletcher asked. His face turned serious.

"I'm still here," Brand said. He faked a smile.

Fletcher grunted and turned back toward Laci. She avoided his gaze.

"You're friend here needs to get in to emergency services right now," Fletcher said. "She may have at least one broken rib and possible internal trauma."

"I'm fine," Laci said.

Fletcher turned and looked at Brand again.

"And you," he said. "You need to come in as well. How long has it been?"

"Just a couple of months," Brand said. "But I've been feeling fine. Really."

"Unlikely," Fletcher said. He shook Brand's hand again and headed for the door. Ren got up and showed him out. Brand took her place beside Laci. Laci turned her head away from him and stared at the TV.

"How're you doing?" Brand asked.

"Shitty," she said. "I'm all knotted up inside, and I can't do anything. Every time I try to stand up, I pass out."

Brand touched her back.

"I'm going to do everything I can to find your little girl," Brand said. "Somehow, we'll find her."

"If we don't," Laci said. "Then I don't want to go on living."

Brand rubbed her shoulder. It was as hard as a rock.

"Just hang in there," Brand said. "Just hang in there."

"Brand," she said.

"Yes?"

She turned her head a bit so that she could see him, and so that he could see into her eyes.

"I don't have any friends or family," she said.

Brand ran his hand through her hair and his mind flashed back to Jule for a moment. Brand's face suddenly got hot and his heart hammered. *Oh my God*, he thought. *I was supposed to meet Jule for coffee this morning.*

Laci bit her lip and then went on.

"Thank you," she said.

Brand stood up and rubbed his forehead. Laci looked him up and down.

"Where are you going?" she asked. Brand couldn't stop thinking about Jule. *Fucked up*, he said to himself. *I am just fucked up.*

"I'm going to visit a friend," Brand said. *I'll have to call Jule later. Fuck.* "She may know something. I'm just flying blind here. Searching. No idea what I'm looking for or what I'll find."

Laci nodded. Brand turned to go and almost ran into Renata. She held out the keys to the Mercedes and dropped them into Brand's hand.

"Take my cell phone too," she said. She stuck her phone into his jacket pocket and then held out his digital voice recorder in the palm of her hand. He stared at it for a moment before she dropped it into his pocket with the cell phone. "And say hi to Krystal for me."

Laci's voice made Brand turn around again.

"Krystal Marshall?" Laci asked.

Brand nodded. Laci frowned and turned back toward the TV for a moment, and then looked at Brand again before her eyes drifted toward the fireplace.

"I've gotta go," Brand said. He walked away with the funny feeling that he was definitely missing something.

TWENTY-FOUR

October 18, 1995 – 11:44AM

On the way to Krystal's, Brand stuck a hearing-aid sized earphone in his ear and listened to the recording from the night before. Most of it was muffled or garbled at best. He listened over and over, trying to pick out something that would help. He almost missed the driveway. Had to slam on the brakes and when he turned his head, the cord from the recorder caught on his arm and yanked the earpiece out.

The Marshall estate looked like a castle. Like Krystal said, the wrought iron gate was hanging open. Brand drove down a long driveway to Guylands Manor, a stately brick mansion surrounded by tall rhodies and weeping willows. It looked like an exclusive country club. Way too big for a family of three. He parked the Mercedes in front of the garage and took a long, slow walk to the front door. There was no doorbell, just a big, heavy iron knocker. Krystal came to the door, still dressed in her blue suit from work. With her stiff hair and heavy, dark sunglasses, she looked like a young Jackie Onassis.

"Gosh, Brand," she said. "Please come in."

She took him by the hand and led him to a parlor just off the main entryway.

"I just got home myself," she said. "Could you excuse me for a moment while I freshen up?" Her house was dark and cold.

Brand nodded but Krystal stood there, staring at him. Brand shifted his feet and glanced around at the coved ceiling and arched doorways. The space was very elegant, very expensive. But lonely.

"Can I get you a drink?" Krystal asked.

Brand swallowed. His mouth was dry but he pressed his lips together and shook his head.

Krystal touched his arm and backed away a few steps.

"Well," she said. "Go ahead and make yourself comfortable. I'll be right back, and I have a surprise for you too."

Before he could ask, she turned and left him alone. He sat down on an overstuffed Victorian couch and squirmed around a bit trying to get comfortable. Someone had set a large glass coffee table too close to the couch, leaving just a tiny bit of room for Brand's legs. He heard Ren's cell phone going off in his pocket. He stood up and fished it out. It took him three rings to get it out and flip it open. He stared down at the coffee table as he pressed the phone to his ear. A large, brown leather photo album sat right in the middle of the table, all by itself.

"Hey Brand," Ren said. "Am I catching you right in the middle of something?"

"No," he said. "Krystal stepped out for a moment."

"So, you got a minute?"

"Yeah."

"Would you like to know who Raevyn's school chums were down at MIT?" she asked.

Brand waited.

"Blankenship called me back. When I asked him about the incident, he refused to talk. I tried to explain, but he just kept cutting me off. Then, about two hours later, he calls me from a pay phone in downtown Tempe. He sounds jittery and nervous, but I got him calmed down and told him about Alicia. Told him everything. He had to hang up and think about it for a while, but he called back. Told me that he was forced to retire last year. Set up with a more than generous pension and a place in Arizona that he never would have been able to afford on his own, on the condition that he never talks to anyone about the lab incident."

"But you got him to talk?"

"Yes."

"So, who were the chums?"

"Well, Trina Marshall was one of them."

"Marshall's first wife?" Brand asked.

"And Kenny's biological mother," Ren added.

"It's a small, small world," Brand said.

"Not that small," Renata reminded him.

"It's like we're in the middle of some kind of evil synchronicity."

"You're in the middle of it," Renata reminded him. "Not me."

"Who was the other?"

"Blankenship didn't know."

Brand sat down hard and tucked the phone between his shoulder and his cheek.

"The bad thing is," he said. "None of this information gets me any closer to knowing who the Dancer is. It's like I'm getting the sound from one channel and the video from another. Nothing fits. Nothing works. Nothing makes sense."

"Everything makes sense if you take the long view," Renata said.

"Long view," Brand muttered. "Longview. Laci said that her husband was working on something at Longview. Funding got pulled. Government funding. Who was chairman of the house ways and means committee the year that Laci Keller torched her husband?"

"I don't have the slightest idea," Renata said.

"I do," Brand said.

"Why doesn't that surprise me."

"Wanna know?"

"Yes."

"Clayton Dash."

There was silence on the other end of the phone.

Brand started flipping through the photo album on the table. He started at the back and moved forward, just like he did with magazines. Bad habit. The yellowed pages crackled as he turned them.

"Mind if I think out loud?" he said.

"Fire away," Renata said.

Brand flipped a page. Wedding photos of Krystal and John Marshall. Happy couple. A young Kenny sulked in the background.

"Jack Raevyn is a star student at MIT. Full ride scholarship. Kind of a genius. Right?"

"Right."

"He's working on an anti-aging drug. Maybe even getting close to a breakthrough. He's got his eyes on the red carpet, but he doesn't really like the red tape. So he does his own testing. Feeds his concoction to a bunch of tame lab rats and monkeys. It makes them go crazy. Very bad reaction. Very bad press."

"But a great story for the Anarchist," Ren added.

Brand flipped another page. Marshall and Krystal at their cabin on Sammamish Lake. She's rowing, they're both laughing. She's got great arms. The sun is shining. Maybe Kenny shot the photo.

"What are you doing?" Ren asked.

"Just looking through a photo book," Brand said.

"Snooping?"

"She left it out."

"What next?"

Brand took a breath and flipped another page. His eyes looked at the picture, but the significance didn't register. He was lost in thought.

"Marshall and Dash let Raevyn take the heat for the rat debacle, but they have some kind of hand in it. Raevyn gets expelled, but even so, he's on top of the world a few years later. Government contract. Maybe they even saw military applications. Who knows? Anyway, Marshall and Dash make sure that Raevyn's research is funded. That was the payoff for Raevyn keeping his mouth shut about their role in the rat eating rat thing. But Dash got tired of Raevyn's blackmail, or maybe Raevyn just wasn't producing results, so Dash pulls the funding under the cover of the Ways and Means committee. Raevyn is pissed, comes home early and finds his wife in bed with her mistress."

"Or maybe Raevyn was successful," Ren added. "And Dash and Marshall wanted a bigger piece of the action."

Brand ran his hand across the photo of Krystal Marshall, beating on a punching bag. For a moment, he thought it was a picture of Laci.

Brand flipped another page, and then another. He stopped on a parchment certificate that awarded Krystal Olivia Marshall with the title of Black Belt, third degree. His fingers touched the letters. His voice was barely a whisper.

"K.O. Marshall."

"Yes?"

Brand turned around. Krystal was standing at the door, dressed in a black body suit, twirling the broken phone cord as if it was her cat's tail. Her feet were bare and the long sleeves of the suit ended just above her wrists. The spandex was so thin and so tight it was almost more revealing than her own skin. Her head was shaved bare and glistened as if she had waxed it.

"You do have a stunning physique," Brand said. "It's a shame you always hide it under baggy clothes and bad wigs."

"Always holds me back at work though," she said. "People think I'm kind of overweight and that I spend too much time on my hair."

"If only they knew." Brand set the phone down and closed the photo album as casually as he could.

"I look better in black," she said. "Black always has a slimming effect."

"Especially tight black."

Krystal wrinkled up her nose.

"Yeah," she said. "That's my favorite."

"Why didn't Laci recognize you?" Brand asked. "You're on TV all the time."

Krystal ran her fingers along the top of the cherry sofa table as she walked around to sit with Brand. She slid over the arm of the couch and dropped down in front of him with her legs spread out. She let one foot creep across Brand's lap while she hugged her other leg against her chest. She reached out and took the phone off the table, stared at the caller ID screen for a moment and then hung it up. While she was occupied, Brand reached into his pocket and his fingers found the record button on the digital. Krystal put the phone down on the table.

"Jack Raevyn busted me up good. I had to disappear for a while. Moved to Portland. Oregon, not Maine. Got my face fixed. Changed my name. I always wanted to be a journalist, so I made up a resume, played down on my luck with the station manager at KATU. Down on my luck, and down on him. Told him I wouldn't tell his wife if he gave me a chance. He did."

She winked.

"Later, I told her anyway. The rest of it was real work though. I came back up her on a transfer. KING 5 is owned by the same people."

"And then you started hunting down Jack."

She nodded. "I worked out. Harder than ever. And then I started roaming the streets at night, looking for trouble. I found it when I found the Griffs. So I started hunting them too. I honed my skills on their pathetic little bodies. Real fighting skills. No the stuff we learn in the dojo."

Her cheeks flushed and her nostrils flared. She slid her pelvis a bit closer to Brand and he could smell her pheromones. Her nipples pointed at him as she closed her eyes and touched her belly.

"God, it was good. Just hammering those boys with my fists and my feet. It was better than sex. Still is."

Her eyes popped open and she smiled.

"Fucking orgasmic," she said.

"You killed Kenny. And your husband."

"And I got this," she said, opening her arms to encompass the estate. "Not bad. It's about time I got something."

She pushed herself back up onto the armrest and tucked her feet into the crack between the pillow and the frame, but she let her knees drift apart so that her thighs were exposed to Brand, beckoning to him.

"All this for revenge," Brand said. Krystal smiled and started swinging her knees together and apart.

"Well," she said. She drew the word out and turned her head a bit.

"Well what?"

Her smile got bigger and she folded her hands together.

"See, turns out that when Laci and I were an item, she'd do that pillow talk thing all the time, and so we knew that Jack was close to a breakthrough. In fact, we knew that he'd done it."

"Done what?"

"What he set out to do."

"Anti-aging drug?"

"Brand," she said. "You're good."

"I had help," he said. Krystal's eyes narrowed.

"Yeah, you would," she said. Brand felt his face get hot. He tried to steer the conversation back to task.

"So, Raevyn invented the drug. So what?"

Krystal's smile returned, but it was more guarded than before.

"Turned out that it wasn't really a drug, but anyway, it worked. In fact, it worked better than anyone could have expected." She took her voice down a notch, as if she were afraid of being overheard. "Not only reversed the aging process, but could even repair and rejuvenate cells. Maybe even keep people alive forever. But Raevyn had the patent. Worth maybe a trillion dollars in residual income. He and two other guys. So Laci and I concocted a plan."

Brand jumped in. "Kill Raevyn and the other two. Laci becomes the sole owner of the patent by way of will or intestate succession."

"Yeah, that was the plan."

"But Laci screwed it up. She can't inherit if she murders the grantor. Against public policy."

Krystal wrinkled up her nose and nodded.

"Yeah. She fucked it up. But I had time to think about it. You know? A trillion dollars. Know how much that is?"

"A lot," Brand said.

"A helluva lot," Krystal corrected.

"So, you came back, wooed Marshall and put yourself in line."

Krystal nodded. Brand glanced over at the photo album again, searching his own mind for the clues he had missed.

"Raevyn must have been testing the drug on himself," Brand said. "That's how he survived the fire."

"Yeah," Krystal said. "The thing has fabulous restorative properties. It's like a goddamn fountain of youth. Works on the eyes first. Really great for failing eyesight."

"But there's a dark side to it," Brand said.

"It makes the user crave protein and amino acids. Basic building blocks of cell regeneration."

"But not just any old protein," Brand said.

"Uh-uh," Krystal said. "Has to be fresh, living or recently dead. And it has to be the same genome as the host. The closer the genetic match, the better. And the best cells are pre-adolescent."

"And you've been taking it too," Brand said. "The dark glasses."

"Yeah. My vision is great, but makes my eyes light sensitive. But other than that, I'm like a god damned twenty year old super-vixen. Tremendous energy and vitality. I can feel it turning back the clock. This is the real thing, the golden elixir."

"How did you get it?" Brand asked.

She shrugged. "I guess I got lucky. Like they say, it's not what you know, it's who you know."

"I don't get it," Brand said.

Krystal laughed.

"It was you up on the needle that night," Brand said.

"No duh," she said.

Brand shook his head. "But you'd have to kill Raevyn as well. And probably Laci."

"Yeah," she said. "It's kind of a mess. Except that Raevyn was already going to kill the others anyway, since they were trying to oust him. I did him and me a favor when I finished off John. Now his Griffs will finish the job on Friday, so I just need to do Raevyn and Laci."

She spread her hands wide.

"And then I'm in the money. The Dancer disappears, and the grieving but fabulously wealthy widow moves to Switzerland. I've always wanted to live in Switzerland. Maybe spend the winters in the Bahamas."

"And what about Alicia?"

"Well," Krystal said. "I guess she's going to have to go too. If she's Raevyn's daughter, she'd be a possible successor too, wouldn't she? And now that you know my little secret, I'm going to have to kill you too."

Brand watched her carefully. She just sat there, smiling.

"But, for now, we wait," she said.

"For what?"

"For my little Laci," Krystal said. She bit on her lower lip and scrunched her shoulders up, adding an evil grin. "We're gonna have a family reunion. Me and Laci and Jack Raevyn and their little Alicia, and you can come too, if you want. Is that what you want?"

Brand nodded.

"Great," Krystal said. She pushed herself forward, supporting her body in mid air with her arms still on the armrest. Her back arched and her knees came so close to Brand that he had to lean back a bit. He hardly even saw her foot as it hit him square in the face.

TWENTY-FIVE

Brand came to sitting on hard, cold concrete with his hands tied behind his back. He blinked a couple of times to clear his head. Light came in from a small, barred window high up on one wall. It looked like it might be late afternoon, and Brand got the feeling that he wasn't in Guylands Manor anymore. Wine cellar. Not well stocked. Lots of broken bottles. Glass strewn everywhere, most of it almost pulverized. Damp air with a gritty smell, like wet charcoal. Probably below grade. The fire hadn't reached here, but the heat had. Even so, not all of the bottles had burst. He could see rows and rows of racks still intact, but they were all empties.

A little girl sat across from him with her hands in her lap. She was staring at Brand. Her blond hair hung in her eyes, and her little night shirt was dirty. She was sitting right in front of two red, five-gallon plastic gas cans.

"I'm cold," she whispered.

Brand just stared at her for a moment, and then past her at the containers, and then back at her again.

"Can I come over and cuddle with you, mister?" she asked.

Brand felt something tighten in his gut, but the girl stood up slowly, teetered a bit, and then staggered across the floor and collapsed onto Brand's lap. She burrowed up against him like a lost puppy and he wished that his arms were free so that he could hold her tight.

"You must be Alicia," he said.

He felt her head nodding against his chest.

"It's nice to meet you," Brand said. "My name is Charlie. I'm a friend of your…"

Brand realized that she probably didn't even know her real mother.

"Are you a friend of my mother?" she asked. She tilted her head back and looked up at him. Brand nodded.

"Yeah. I am."

Alicia's eyes brightened.

"What's she like?" Alicia asked.

Brand took a deep breath.

"She's very beautiful, like you."

Alicia shook her head.

"Oh, no," she said. "I'm not beautiful at all."

Brand frowned.

"Of course you are," he said. His frown turned to a smile. "You are quite beautiful. Just like your mom. And I'll bet you're strong too. Your mom is very strong. And brave."

"How come she never comes to see me?" Alicia asked.

Brand took another deep breath and let it out with a sigh. He shook his head slowly.

"Sometimes mom's get taken away," Brand said. He knew it was inadequate. How do you explain social services to a four year old?

"Does she love me?" Alicia asked.

Brand smiled again. "More than anything," he said.

"Then how come she doesn't come see me?"

"She'd like nothing better in the world than to be with you," Brand said. "But sometimes we just don't get to do the things we want to do."

"How come?"

"I can't explain it."

"Why not?"

Brand almost laughed. There was silence for about three seconds before she spoke again.

"I'm hungry."

"Me too," Brand said. "As soon as we get out of here, we'll go get you some pancakes."

"And sausage?"

"Yep."

"And milk?"

"Yeah. A big glass of milk."

Alicia put her head back down.

"That sounds really good, Mister Charlie."

"Just Charlie."

Brand sat quietly for a while, hoping that Alicia would fall asleep.

"Alicia?" he whispered.

"Yes?"

"Why aren't you sleeping?"

"Too cold."

"Get up for a minute," he said.

"Uh-uh."

"Please," Brand insisted. "I need you to do something for me."

"Uh-uh. I'm cold."

"Come on," Brand said. He rolled over a bit, dumping Alicia on the ground next to him. She whimpered and started to cry.

"Hang in there, Alicia," he said. "I just need you to look at the way I'm tied up here, okay?"

He turned around and showed her his wrists. She stopped whimpering.

"Does that hurt?" she asked.

"Yes. Can you pull it off?"

Silence. Brand looked over his shoulder. Alicia just stared at him.

"Can you tell what it's made of?" he asked. "Metal? Plastic?"

"Looks like plastic," she said. He felt her fingers playing with the cord that bit into his wrists.

"Alicia, listen to me," he said. "I need you to go over there and get one of those big bottles from the shelf. Bring it here."

Alicia stood up slowly and plodded over to the nearest wine rack. She picked a bottle from the lowest shelf and carried it back with both hands. She put it on the floor and squatted in front of Brand.

"Do you know that glass is sharp?" Brand asked.

She nodded.

"I want you to break that bottle," Brand said. "And then use a piece of broken glass to cut through the strap around my wrist, okay?"

She shook her head.

"You have to do it," Brand said. "I can't get us out of here unless my hands are free."

She shook her head again and started to cry.

"I'm scared," she moaned.

"Alicia, honey," Brand said. "As soon as my arms are free, I'm gonna give you a big hug. But you need to cut the cord."

"But you're bleeding," she sobbed.

"I know. I know. We'll get a Band Aid to stop the bleeding as soon as we get out. Now come on, you can do it. Just break the bottle and be careful so that you don't cut yourself."

Alicia tapped the bottle on the ground softly, weeping as she did.

"Harder," Brand insisted. Alicia hit it against the concrete, but the heavy bottle refused to break.

"Lift it up and slam it down," he said. She did, and it broke into a dozen pieces.

"Grab a shard," he said. "A piece of broken glass. One of the big ones. And then use it like a knife to cut the strap around my wrists."

Alicia picked up a big, nasty looking piece of glass and Brand shuffled around so that the little girl could see his hands better. He felt her plucking at the nylon cord for a moment, and then she stopped and started crying. He pulled his legs under him and came to a squat, turning around as he did. Alicia dropped the glass and stared at her hands. They were covered with blood. Brand's heart pounded in his throat.

"Did you cut yourself?" Brand asked.

Alicia nodded. Her face was frozen in a gasp of fear and pain. Brand twisted his hands but still couldn't get them free.

"You have to try again," he said. "Please, try again."

She was crying full bore now, with tears dripping down her dirty cheeks. Brand fumbled with his fingers on the floor until he felt a piece of glass. He tried to saw the bindings himself, but couldn't get an angle. As he concentrated, he momentarily lost track of Alicia. Suddenly, her felt small fingers touch his. Alicia took the shard from his hands and started working at the strap again. Her wailing turned to sobs and then Brand's arms popped free. He brought his hands to the front of his body and grabbed a wide gash that was coursing blood.

"You did it," Brand said through clenched teeth.

"Can I get my hug now?" she asked. Brand picked her up and held her tight for a moment. Then he set her down and checked her hands. Her left index finger was cut to the bone, and the flesh part of both hands had deep gashes as well. The sight of meat and blood made Brand's eyes sharper, his sense of smell more acute, and he felt the change coming on.

"We don't have any time left," he said.

He tore off his coat and then his black shirt. He ripped the shirt into ragged strips and bound one around his own gushing wrist before he wrapped Alicia's little hands. He sat her down in his lap and started cutting through the GPS wristband. His grimace turned to a smile and back to a grimace again as the glass cut into his other wrist. He kept at it until the GPS device dropped to the floor. He used another strip of black fabric to wrap his bloody wrist, and then he pulled Alicia against him tight, holding her with his arms and nestling her into his lap between his bent knees and his chest. He started to shiver, and started thinking about searching for a bottle of red wine, convinced that there had to be at least one survivor. He licked his lips and held the girl even tighter. Every few seconds, her body was racked with a deep sob. Brand cleared his throat and closed his eyes. His body told him that it would not be much longer.

"Jesus Fucking Christ," he said.

"Is Jesus going to save us?" Alicia whispered.

Brand just closed his eyes again and tried to stop shaking.

TWENTY-SIX

October 18, 1995 – 6:29PM

The temperature dropped till Brand could see the vapor of his breath, and then the sun went down and cold turned to frigid. Alicia's night shirt was damp and he couldn't hold her tight enough to keep her from shivering. Brand took a chance and pressed the button on the side of his watch. A green glow lit his face. Six fourteen. He started praying again and was answered by the sound of cracking wood somewhere above him and far to the right. A heavy thump and another crack made Alicia jump and suck in her breath. Brand sat stiff and tense. Two beams of light stabbed into the darkness, playing off the broken and tipped racks around them. Brand held his breath. Alicia whimpered again.

"Shhh," Brand said as quietly as he could.

"Brand?" came a deep voice.

"Joshua?" Brand called out. One of the beams bounced quickly in his direction. The other followed more slowly. Brand winced and turned his head away as the bright light washed over his face.

"What the hell are you doing here?" Joshua said.

"I don't even know where I am," Brand said.

Another voice joined in, along with a second beam of light.

"You found the girl." It was Renata.

"Ren," Brand said. "What are you doing here? You have to get out of here."

Joshua crouched down and put his hand on Brand's shoulder.

"Can you get up?" he asked. Brand nodded.

"Where are we?" Brand asked.

"This is the old Raevyn estate," Renata said. "Joshua followed the GPS signal here. Nothing left upstairs but a burned-out shell. Looks like it was never rebuilt."

Brand was up on his feet now, still holding Alicia. She hung on him like a starfish to a rock. As he brushed up against Ren, her camera swung around, and the lens poked him in the side. He frowned for a moment but brushed it off. Always a professional photographer. He realized he still had his digital recorder in his pocket too. He would have laughed at the irony of it if he wasn't so cold and scared.

"Krystal is the Dancer," Brand said. "She's dangerous and she's on the warpath."

"Hold this," Joshua said. He handed the flashlight to Brand. Brand shifted Alicia to his hip and took the heavy Durco from Joshua's hand. Joshua pulled out a big nine-mil Berretta, the kind that held fifteen shots. He'd scoped it with a narrow beam light. He held it with both hands, moving it slowly from left to right. Ren and Brand swept the dark basement with their beams as well.

"Let's see if that bitch can dodge bullets," Joshua said. "Come on."

He started moving forward, retracing his steps to the door. Ren moved her flashlight along the rickety wooden stairs that led up and out. She stopped as she lit up the door at the top. It was closed.

"Did you close the door?" Joshua asked her.

"No," Ren said.

"Take this," Joshua said. He handed the gun to Renata. She took it and bent her legs, holding the fat nine mm in an isosceles stance like a pro. Joshua stared at her.

"You look like you know how to shoot," he said.

He eyes flicked toward him.

"Surprise you?" she asked.

He chuckled. "Not at all."

Joshua took the stairs slowly, staying toward the wall on the left. Brand's teeth chattered softly, and he could feel Alicia trembling against the side of his chest. He had one arm around her little butt, and she had her legs wrapped around his waist. He shifted her up a bit and tried to hold the lamp steady, but it kept shaking. Joshua reached the top and pulled on the door handle. The door didn't budge. He rattled it back and forth and pulled harder. Still nothing. He turned and shot a concerned look back down toward Ren.

"I thought we busted this handle," he whispered.

"Get back down here," Ren said.

"Nah," Joshua said. "I can get this open."

"No," Ren insisted. "Get back down here. We'll find another way."

"That's just what she wants us to do," Joshua hissed.

"She's using Alicia for bait," Brand said. He kept his voice as quiet as he could.

"Bait for what?" Ren said.

"For Laci and Raevyn."

Ren glanced at him but kept the gun pointing upward toward the closed door; her breath came quick and shallow.

"Have you ever shot someone before?" Brand asked. Joshua was pulling on the door handle again, rearranging his stance on the stairs so that he could get more leverage.

"Not with a gun," Ren said.

The door popped open and for a split-second Brand thought that Joshua had done it until her realized that the big man was off balance. Something dark and fast shot through the door and Ren unloaded three rounds into the ceiling. The thing wrapped itself around Joshua like a dark cloud and Brand heard the big man grunt and then gasp, as if something had been sucked out of him. Ren fired again. Alicia cringed at the sound of the blasts, and Brand's eyes were full of spots from the muzzle flash.

"Run," she hissed.

Brand's light caught Joshua struggling with something big and dark. The tendons on Joshua's neck stuck out like tent wires, and he turned his head slowly toward Brand. His eyes looked like they were about to explode. Joshua was holding on to Raevyn, hugging him with both of his bulging arms, but his mouth formed the word run, and the life in his eyes was like a fire going out. Brand threw his flashlight at Raevyn and grabbed Ren by the shoulder, pulling her back into the cellar. As Ren backpedaled, the gun bucked over and over in her hands until it froze open on an empty clip. Ren threw it and screamed like an enraged lion. Brand yanked on her arm again and the three of them tripped over a flimsy wooden bookshelf, landing in a heap on the floor. Alicia started crying with fear and pain. Brand pulled her back against his body and reached for Ren. They scrambled to their feet and stood in the blackness, unable to move. The cellar was quiet again. One flashlight beam cut a shaft of light from the floor to the ceiling at an odd angle just at the foot of the stairwell. The stairs groaned, and Raevyn appeared, stepping over the light and melting into the darkness again.

Brand almost sprained his neck as he turned toward the sound of breaking glass. A road flare came spinning across the open room, bathing everything in a sputtering red light. It landed in a pool of red wine, sending smoke and steam into the already putrid air. Something slipped in through the broken cellar window like a cat, dropping down and vanishing behind a rack of unbroken bottles. Brand glanced around for Raevyn, but saw nothing.

"Laci?" he called out. "Laci, be careful. Raevyn is here, and so is the Dancer."

Only silence spoke back to him.

Brand's eyes were drawn to the now open window. It looked big enough for Ren and Alicia. Maybe not Brand. He nudged Ren and whispered.

"You have to get over to that window." As he spoke, his stomach clenched into a knot, feeling like a truck ramming into his solar plexus. The flare hurt his eyes now, but he could see into the dark corners, see movement and heat. He could smell Ren's fear and the light sheen of sweat on her forehead, even tough the acrid smoke of the flare filled his nostrils.

"It's starting," Brand whispered.

Ren's eyes were wild, but she nodded as if she understood. Even so, they both just stood there, uncertain of what waited between them and escape. Brand looked down at his feet. He tried to move a bit, but the clutter of the broken shelf clattered like a roomful of broken dishes. His foot hit a tin mop pail and he stepped back onto an old broom handle. On impulse, he squatted down, still holding Alicia tight against his left side, and picked up the broom. The business end was long, like a sidewalk sweeper. It was loose, so he twisted the handle a few times until the broom end fell off. He nudged up against Ren and pushed Alicia into her arms.

"Take her," Brand said.

Ren glanced at the puny little stick that Brand was holding, and he could tell that she didn't have much confidence in his ability to fend off and attack with it. Brand looked at it and grimaced. It felt like fir and weighed less than a pound. One good kick would split it right in two. He glanced at the ground for something else, an axe, a crowbar, anything. Nothing but dust and broken wood and an old metal pail. The stick was the best he had.

"Come on," he whispered.

Just as he started to move forward, the door burst open again and Krystal stepped casually down the stairs as if she was shopping at Saks, graceful, seductive, dangerous. She stopped right at the base, tipped her head down as she glanced at Joshua's body, and then stepped over it. She stood in the middle of the cellar with her legs spread wide, nothing more than a dark shape against a darker background. The flare sputtered and died.

"Come on Raevyn," she said. "Let's dance."

Brand's eyes shifted to the right and searched the shadows for something that looked like a man. Nothing moved. Nearby, the flare still fumed and sputtered. Krystal waited as if she had all the time in the world. She was like a panther in the deep woods, waiting for her prey to arrive. Laci stepped from behind a thick post and stood ten paces from the Dancer, staring at her.

"Hello, K.O.," she said.

"Hello, Laci."

"We have company," Laci said.

"I know."

"What's your plan?" Laci asked.

"My plan," Krystal said. "Is to kill you all."

"All I want is my daughter, and then I'm gone forever," Laci said.

"You should have taken her and ran a long time ago," Krystal said. There was a sneer in her voice.

Brand's eyes kept searching along the far wall and his body wouldn't stop shivering. The knot in his stomach almost doubled him over, but he resisted, holding the broom handle in front of his body with both hands, standing in front of Ren and Alicia.

Krystal tipped her head back and yelled at the ceiling.

"Raevyn," she called out. "Come join us."

He slipped out of the shadows like a ghost, from a place that Brand had scanned again and again, but even with his acute vision, he hadn't seen Raevyn there. Now the three of them stood in the center of the cluttered basement, grouped around the sizzling flare like evil campers. Only Laci looked human, in jeans and a dark tee shirt. The Dancer and Raevyn were like black monsters, waiting to suck the life out of whatever they touched.

"I'm scared," Alicia moaned. Her voice was muffled against Ren's jacket. Brand braced his legs and waited.

"Well," Krystal said. "Time to tango."

She struck at Raevyn first, whirling like a tornado. Raevyn fended off her first two kicks with his arms before she landed a crossing punch to his head that sent him sideways. Laci stepped in and threw and left right combination at the Dancer, but K.O. just laughed and brushed her off like an annoying pest. Raevyn came back and hit K.O. hard, right square in the face. The blow sent her off her feet and her back hit one of the big support posts, sending a shower of dust down on her head and shoulders. She bounced right back to her feet and swung her head from side to side. Brand heard her shoulders pop back into place as she resumed her fighting stance.

"I'm gonna need some help, lover," she said. She was facing Raevyn with her hand held up like knives. Brand caught a glint of light off her palms and his mind flashed back to the way she cut her husband's throat with a swipe of her fingers. Laci took a deep breath and rotated toward Raevyn. The two women stood side by side, locked in position like twins. Raevyn chuckled.

"This is going to be just like old times," he said.

He lunged in like a bolt of lightning, turning as he moved. His cloak flipped out and up, flapping at Laci's legs. Something along the hem caught a glint of orange light as it cut through Laci's jeans, opening deep gray slits in her upper thighs. She gasped and stepped backward, staring down. Blood started running out as Raevyn's stuck his fist into the air next to Dancer's head. She bobbed to the side and raked her hands across his stomach and chest, ducking under his arm and springing into the middle of the room again. Laci backed up against a shelf of bottles. They rattled and chinked together. Her eyes were wide and her hands dropped down and away. Raevyn stepped toward her and hit her hard on the chin with the heel of his hand. Her head snapped back and the shelf went over backward with Laci on top of it. It came to a crashing stop and her feet stuck up in the air. One leg twitched rhythmically for a few moments and then stopped.

"Looks like it's just you and me now," the Dancer said. Raevyn was still facing Laci's feet. He swung around and crouched low.

"Let's finish this so that I can get back to work," he growled.

They charged each other. The Dancer was quicker, faster, but Raevyn was stronger and stood his ground. She darted under his defense and the blades on her hands tore across his face, but he wrapped his arms around her and hoisted her off the ground. Her back arched and the back of her head looked as if it was going to touch her feet. She brought her head forward again, striking like a snake. Their foreheads cracked together and Raevyn staggered backward, but he tightened his grip on his attacker. Dancer gave him another head butt, and then another, but Brand saw each one getting weaker. Raevyn squeezed harder, and the Dancer started howling with anger and pain.

"You underestimated me," Raevyn said. "I thought I taught you to never underestimate your opponent."

The Dancer's back arched again and she screamed, but this time her head stayed back. She kicked her legs as if she was trying to swim away, twisting her torso back and forth. Raevyn hugged her harder and then he leaned forward, farther and farther. Brand heard K.O. gasping for breath and almost sobbing, and then she yelped once, like an injured puppy, as her back snapped. Raevyn held her there for a moment, bent in an almost impossible reverse curve, and then he dropped her. She landed in a pile on the floor, next to the flare, with her legs folded under her buttocks and her feet almost touching her shoulders. Her head and arms stretched out across the floor. She looked like a doll that had been painted black and folded backward before being thrown away. Brand's stomach rolled. He looked at the stick in his hands, tempted to throw it away. Instead, he clenched his teeth and brought it down hard on his knee. It split lengthwise along the grain, leaving him with two sticks, each one tapered to a point. The sound of the snapping wood brought Raevyn toward them.

TWENTY-SEVEN

October 18, 1995 — 7:00PM

Brand pressed his back against Ren and Alicia, pushing them both against the wall. Raevyn stalked forward like an angry gorilla, his chest heaving and his breath coming hard and heavy. He reached up and pulled the thick black mask off his head. Ren turned away and pulled Alicia's head down so she couldn't see. Brand put his arms out as if he could somehow shelter them from harm. Even in the darkness, Brand could see that Raevyn's face and scalp were a mess of angry red scar tissue. He snarled at Brand, showing chiseled yellow teeth and pale gums. Brand's stomach turned over and he tasted bile in his mouth.

"Your elixir of life isn't working very well," Brand said. His voice growled inside his throat. Raevyn moved closer and spoke in a hushed tone.

"Do you know how much genetic material I have to consume just to stay alive?"

Brand shook his head.

"My wounds are deep," he said. "And my hunger is insatiable."

Brand felt Alicia cowering behind him.

"Leave the little girl alone," Brand said. "She's innocent."

"No one is innocent in this life," Raevyn said.

"Laci told me that she wasn't your child," Brand said.

"She is," Raevyn countered. "Laci lied to you."

"Why?" Brand asked.

Raevyn's smile was like a sneer. "Because she needs that child as much as I do," he said.

"Laci would never hurt her own child," Brand whispered.

"She can't help it," Raevyn said. "Any more than I can. I'm a monster, Mr. Brand. And so is Laci."

He took another step closer and then stopped. He stood up straight and tipped his head from one side to the other. Brand could hear his joints popping as he stretched his neck. The hard, red, wrinkled skin glistened like plastic.

Brand laughed. "You think you're a monster," he said.

Raevyn was on him in two strides. He hit Brand in the stomach with a hard fist and Brand dropped the half-handle in his left hand. It bounced once and clattered to a rest at his feet. He held the other piece in his right hand as he doubled over. Raevyn stepped in and grabbed Brand by the throat, lifting him onto his toes. The monster glared into his eyes. Brand felt the world going white, and a steady whine filled his ears.

"I am a God," Raevyn whispered. "I am the next evolution of mankind."

Brand's head felt as if it was going to explode, and yet the whining sound seemed to come from outside. Everything stopped for a moment as he realized what he was hearing, and he couldn't help but smile. Raevyn's glare turned to confusion for a moment and Brand raised his eyebrows as if to say 'see, I told you so.' He felt Ren squirm behind him and he pushed against her and away, giving her just a bit of room.

Brand managed to squeak out a hoarse sentence.

"I think you'd better take a look at what's behind me," he said.

Brand closed his eyes tight just before he heard the pop of Ren's flash. Raevyn grunted a curse. Brand took the stick and jammed it upward as hard as he could. Raevyn grunted again and one hand let go of Brand's throat. Brand pulled the stick back and opened his eyes. Raevyn was still blinking away the effects of the flash as Brand jammed his makeshift weapon into his attacker's face. He hit Raevyn's left eye dead on and pushed as hard as he could. Raevyn screamed, dropped his grip on Brand entirely and staggered backward. Brand pulled the broken broom handle back and lunged again, sliding it up and under Raevyn's ribcage.

Brand swung his head around toward Ren and she screamed.

"Run," he hissed.

Raevyn stepped back again and grabbed the end of the stick, but Brand beat him to it, ramming it with his knee, planting it further up inside the Raevyn's torso. Raevyn careened backward again, and Brand landed a sideways kick to the last bit of the rounded end of the shattered handle. The impact sent the base of the stick clear into Raevyn's body and he fell against an empty rack, toppling two others and landing next to Krystal's body, still bent in a grotesque and unnatural arabesque.

Brand felt the change come over him like a strike of lightning, raging through his body, orgasmic in the unleashing of its raw power. He tore at his clothes with claws that raked his chest, spewing his own blood onto the floor. He sensed some life left in Laci, nothing in Krystal, the woman and the girl behind him, fresh and warm, and the man, hard and tough and heavy, full of blood and something else, a hotness that made Brand's hackles rise and stiffened his long back. He growled and pounced without thought, tearing and ripping and howling with rage, felt the man pummel him, heard the man screaming, tasted blood and meat and felt the black love of murder surround him.

TWENTY-EIGHT

October 19, 1995 – 7:15AM

Brand ran, on his hands and feet, like a dog, but his limbs tangled and he fell, tumbled, rammed his shoulder against a hard piece of turf, maybe a rock. He stopped rolling, found himself laying in the cold grass. Came to hands and knees, threw up, vomiting blood and bits of tendon, things that no man should find in his gut. He crawled toward the house, a dim outline against an effusive pre-dawn. It was Brand's first real look at the outside of Raevyn's burned home, still nothing more than a charred skeleton after all these years. The only part that had survived was the wing over the wine cellar. The paint on the white clapboards had bubbled and peeled, and black soot covered the siding above the windows. As he sat there in the grass, flames began to move out of the basement to finish the job that Laci had started so many years ago.

"Ren," Brand whispered, his voice nothing more than a hoarse growl. He could still feel the animal writhing inside of his soul, but he looked at his hands and saw human flesh. A hand touched his naked shoulder.

"Charlie," Ren said.

Brand pushed himself to his knees. Ren was holding Alicia in her arms. She stepped back, creating some distance between Brand and Alicia, and then she noticed that Brand was watching the tendrils of thickening black smoke coming from the wine cellar.

"Laci," Ren said.

"Where is she?" Brand asked.

"In there. With him."

Ren closed her eyes and Brand could feel her anguish at what she must have seen, knew that Laci had chosen to stay with Raevyn.

"Is he dead?" Brand took a deep, shuddering breath.

"Yeah," Ren said. "This time, he's dead."

Alicia put her arms out to Brand. He stood up and took her from Ren, who let go carefully. The little girl hugged him hard around the neck and trembled. "Charlie," she whispered.

"Yes," he replied. He felt his strength slipping away.

"You are a very bad dog."

The three of them staggered to the Jeep. Ren took the driver's seat. She started it up and turned on the heater, but she just sat behind the wheel staring into the night. Brand took Alicia over to the other side and opened the door.

"Blanket in the back," she said.

Brand reached behind the seat and found a soft, light throw, red and black plaid. He held Alicia with one arm while he tied the little blanket around his waist. He sat down, Alicia still clutched to around his neck. Fastened the safety belt around her, around them both, and then sat, staring out the window, watching nothing.

"Did you see it?" Brand whispered.

Ren shook her head. "We ran." She paused for a moment and then spoke quietly, almost to herself. "Joshua was my friend."

"I'm sorry, Ren."

She sat like a stone. The heater blew cool air, but it was warmer than anything Brand had felt for hours. Alicia was strangely quiet. Brand looked over at the remains of Laci's home. The flames danced up the outer walls now, licking and caressing it like a lover's touch. He closed his eyes and held Alicia tight, feeling in her all that was left of Laci and her pain.

Ren put the wrangler in gear and kicked up gravel as she drove down the lane.

"We need to get to a phone," she said. There were tears in her eyes. "God, Brand," she said. "I wish I'd never met you."

They stopped at an Exxon and Ren called 911. They sat there in the Wrangler and waited. Ren started to sob, and then her sobs turned to crying. Brand held Alicia tight to his body as Ren pounded on the steering wheel.

"I'm sorry," Brand said.

Ren put her arms across the wheel and let her head fall forward. She rolled it back and forth for a moment and then sat back and took a deep breath.

"I'm sorry," Brand said again.

She nodded. She wiped her face with the back of her hand, leaving a black streak of soot across her cheek.

"Brand," she said.

"Yeah?"

"There's something I didn't tell you."

Brand waited.

"Blankenship said that the rats had been infected."

"Infected by what?" Brand asked.

She shrugged. "Some kind of parasite," she said. "He told me that the ones that did the damage were extensively infected. Some kind of tape worm, only it was everywhere inside them, like cancer. Through the lymph system, arteries, veins, spinal column, even in the brain. He thinks that the worm, or whatever it is, is producing the toxins that drove the rats crazy."

Brand frowned.

"So you think that Raevyn and Krystal and Laci were infected with this parasite?"

Ren shook her head.

"I don't know anything," she said. "I'm just telling you what Blankenship said."

"How is it transmitted?" Brand asked.

"Blankenship thought it might be blood born. Or maybe any fluid transfer. Probably blood though. Or maybe saliva. Maybe even by a bite."

It was Brand's turn to shake his head.

"Great," he murmured. Then, out loud, "Sounds pretty far out there. How old is Blankenship?"

"Not old enough to suffer from dementia," Ren said. "He sounded scared, but not crazy."

In the distance, a lonely siren started to wail, and was joined by another. Ren started the jeep and put it in gear. The station owner watched them from inside the glass booth as Ren hit the gas and sped away.

"What are you doing?" Brand asked.

"Leaving the scene," she said.

TWENTY-NINE

October 19, 1995 – 7:29AM

Ren took them to her house and straight to the kitchen, leaving them there for a moment while she bounded up the stairs. She came back with a first aid kit and a robe for Brand. She peeled the black rags off Alicia's hands and the little girl cried as the coagulated blood pulled away. Brand gripped her arms while Ren dabbed her wounds with a damp cloth. Ren grimaced and bit her lower lip as she examined the cuts.

"These are going to need stitches," she said. Alicia's kicking and screaming doubled when Ren poured hydrogen peroxide over the cuts. It fizzled and dripped in the sink. It was all Brand could do to hold her without hurting her. Ren squeezed a whole tube of antiseptic onto Alicia's hands and then gently them in wrapped white gauze. Brand let her go and she wrapped her arms around his neck, sobbing. Together, Brand and Ren stripped off her nightgown. Alicia reached out with one hand, tears streaming down her cheeks, as Ren held the tattered cloth at arms length and dropped in into a wastebasket.

Brand wrapped Alicia in a small blanket and took her to the guest room while Ren put a call in to Devers. Alicia sobbed for a while and then drifted off to sleep. Brand came downstairs and found Ren cleaned up and dressed in jeans and a baggy sweatshirt. Her clenched hands pushed against the counter top and she stared into the dining room, past Brand, as if he wasn't there.

"I could have killed you," he said.

"I know." Ren gave him a tight smile as she reached around her back and pulled a Smith and Wesson snub-nosed revolver from under the tail of her thick shirt. She flipped open the cylinder and dumped six shells on the counter. Three were spent. The others showed gleaming bullets still crimped into the shoulders of the casings.

"I think I missed, all three times," she said. "But you ran."

"You think those could kill me?" Brand asked.

Brand touched one of the empty casings with his finger and felt a knot in the pit of his stomach. He glanced at Ren. She sighed, scooped up the cartridges and disappeared into the den for a moment. When she came back, she sent Brand upstairs to use the shower in her room. While he let the hot water soak through him, she laid out a pair of jeans and a blue U of W sweatshirt, white socks but no underwear. Brand glanced at the clock as he dressed. It was half past seven in the morning.

I was out that long, Brand thought.

Devers showed up thirty minutes later with two uniformed cops. Ren let them in and led them into the living room. Brand sat on the couch with his elbows on his knees and his head hanging forward. Ren put her hands behind her back and leaned against the wall, staring at the floor.

"So," Devers said. "What happened?"

Brand filled him in while his two buddies stood by the door. Devers didn't take notes, he just listened. Brand started with Joshua, and then Laci, and the Griffs and the Underground, Marshall and his military operation, Alicia and Krystal and Raevyn. He did his best to make all the pieces fit without describing his part in it.

Devers stood through the whole thing with his arms crossed and a scowl on his face.

"You don't believe a word of it," Brand said.

"We're having trouble identifying bodies out of the bone yard," he said. "But, yeah, we did find what looks like John Marshall, or at least what's left of him. And a whole hell of a lot of bones."

"What about the Griffs?" Brand asked.

"Can't locate a single one, except the dead ones down below First Avenue."

"And the fire out at the old Raevyn place?" Brand asked.

"No bodies," Devers said.

Brand stood up and Ren came off the wall. Brand could see the fear in her eyes.

"It's still an oven over there," Devers said. "We won't be able to get in for at least a couple more hours. At least. Maybe days. I don't know."

Brand and Ren both relaxed a bit, but exchanged glances. Neither one gave the other any comfort.

"Where's the kid?" Devers asked.

"Upstairs," Ren said.

"We'll have to call social services," Devers said.

"Can you give her just a little more time," Brand asked.

Devers stared at him for a moment and then nodded slowly.

"I keep thinking I should take you back in for something," Devers said.

Brand was too tired to argue.

"But I can't quite figure out what the hell you've done," Devers continued. He stood with his hands on his hips and chewed on his lower lip a bit. He glanced over at Ren and then back toward Brand. Just then his radio crackled, and he picked it off his belt. He stuck an earpiece up against his head and held it with one finger. His concerned look turned to a frown, and then to a look of disbelief. He shook his head.

"Yeah, O.K.," he said. "Yeah, I got it." He looked at Brand.

"I've gotta take you downtown," he said.

"For what?" Brand said.

"For a while," Devers replied. "I'm gonna leave these two officers here with you, Ms. Rhodes."

"Thank you," she said. "What's going to happen to Charlie."

Devers smiled and shook his head.

"I have no idea," he said.

Devers stuck Brand in the back of a white Interceptor but didn't cuff him. They rode in silence all the way downtown to the Marriott. Devers let Brand out and two guys in black suits took over, leaving Devers standing by the car like a cabby. A few hotel patrons meandered past the cruiser as Brand walked away. The pavement glimmered with moisture. Above them, the streetlights made the lower reaches of the city look like day.

"Where are we going?" Brand asked. They passed by the main doors and headed for a loading dock in the back. His two companions were mute. They stepped into a large, brightly lit open space filled with stainless steel racks. Rows and rows of fresh sourdough loaves cooled alongside stacks of boxes filled with tomatoes, lettuce, and flash frozen chicken breasts. The doors were guarded by more black suits, and no one else was around. Brand's buddies led him past the produce and poultry and left him standing beside a stack of wooden pallets. Brand took a breath and leaned against the wall. He waited for almost a half hour before his two escorts showed up again. They took positions at either end of the short bay. The taller of the two spoke into a mike on his lapel and then they stood like statues with their hands clasped in front of their waists.

"Charlie Brand."

Brand turned slowly and watched Clayton Dash approach. The VP stopped in front of Brand and crossed his arms.

"Mr. Dash," Brand said.

Dash studied Brand for a moment and then smiled and stuck out his hand.

"It's nice to meet you," he said. Brand shook his hand. Dash held on hard and long, like an alpha dog establishing his dominance. Dash wore his smile like the ballroom dancers back in the seventies, big and broad and plastic.

Brand cleared his throat and waited.

"Not much for small talk, are you?" Dash asked.

Brand shook his head. Dash clasped his hands and pressed his lips together. He stared into Brand's eyes for a while before he spoke.

"You've been on quite an adventure these past few days," Dash said.

Brand nodded.

"How long have you been following me?" Brand asked.

"You came into our sights the night you followed Laci Keller to her daughter's house," Dash said.

"And what's your interest in Keller?" Brand asked.

"You're not much of a reporter if you have to ask me that," Dash said.

"I always assume that I know nothing," Brand replied.

"And how often are you right?" Dash asked.

"Most of the time."

"Well," Dash said. "What do you think you know?"

Brand rubbed his chin.

"Well," he began. "Jack Raevyn and Trina Marshall were buddies at MIT. Jack was working on some kind of youth serum, but the research went bad. Turned a lab of rats and monkeys into monsters. Marshall must have gotten a sense of the military implications, so he convinced congress to fund Raevyn's research. Y'all set him up here in Seattle to continue, despite the fact that he'd gotten the boot out of MIT."

Dash kept his eyes locked on Brand's. Brand kept going.

"Jack got far enough for you two, so you pulled the funding and Marshall covered your tracks by burning the lab. Only thing you didn't count on was that Raevyn was experimenting on himself. He escaped. But one thing he didn't count on was his wife. She was tired of being beaten, so she torched him. Even then, he survived. But now he's got a grudge against a whole lot of folks, you included. Meanwhile, Marshall gets hitched up with a gal, and she's got an idea. She figures out that you and Marshall and Raevyn own the rights to Raevyn's formula, and she's smart enough to know that if she's married to Marshall, and if all three of you are dead, she'd end up with the patent and the money. Have I got it right so far?"

Dash nodded. "Mostly."

"So, she's out to kill everyone. But, when the dust settles, Laci and Jack Raevyn are dead, Senator Marshall and Krystal are dead, and so is Kenny."

"Seems like the only other survivor is little Alicia Keller," Dash said.

"Touch her and I'll see you burn in hell with your buddies," Brand said.

Dash chuckled. "I could have you imprisoned for life just for saying that," he said.

"But you won't."

Dash shook his head.

"Do you know who set me up in prison with the Griffs?" Brand asked.

Dash shook his head again.

"We think that Raevyn had his claws into all kinds of things," Dash said. "We're talking here about a guy with a corner on the next trillion dollar market. He makes Bill Gates look like a dirt farmer from Kansas."

"Do you know what it does?" Brand asked.

Dash nodded.

"Yeah," he said. "I do. That's why I pulled the funding and had the research confiscated."

"And burned the lab to the ground?"

"Uh-uh. That must have been Marshall."

They stood there, staring at each other for a moment.

"Why am I here?" Brand asked.

Dash's bright smile crept back across his face. "Well, you're a writer, right?"

Brand nodded. Dash continued.

"Seems like writers are always dreaming up stories. Article, books, exposes."

"Yeah," Brand said. "That's what we do."

"But this is one story that's going to get left on the cutting room floor," Dash suggested. Brand watched him carefully.

"I'm not planning to write any stories," Brand said.

Dash nodded.

"I could have had you terminated," Dash said.

Brand waited for more. Dash waited as well.

"But?" Brand asked.

"Renata," Dash said.

Brand felt his hackles go up.

"What does she have to do with this?" Brand asked.

Dash chuckled.

"She's not in any danger," Dash said. "I love that kid."

Brand almost laughed.

"What the hell are you talking about?" he asked.

Dash slapped Brand on the shoulder and turned him toward the door.

"Ren's a good friend of mine," Dash said. "A long-time friend, if you get my drift."

"She hates you," Brand said.

Dash shrugged.

"Whatever," he said. "Anyway, she and I go way back. She asked me to keep track of you. Help you out if need be."

Dash let go of Brand and the two men turned to face each other again. Dash's face went serious in an instant.

"We're going to contain this situation," Dash said. "Taking whatever steps we deem necessary in the interests of national security. Regardless of what Renata wants or wishes. Do you understand?"

Brand nodded.

"So, maybe you should keep a low profile for a while," Dash said.

"Yeah," Brand said. "I'll do that."

"Well," he said. "I'll be watching your work."

"I'm sure you will," Brand said. "Can I go now?"

Dash nodded and motioned toward one of his secret service goons.

"Get him out of here," Dash said. He turned and spoke as he walked away. "Nice to meet you mister Brand. I hope you vote for me next election."

Brand let the suits usher him back to the sidewalk. They left him there. He found Devers still waiting out front.

"Can I ride up front?" Brand asked.

Devers gave him a look, but opened the passenger door for him. As they pulled out of the turnaround, Brand glanced out the window. Silver pools of light spilled across the shining pavement. In the shadows across the street, something moved. Brand looked harder, peering into the darkness. As he watched, a flame sputtered to life, lighting a cigarette. In the soft glow, shielded by a black-gloved hand, he saw a familiar beaked nose. A white face rose up in the orange light and dark lips parted in a wicked smile. Devers' eyes were on the road in front of him as he hit the accelerator and pulled away. Brand craned his neck around, but the apparition was gone, melded back into the dark morning from where it came.

"Good luck, Mr. Dash," Brand whispered.

They drove through the tunnel and out onto the floating bridge before Brand spoke.

"Thanks, Devers," he said.

Devers grunted. He dropped Brand off in Ren's turnaround and drove off. The two cops were sitting at the dining room table drinking coffee. They stood up when Brand came in. The bigger of the two put his hat on and nodded at Brand.

"We're out of here," he said.

Brand and Ren watched them go and then Brand collapsed into an armchair. Ren took a seat on the couch across from him.

"They're sending a social worker to pick up Alicia," Ren said.

"At six in the morning?" Brand asked.

Ren nodded. They sat in silence for a while. The only sound in the house was the ticking of a clock. Brand stared at Ren. She stared into the empty fireplace. After a while, she turned her head toward him.

"How are you doing?" he asked. It took Brand a moment to realize that Ren was looking past him toward something in the hallway. He turned around and found Alicia standing there.

"I'm hungry," she said.

Ren glanced at Brand. They both turned at the sound of a knock on the front door. Ren stood up and Brand grabbed Alicia. Ren peered out through the peephole, frowned, and then opened the door. A thin, dark-haired woman slipped in and stood just inside the door. Ren had to nudge her gently forward a bit to get the door closed behind her. She glanced back as if she was annoyed, and then turned her attention to Brand and Alicia.

"I'm Judy Stayberg," she said. "I've come for the little girl."

THIRTY

"Where will you take her?" Brand asked.

"We can't disclose that," Stayberg said. "But she'll be safe. Don't worry about that."

"Can I see her again?" Brand asked.

Stayberg shook her head. "I'm afraid not. It wouldn't be good for the girl."

She reached out and pulled Alicia out of Brand's arms. The little girl's face contorted with pain and she reached out toward him. Stayberg held the girl like pro, braced against little struggling body. The social worker took a step backward and Ren slowly opened the door. Stayberg stepped out into the night. Even as the door shut, Brand could still hear Alicia wailing. The sound of a car door shutting muffled the cries even more, and then the car drove off and the house was silent again, except for the ticking clock. Ren and Brand just stood there in the foyer with their arms hanging limp at their sides.

"Ren," Brand said.

"Um-hm."

"Did you ever have kids?"

"No."

"Ever thought about it?"

"Yeah. Once or twice." She paused for a moment. "Are you making a suggestion?"

Brand shook his head.

"No," he said. "I wouldn't want to bring a child into this screwed up world."

"You would have been a good father," Ren said.

He turned his head and gazed through the gossamer curtains into the empty courtyard beyond. He squeezed his eyes shut, and for a moment, he could feel Alicia, huddled against his chest, could see her blue eyes staring into his, trusting, needing, grateful, not for protection, but just for being held when everything else seemed hopeless. Brand sucked in a lungful of air and blinked the tears from his eyes. Ren came over and slipped her arms around him, and they hugged each other hard. A series of sobs racked Brand's body.

"Charlie Brand," Ren said. Brand squeezed his eyes shut and prayed that she was not about to say what he thought she was going to say. Brand pulled away and looked out the window again. Ren smoothed the front of her sweatshirt and looked at the ground.

"I guess I'd better get home now," he said.

She nodded.

"I'll drive you," she said.

The Wrangler reeked of smoke and something else that made Brand's nostrils flare. Brand rolled the window down and stuck his head out. He kept thinking about bites and parasites and Alicia, and he rubbed his shoulder where Laci had bit him. But she hadn't bit him. It was just a dream. A vivid dream. And then he wondered what would have happened if Laci had gotten pregnant after she was infected with the parasite. Would the child be infected? He wondered about himself now, what he might be carrying inside his already cursed body. He pulled his head back inside the car and closed his eyes.

"You OK?" Ren asked.

"Yeah," Brand said. "As good as can be expected."

The city was dead when Ren dropped him off up on the hill. Brand stared up at the old apartment building and waited till Ren drove off. He walked over to the corner store and went inside. An old man sat behind the counter reading a magazine.

"Is it too early to get a beer?" Brand asked.

The old man glanced up at the clock and nodded.

Brand looked out the glass windows toward the city beyond.

"Mind if I just hang out and wait?" he asked.

The old man shrugged and went back to his magazine. Brand sat down on a bench with his back to the window and closed his eyes. The clerk looked over the top of his magazine.

"You just want one beer?" he asked.

Brand turned and stared at him.

"Why?" Brand asked.

"Because," he said. "If all you want is one beer, I'll just give you one. You can go home and then I don't have to worry about you."

Brand laughed.

"One beer won't do it, pops," he said. "And you don't have to worry about me. I'll be fine. I'll be just fine."

"Well, I have a rule against loitering," the old man said.

Brand leaned back and closed his eyes.

"I won't bother you," he said. "I promise. I just need some company till I can get a drink. Then I'll be out of you hair. I promise."

Brand heard the old man grunt. Brand cracked one eye open and glanced at him. The old man picked up a magazine and started flipping through it from back to front. Brand closed his eyes again and let out a long, slow breath.

"Know what?" Brand asked. The old man just grunted again.

"The whole world is just fucked up," Brand said.

"You said it," the old man replied. He stared at Brand for a full minute, and then said, "I know you. Seen you around. You're looking better today though. Almost human."

Brand took another deep breath but let it out quickly this time. He tried not to think, but his mind disobeyed him. He kept thinking about Jule, but it was Laci's face that popped up, and it was the feel of her hard body under his that he couldn't shake, even though he wasn't even sure if it had been real. He felt cheated, like he should have had more time with her, and yet he kept seeing her there in the fire, standing over Raevyn, with long, tape-like worms writhing out of their bodies, tangling together in the agony of the flames. And he kept seeing little Alicia, with her sad, blue eyes, but they turned into red, burning flames too, and when she smiled, her pointed teeth dripped with blood. He shook it off and tried to focus on the taste of a cold beer. *Beer will be good to start*, he thought. *When the liquor stores open, I'll go down and get a bottle of the good stuff. Haig and Haig, in the pinch bottle. Or maybe I'll go down to the Mayflower and just sit in the bar and have them flame a Grand Marnier for me. Yeah, that'll be good.*

Brand heard the sound of the morning edition getting loaded into the newspaper bins outside, and even though his eyes were closed, he followed the old man's movements with his ears. The clerk went outside and came back in with a paper, rattling it like a kite in the wind.

"Another lady gone missing," he said. "Out along Lake Road this time. And you'd think that'd be a nicer neighborhood, you know?"

Brand tapped the back of his head against the glass window behind him. A siren wailed in the dark distance, echoing off the hardscapes of the city.

Post Script

As we finished transcribing this particular set of notes and papers, Kate found, on the last page of one journal from which several pages had been ripped, a single line written in Brand's scrawling cursive:

I need to get out of this fucking town.

We both looked at the piles of boxes that now sat scattered across my office floor, once nothing more than a small nuisance, but now opened, like Pandora's famous box, a chaotic puzzle that seemed too large for my quarters.

I remember stepping out onto the pavement that night, waving good-bye to Kate, wondering if I would see her again, wondering why I wondered that. New York was cold, and a continent away from Seattle and all that Brand spoke of and wrote of. And yet, as I said in the beginning, nothing in my world seemed safe again.

I stopped for a cup of coffee at the Perk, just down the corner from my office. It was late, but the café was full of students from the village, and I sat next to a man who was proselytizing to a young woman, going on a on in a somewhat loud and pervasive voice about Jesus and God and the power of scriptures, the evils of hell and damnation. His words grated on me, nothing sounding rational or real, despite his thorough knowledge of the Bible and his particular religion. I could not pinpoint the source of my angst, other than the simple fact that I had read the journals of Charlie Brand, had distilled from them what thread of life I could find, and in so finding, had believed. Such belief, far from making me even more of a skeptical agnostic, did the opposite. I found myself incensed at this expert's simple faith, and yet hoping, with hope beyond hope, that there might really be a God, or some power for good, for in my heart I knew that evil does indeed exist. And it is as close to us, even now, as our very breath.

Joe Cooke makes his home in Santa Fe, NM teaching, writing and playing music. He's also an accomplished ballroom dancer and enjoys skiing and riding his Harley.

You can find him on-line at www.joecookeauthor.com

www.ingramcontent.com/pod-product-compliance
Lightning Source LLC
Chambersburg PA
CBHW030515020726
47494CB00004B/1098